Destiny Rejected

Felicia Jedlicka

Book 1

Copyright © 2016 by Felicia Jedlicka

All rights reserved.

Cover design by Felicia Jedlicka
Book design by Felicia Jedlicka
Editing by Silver Jay Editing

No part of this book may be reproduced in any form
or by any electronic or mechanical means including
information storage and retrieval systems, without
permission in writing from the author. The only
exception is by a reviewer, who may quote short
excerpts in a review.

This book is a work of fiction. Names, characters,
places, and incidents either are products of the
author's imagination or are used fictitiously. Any
resemblance to actual persons, living or dead, events,
or locales is entirely coincidental.

Felicia Jedlicka
Find me on Facebook: www.facebook.com/feljedauthor
Visit my website feljedauthor.wordpress.com

For the Bacchae; my first fan.

More titles by FELICIA JEDLICKA

DESTINY REJECTED
DESTINY RECLAIMED
DESTINY RAZED
DESTINY RESTORED

DÉJÀ VU

SAVE THE HUMANS

THE NECROMANCER'S CHILD

SISTER WITCHES
THE DEVIL'S SHADOW
THE DEVIL'S SOUL

THE NEBRASKA APOCALYPSE NOVELS
CORN COWS AND THE APOCALYPSE
COW TIPPING AFTER THE APOCALYPSE
CORN HUSKING AFTER THE APOCALYPSE

THE WARDEN SERIES
SUCCESSORS
RIVALS
LOVERS AND LIARS
BAD BLOOD
TENANTS AND TYRANTS
THE RING BEARER
GODS AND MONSTERS
BEASTS AND BURDENS
MAGIC AND MAYHEM
FORK IN THE ROAD
DETAILS AND DEADLINES

Destiny Rejected

Felicia Jedlicka

Shopping

I told Ayil shopping at the galaxy's largest shopping mall was a bad idea, but he insisted he would not miss a sale this big. Especially if he could get banded jeans for less than 500 dosh. He wasn't wrong, and I had to admit we both did look rather *parch* in the tight blue stripes, but unfortunately I wasn't wrong either.

The minute my credit stamp showed up on the computer, we were on the planet's most wanted list. And since the planet—aka semi-atmospheric asteroid—only had about forty square miles of surface area, escape was about as unlikely as someone waking up from a ten-year hypersleep coma, but I still had my fingers crossed on that one too.

"Kit!" Ayil screamed and sideswiped me, sending me into the path of a midway vendor. Thankfully, he was selling stuffed toys, or it might have hurt more.

The electromagnetic blast wave he was saving me from nicked his shoulder. The lingering yellow radiation begged to attach to anything metal. Ayil grunted as the drainage grate we had recently passed slapped against his back.

"Ayil!" I squirmed out of a pile of squeak toys and jumped to my feet again. I ignored the vendor's complaints and ran off with several Velcro Cephalopods attached to me.

Another shot fired less than a block in front of us, but a well-timed back bend on my part kept me from being irrevocably attracted to metal objects. I crawled the remaining distance to Ayil and assisted his efforts to stand. The iron grill was enormous, and it took both of us to lift it so he could continue to move.

Once we were upright, Ayil bent forward, carrying the weight like Atlas. "Come on." I pulled on his arm and he did his best to run in his new hunchback condition. "Faster!"

"Easy for you to say," he grumbled as we ducked into an alley. There were still more vendors, and it was hard to distinguish between them and the transient population that wasted their money on them. The excitement over the denim sale created a sea of banded legs, hiding us in plain sight. The drainage grate, on the other hand, could not be disguised as fashion no matter how we played it.

I stopped halfway through the alley. I could see the other end clearly enough to recognize the influx of bounty hunters. The group looked familiar, and I didn't have to see the one familiar face to know it was Terrin's men. The man responsible for the bounty on my head. The man my parents entrusted with my protection and containment. The man I had tricked and escaped from over six years ago.

Oh, he was going to be so pissed.

"What is it?" Ayil panted beside me.

I turned to him and stared into his gorgeous pale brown eyes. His Old-Arabic heritage gave him silky black-brown hair with lazy curls. His smooth skin had a bronze tone, and his youthful physique captivated young ladies on every planet we visited. If he were a few years older and not a brat, I might have indulged in that adventure myself. However, as things were, I only thought of him as my smart-ass sidekick.

Truthfully, the only reason we were traveling together was mutual convenience. I saved him from a life of boy-toy slavery, and he lifted heavy stuff for me.

"What?" he asked again, no doubt seeing the concern on my face.

I frowned and pulled a key card from my pocket. The antiquated device was basically a rectangular piece of metal with a puzzle matrix cut from it, but it was the only thing that would start my rust-bucket of a ship.

I placed it in his hand. "Take it. Go. Get out of here."

"What are you going to do?" He glanced toward the other end of the alley.

"They're here for me. I'm going to turn myself in."

"You're kidding."

"No, it's Terrin. You should save yourself."

He stared back at me, questions lining up on the edge of his lips. "Oh, my God!" he eventually blurted out and rolled his eyes. "You are such a drama queen!" He forcefully turned me around and shoved me into an emergency ladder lining the side of the adjacent building. "Climb the damn ladder!"

"Ayil—" I objected, but he shoved me hard. If I didn't want his hand to remain digging into my ass, I would have to climb higher and faster.

I came up to an enclosed portion of the ladder, but before I could express concern, Ayil switched his ascent to the outside to avoid getting his metal appendage lodged. His speed surprised me, but he was a constant competitor. He was likely internally challenging himself to beat me to the top despite his handicapping weight.

He reached the roof and pulled me up the rest of the way. A shot fired behind us, grazing my foot. Ayil dropped me and ripped my shoe off. He threw it, but the radiation had already surrounded it and it boomeranged back, slapping him on the shoulder.

"Run!" he scolded me when he discovered I was still on the ground where he had dumped me.

I stood and ran half-barefooted across the roof with him at my side. "Ayil, he won't give up!" I explained. "It was his duty to my people to keep me safe. I shamed him terribly by fleeing from him."

Ayil skidded to a stop, and I stopped with him.

"Do you want to go with him?" His annoyance was justified, but the glare he was giving me seemed unnecessary.

"No, of course not."

"Then move your ass, woman!" He ran to the end of the roof and leaped across to the next one with ease. I wasn't sure I would fare as well, so I backed up a little more to get some speed. "Kit!" Ayil screamed at me. "Run!"

I should have just run, but every human instinct demanded I look back to see exactly how much enthusiasm I should put into my leg movement. I turned and saw Terrin standing behind me. His leathery green face was not as angry as it should have been. He almost looked relieved to see me, rather than livid. Perhaps he had missed me as much as I missed him.

"Hello, Mallory," he whispered. It had been a while since anyone had called me by my other name (I'll explain later). His black stubbed horns bowed slightly to me. He kept them short for practicality, but ever since I had commented that they made him look dangerously handsome, he started growing them out a little longer. I was pleased to see he still took my opinion into consideration.

My mouth tipped up into a slight smile. I opened my mouth and spoke the words I had been waiting to say to him. The words that two years of friendship had deserved and earned. "I'm sorry," I whispered.

He gave me a nod. "Me too."

"KIT! RUN!" Ayil screamed behind me.

Even from a distance, Ayil had seen the movement before I had. This time, I didn't hesitate to follow his command. I shifted—seemingly in slow motion to my mind. I glimpsed Terrin pulling the gun from behind his back before I was facing Ayil again. He was still screaming at me, infuriated by my hesitation.

My legs took stride. Tiny long jumps, one after another. I could feel my heart in my ears and hear the rasping of my breathing. I knew what my options were: freedom or captivity.

Granted, my freedom was a pain in the ass, and I had far more luxuries in my captivity, but let's face it, I know why the caged bird sings.

It's because she's so freaking bored.

I followed Ayil's instructions as he coached me with derogatory encouragement. I heard the familiar *plooff* of a weapon's discharge and I jumped before I had reached the edge of the building.

Ayil's eyes bulged as he calculated the three feet that were lacking in my jump. Thirty-six inches of impending doom swarmed my thoughts, and I looked down to see if there were any giant stuffed animal vendors to save my life.

The blast hit my back dead on. No shock there. Terrin never missed his target. I was relying on that.

I felt the impact push me forward. It was enough of a boost to give me a solid surface to land on, but I didn't plan my tuck and roll before I hit the roof. The magnetic field whipped me around and attached me to the grate on Ayil's back.

He grunted and coughed, followed by a sorrowful laugh. "Ouch," he moaned.

"Sorry."

"You'd better be as light as you look." He lifted his body, with me, the metal grate, and my shoe attached to him like a backpack.

I could see Terrin behind us, contemplating whether to follow us across the roof scape, or take the ground path and wait for us to come down. He spoke into his wrist communicator and took the low road. That didn't mean I was out of trouble, only that he wouldn't risk a rooftop pursuit.

He was probably certain I was as good as caught. Given that I was no longer in control of my mobility, I had to agree with that assessment. Still, I didn't want to deny Ayil the opportunity to give him a good hunt. He was so competitive, after all.

But before I get into the rest of the chase, I should introduce myself.

Two Households

My name is Kit Mallory, or Mallory Kit, depending on which biological parent you ask. I would love to say I come from a broken home, but technically my parents got divorced before I was born. I've never known a whole home. I prefer to say I come from two homes.

Their divorce was a bloodbath of litigious bullshit, so it wasn't a surprise that neither of them was willing to agree on a name for me. My mother, Susan Mallory, wanted to name me Alexandra Olivia Mallory. My father, Richard ("Ri-card") Kit, wanted me to be Elizabeth Eleanor Kit, after his grandmothers.

There were even discussions about nicknames: Lexy, Olive, Lizzy, Lenny. Frankly, I think I dodged a bullet when they couldn't agree. The lawyers eventually labeled me "Kit/Mallory child" and "Mallory/Kit child" in their files. Consequently, I became the first person to legally have a name that could change, depending on which parent I was with. When I was with my father, I was Mallory Kit, and with my mother, I was Kit Mallory.

To make my childhood more confusing and disruptive, my parents couldn't even stand living on the same planet as each other. I wasn't the first child to be subjected to an interplanetary commute. However, I was pretty sure I was the only one to do it on my birthday. It was a conciliatory agreement to have me spend one year on each planet, so there was no argument about holidays. Because my birthday remained an issue, they stipulated I travel on that day. A sort of "if I can't have her, no one will" clause.

So that's what I did, every year on my birthday. From year one and up.

Before you start to feel sorry for me and my tragic forgotten birthdays, I'll let you know I love space travel. Three days a year, I got to travel the stars, passing planets, and exploring what I called the *black oceans*. I loved my birthdays and if I could have reprogrammed the taxi ship and run away from home, I would have left my family a lot sooner than at seventeen.

But before I get into my escape from joint custody, I must tell you about my handsome, green bodyguard, Terrin. And why my father requisitioned him for me at age fifteen.

Tꜣe Green Guy

I was hanging upside down in a tree when Terrin arrived at my father's estate. (Oh, I should probably mention my father is the president of his planet. Yeah, I suppose that's sort of important.) Even upside down, Terrin's abnormally broad shoulders and thick neck intrigued me. I was only fifteen, but my hormones insisted I was twenty-something. I wanted to marry every handsome man I met, from the gardeners to the lawyers, but this was different.

Although gattaw were a decidedly unattractive green color, they were almost always tall and robustly muscled. Because of their upper body strength, people often hired them for physical labor and security. Their reticent behavior often came across as unintelligent, but nothing about Terrin's behavior seemed oafish to me. He glided along the columns of my father's atrium with an ease of sophistication. The thick boney combs that trailed his horns, down to the base of his scalp, were unobtrusive, blending perfectly with his skin tone.

My father pointed me out across the yard, and he looked at me. His cool gaze examined me like an interesting specimen in a petri dish. It was then I became acutely aware that my dress had long since shifted down to my stomach and I was basically showing the hot new stranger my panties.

I gasped and released my legs. Despite not planning my arrival to the ground eight feet below, I landed on my feet. However, my long beige-tinted hair got tangled in the branches on the way down. I scrambled to unwind my tendrils, but of course, that only made it worse. My ladies in wait—aka hired friends—couldn't get me undone, so they called for help. The attention drew my father, and naturally, Terrin followed him.

Father arrived, shaking his head at my childish antics. He said something about a monkey, but I didn't hear him. My gaze remained fixed on the almost reptilian skin behind him. Perhaps it was because he was exotic to my budding hormones, or maybe it was the way his eyes locked onto mine as hard as mine did his. I couldn't look away, nor was he uncomfortable with my outright stare. At the time, I had hoped he was feeling the same attraction I was, but in my maturity, I now know he was merely evaluating me.

Like a bug.

"Cut the branch!" My father waved his hand, making the bells on his wrist ring—an intentional fashion choice, albeit annoying as hell.

"Nonsense!" Terrin announced, stepping in front of my father. His eyes never left mine as he did. In fact, he never broke eye contact until I did, and then it was a fight to get it back. "The tree has done nothing wrong. It is the child who has tangled herself. Let her accept the punishment for this foolishness, not the tree."

"It's only a branch," my father gently insisted, glancing between the two of us. Apparently, he had never seen his daughter so attentive.

"It is not only a branch." Terrin's dulcet words poured over me. "It is life. It provides fruit, shade, and shelter."

"This isn't a fruit-bearing tree," my father commented, trying to figure out why his companion had suddenly become an advocate for saving trees.

"We must not cut the branch," Terrin continued, employing his Zen logic. "We must cut the hair." His words spilled over me, meaningless in purpose, but so poignant in their baritone beauty.

"I think the branch is dead," my father pointed out, timidly trying to add his own logic back into the mix.

"Allow me," Terrin said as he drew a long copper half-sword from its sheath on his hip. I inhaled, feeling as much tension in that moment as a first kiss. It was at that moment I was truly in love with him.

"I don't see why this is necessary, Terrin." My father attempted to reason with him, but his objections were hesitant. He was no doubt reluctant to antagonize the *gattaw*.

My friends frantically tried to undo the locks of my hair, which were stretched to full length by the pull of the branch. Terrin raised his sword, and the women squealed and scrambled away. Even my father took a graceless step backward to avoid being hurt.

The sword crossed with nary a snag against my tresses. All the while, my eyes remained on Terrin. The branch released and feather-light strands fell into my face, blocking my view of the beautiful stranger I now knew as Terrin.

I looked away to swipe the hair from my eyes, but when I looked back, his attention and his ardor-inspiring fire-brown eyes were gone. He was already discussing business with my father and walking with him back to the house.

I watched him go, silently begging him to look at me once more. To breathe life back into my intolerably boring existence. To love me, marry me, and have beautiful lime green babies with me.

It was nearly five minutes after he left that my revelry evaporated and I realized I had lost eight inches of my long silken hair for a damn dead branch. My visceral castigation of Terrin resounded across the courtyard and, no doubt, well into the mansion's interior.

"Son of a bitch!"

Some Dumb Prophecy

"No, I don't understand because you are not explaining it to me like I am an adult," I insisted as I sat across from my father at our dinner table. I glanced over at Terrin, but he hadn't looked at me since I sat down, and that was only to simper at my *new* hairstyle—a rather creative up-do that hid my shorter strands.

It had been a few days since our first meeting, but he had technically not left the mansion since he arrived. I had wanted to admonish him for his disgraceful regard for my hair—aka scream at him—but I kept missing him. He was either cleverly avoiding me or... Yes, he was most definitely avoiding me. The only reason I hadn't berated him over the appetizers was because father had kept me busy explaining the root system of plants. I felt like a five-year-old learning about botany for the first time.

"Just tell me why he is here." I pointed at Terrin. "It was a simple enough question, I thought," I murmured as I pushed around the last of my peas, which were too stubborn to get on my fork.

"Yes, it is," Terrin interjected. "I am your chaperone."

"Chaperone?" I looked at him and he finally looked back at me. I held his eyes for a moment, but I didn't want to get caught up in his hypnotic gaze and lose an ear, so I returned my attention to my father. "Why do I need a chaperone? I never go anywhere."

"You are getting to that age, my dear, and I can't leave your marital choices to chance."

"Oh, geez. You seriously want me to date with the Green Gateau on my heels?" Terrin perked a brow at me, unable to interpret my insult.

My father looked down at his hands. "You carry a very specific DNA set. A child with a complete, undamaged DNA profile is predicted to be born in my lineage."

"Don't you find it strange that you're referencing a thousand-year-old myth in the same sentence you're talking about DNA? I mean, science or fantasy—pick one. This whole cross-genre stuff is ridiculous."

Richard flushed and opened his mouth to yell at me for my sacrilege, but Terrin touched his arm. "It's not just a religious prophecy," Terrin explained. "Genealogists have marked several times in history when human DNA has coalesced in individuals. The lineage following these... superior humans have little to no health problems, longevity, and above average intelligence. Many families stemming from this broadened DNA pool have been exceedingly intelligent and physically dynamic."

I shook my head. I knew most of this already, but I just didn't believe it. "There is no proof *I* will have a baby with superior DNA."

"That is where faith comes into play," my father said. His tall forehead had creases and his blond hair looked increasingly whiter as the years passed. He didn't look like the harbinger of a grand lineage, but then again, who was to say that beauty was a guarantee of superiority?

"What exactly are you suggesting I do with this gift of potential DNA? Should I mate with someone of equal potential like you and mother and then divorce the minute the pregnancy is successful?"

Richard frowned and pushed his plate away. "I have explained that many times, Mallory."

"Yes, you have, and each time the story of you being a devoted son sounds more and more like *weakness*!" My father's bright blue eyes dimmed and I instantly regretted my jab at his proudest accomplishment.

"Let me speak with her alone," Terrin said.

I rolled my eyes at the suggestion. He was no one to me; what could he possibly say to convince me to tolerate this ridiculous scenario?

Richard glanced at him and stood. He left the table with little more pause than to remove the napkin in his lap. After he was gone, Terrin slipped across to his seat and leaned back to observe me. He raised his hand, dismissing the servants with a wave.

We were alone.

I had never been alone in all my life except during my travels from planet to planet. I had certainly never been alone with a man outside of my relation. As tantalizing as it was, it was also terrifying. Especially after he swiped his arm across the table, dragging every dinner plate and fork down to the floor with a crash.

I jumped at the explosive introduction and glanced at the doors. No one came rushing back in. Not my father. Not my servants. I looked back at Terrin, trying to discern his temperament. Was he mad? Was he amused?

He was neither. He was just observing me, gauging my reaction.

"What the hell?" I pointed to the broken dishes.

"I wanted you to see who is really in charge right now."

"In charge of what—the longevity of china?" I squawked.

He stood abruptly and moved to my side. My heart raced as his belt buckle pushed against my shoulder. "I don't have the luxury of patience." His voice was as smooth as ever, but the threat was unmistakable. "Your father wants to ease you into this, but he has no authority over you anymore. I am not your chaperone. I am your guardian. I am here to keep unsavory characters from impregnating you and wasting your eggs. More importantly, however, I am here to make sure you bear a child, or several, if necessary. The government wants that DNA, and I will ensure its creation.

"What are you going to do, turn me into a breeding cow?" I grimaced.

Terrin leaned down, putting his face mere inches from mine. "I will decide who you can and cannot mate with, but no, I will not force you to be with anyone. That is where fate will still hold true." He stood tall again. "It is a great honor to serve in this capacity, and I take it very seriously. So." He walked over the plates, crunching them into tinier pieces with his weight. "You will do as I say. You will not back-talk me. And you will abide by the rules I create."

"What rules?"

"Rule number one! You will not interrupt me. Rule number two! I will be in your presence at all times, except for personal moments, in which I will submit to having a door between us. Rule number three! We are not friends or family... or lovers." He looked back at me, breaking my still naïve heart with the perceptive accusation. "Rule number four! You will behave respectfully in my presence. Rule number five...!"

Let me just skip the rest of this because it went on for almost ten minutes, specifying the food I should eat, and the amount of outdoor activity I should take part in. I was basically a cross between a houseplant and a farm animal by the time he was done.

Let's fast forward about a year. To the point in time where most of his rules had gone out the window because spending that much time with anyone is bound to break down reservations, no matter what species you are.

Fatal Loins

"**D**o you see that one?" I asked, smooshing my face against the triple-layer glass to see the planet we were passing. "That one is uninhabitable, but I heard they installed a reading station in the upper atmosphere to monitor the weather and measure the chemical content of the air."

"Why do such a thing if no one will ever live there?" Terrin asked in a sullen tone.

I looked over at him. He looked greener than usual. "What's wrong, horn-head?" I grabbed one of his three-inch stumps and shook his head.

"Do not touch the horns," he rumbled.

"Why? Does it turn you on?" I asked, falsely seductive.

He turned his head slowly and glared at me. It only made me smile. "You kept them long," I pointed out, tapping the rounded nubs. From what he had told me, the horns grew from the inside out, so he had to file them down regularly to keep them from getting a sharp tip.

He noted my attentions as usual, but also as usual, he did nothing to encourage them. "How much longer until we reach your mother's planet?"

"Bra-ha-ma," I pronounced again with a giggle. "Come on, Terrin, you can say it." I leaned over in front of him, my freshly colored coral hair draped down across his knees.

"I will not demean myself by offering you entertainment."

"Oh, but you do that every day, just by being you."

"Look at your stars, girl, and leave me alone."

"Why won't you stargaze with me?" I asked, sincerely hurt.

He sighed. "I am not accustomed to space travel. The shifting of gravitational forces tends to unease my digestion."

I snorted. "You're getting seasick... or space sick."

"Yes."

I laughed, but I could see he wasn't joking. He looked ill, and he was even breathing through his mouth, which meant he was feverish. He didn't have sweat glands, so there wasn't much he could do to cool down, aside from outright panting like a dog, and he would have to be very near death to resort to that indignity.

"Why didn't you opt to sleep through the journey?" I asked. He looked at me, answering my absurd question with his narrow-eyed stare. "Is there anything I can do to help?"

"It will pass. It just takes some time. A few more hours should do it. I can't express how happy I am that you only do this once a year."

"Well, I guess that settles it." I slumped down next to him with my back to the long bench seating lining either side of the passenger cabin. They served as both seats and beds during long-term travel.

"That settles what?" he finally asked when it was clear I wouldn't tell him until he did.

"I can't marry you."

He turned slowly to face me, and I expected the usual disciplining scowl, but he was smiling flirtatiously at me. I smiled back, unable to resist his charms when he actually used them.

"Do you know why they chose me to watch over you instead of a human?" he asked with baited enthusiasm lingering in his tone. "Have you ever seen a human woman and a male gattaw in a relationship?"

"I have seen no one in a relationship. I live in a secure facility laughably called a home."

"Well, allow me to illustrate why we are not compatible."

"What, you don't like me?" I whined, giving him my best pouty lips.

"We are not sexually compatible," he specified. I made the mistake of looking over his body, trying to find the incompatible parts. "I suppose I should say that our genitals are well-suited for each other." My mouth went dry somewhere around "genitals" but it wasn't until my focus returned to his face that I thought he might actually be flirting with me. My eyes danced over his, searching for some signal to begin my lean in for a kiss.

"We are?" I gulped and licked my lips.

"Oh, yes, I think we would fit nicely together. And at first you would enjoy the feel of my swelling member inside of you, throbbing with the beat of my heart."

My eyes widened, and I almost choked on my spit. Completely dismissive of the obvious impropriety of the conversation, I started to pant and imagine what I had only read and dreamed about.

"Unfortunately, at full arousal, the splaying of my penile spurs would shred your cervix, decimate your chances of having children, and possibly kill you before the act concluded."

I stared at him with a horrified grimace. He wasn't joking, and he wasn't saying it to tease me. He wanted me to understand that we *literally* were not compatible. This was a lesson I was old enough to learn. Or perhaps my love-starved flirting had finally annoyed him enough to do something about it.

I put away thoughts of first kisses and romantic trips to and from my homes. This was not the makings of a love story, no matter how I angled it.

Rather than admit to how heartbreaking that was to my still adolescent ideals, I let out a dejected exhale and exaggerated my frown. "So, you're just not that into me?"

He chuckled, which sounded strange for two reasons: one, his throat gurgled when he did it, and two, he never laughed at my jokes. "No, Princess, I'm not *that* into you."

"Oh, God, don't start the royalty stuff already. The last thing I need is you calling me 'your highness' and bowing."

"I will do what is appropriate."

I frowned at him. "What is appropriate is for the only constant in my life to continue being constant."

He nodded. "What name *do* you prefer? Kit or Mallory?"

"I don't know, but I like the way you say Mallory."

"Then I will continue to call you Mallory, but in the presence of your queen mother, I will call you Princess Mallory."

"Fine, but for the record, I hate it."

"Noted. Now, if you'll excuse me, I am going to expurgate my most recent meal."

"Hurl away, my friend." I waved him away and went back to looking at the stars.

The Queen

I suppose you were wondering about that. Yes, it's true, I'm a princess, but it's such a hackneyed plot base I didn't want to bring it up until it was absolutely necessary. Not that it matters; my father is practically a king, anyway. And you also have to remember these are minor planets, with small populations. Nothing like our Earth origins.

Oh, hell, why do I bother? You've already deemed me to be a spoiled brat, no matter how I explain it. So, let's just move on. The pampered princess comes home to her palace to be pimped out by her parents because of a pointless prophecy.

"Kit!" Susan ran, or rather swept, across the marbled entryway and smothered me in her ample bosom. I had so often wished I could grow faster so I could escape the barrage of mom boobs, but I was pretty sure she was wearing higher heels to compensate for my growth. "Oh, how I have missed you." She cried, squeezing my cheeks and kissing my head in every spot except my lips.

"Mmm-ver, ay I pee-sent," I raised my hand to Terrin. "Te-in—"

"Oh, never mind that." Susan pushed me away and looked over at the green stranger in her foyer. "Darling, why don't you run along to the drawing room so I can have a chat with your bodyguard?"

I glanced at Terrin. He was already prepared to object to the separation. "I can't, Mother," I interjected quickly to keep things civil. "He is my guardian; he won't leave my side. And I won't leave his," I added as a gesture to make my mother understand where I stood on the subject.

Terrin glanced at me; pride written all over his face. By this point in our relationship, it was hard to decide who was in charge. He gave all the orders, but in the end, everything he did served me.

"This is ridiculous. Your father is taking a prophecy and turning it into a scientific endeavor. Just like he did with us. I tell you, girl, you can lead a horse to water, but you can't make her marry an ass."

I glanced at Terrin, hoping he had understood that logic, but he seemed to search me for the same answer. We walked on behind Mother as she led us into the drawing room. I hadn't been prepared to meet anyone, but inside the sunny fabric-smothered room were eight men.

"Oh, shit," I muttered and took a step backward. I hit Terrin's firm chest and decided it was as good a place as any to hide.

"Darling, these are the eight most eligible suitors in the district." My mother waved her hand over the selection. She introduced them even though I didn't hear or remember any of the names. My eyes swept over the cheerful, handsome faces, searching for one that wasn't intent on impregnating me before I left the room. "They will be your escorts for meals, gatherings, and dances. You may alternate them as you like, but I want you to spend some time with each one of them before you dedicate yourself. You never know where you'll find love."

When the green man behind me didn't saddle up his white horse, I kicked his shin. He shifted to attention and stepped beside me. "With all due respect, Your Majesty, these men will have to be tested for DNA viability. I can't allow Princess Mallory to—"

"Kit," my mother said, breaking Terrin's cardinal rule. "You may call her Princess Kit."

Terrin looked over at me. His amusement was evident. My mother was trying to bully him, but of course, that didn't work with him.

"May I speak to you outside, Highness?"

"I thought you couldn't leave Kit's side?"

"I would be happy to explain the specifics of our rules, but first you and I need to clarify a few things."

My mother's mouth twisted with wicked amusement. "Yes, I think we do." She stomped out the door we had just come through.

"Terrin—" I objected.

"Sit here," he commanded, and I sat on the polka dot chaise lounge.

"My mother is not as easygoing as my father," I warned.

"Nor am I as gentle as I was with you and your father. Your mother will soon learn who is really in charge here."

"Yes, yes, the speech, the rules, but she has an army."

He leaned in next to my ear and whispered, "So do I." He drew back and looked at the men awaiting my attention. "You! All of you! She is off limits until I have approved you. Understood?" The men nodded in staggered unison.

I stood, but Terrin shoved me down. "Sit here. I will not say it again."

I stared at him coolly and crossed my arms, but I didn't get up. Out the door he went, and the excitement began. The yelling was impressive, but after a half hour, my mother lost her voice, and then it was only Terrin spouting his rules.

His endless, endless rules.

Rules

I sat on the edge of my mother's wading pool with my feet in the water. The little fish nibbled at my toes, tickling them. It usually made me giggle, but I was not in the mood for hilarity. I stared out onto the waterscape, wishing I could truly be alone.

"Are you still mad at me?" Terrin's bare feet plopped into the water, scaring the fish away completely. I glanced over at his leathery green feet and black claws.

"They think you're a crocodile. You scared them all half to death."

"Answer me."

"And what if I don't?" I twisted to face him. "What if I break your rules? What if I run off with Jeffrey, the unapproved-DNA guy?" Terrin's expression remained stoic, still waiting for his answer. "Yes, I'm still mad. You humiliated me. You treated me like your pet."

"I can't help but think this argument would not be happening if I hadn't told you we couldn't be a couple. I think I preferred you slightly smitten."

"I don't care what you prefer." I shook my head. "This is my life. Do you hear me? I thought we had an understanding, a friendship of sorts."

"Rule number three. You should have listened better."

"Is that what you want? You want us to be nothing. We will spend every waking moment together, eating and sleeping in the same room for another year or until I find a suitor, and you want us to be nothing to each other?"

"You knew the rules."

"Screw the rules!"

"Quiet. I will not tolerate disrespect.

"Or what?" I taunted him. His hand was on my face before I could question his angry expression. My cheek burned, though not as hot as I know it could have. He was holding back. He just wanted to keep control of the situation. Though I knew it would only take one mention of the assault to my mother to get him fired—or worse, I didn't actually want him gone. "Go on," I said, turning the other cheek to him.

He looked away, directing his gaze to the water. He seemed disappointed in himself. He wasn't the type to rile easily, certainly not because of a human girl. "You try my patience so much, Mallory."

"I know," I admitted, rubbing my cheek.

"I do not want to hurt you, but you must understand this is my duty. It is something which I cannot do casually."

"Your *duty*..." I cringed, feeling my tears come on. "...is also a human being. And I'm not pointing out my species. I mean, I am a person. This might be your duty, but this is also my *life*, and everyone has been trying to ruin it since I was born. Do you know how much I want to pack my bags and leave this all behind?"

"Mallory—"

"Don't tell me it will all be okay!" I sniffled and wiped my nose before I realized I had interrupted him. "I'm sorry. What were you going to say?"

"I was going to say that there is not a circumstance in this universe in which you could escape my side. And if there was, you would not get far, because I would hunt you down and return you to your obligations."

I stared at his cold, hard gaze, trying to figure out which part of the reddish-brown eyes I had ever found compassion in. I mistakenly believed we were friends, but he was actually one of my jailers. "From now on, I want you out of my sight," I said, my eyes freshly dry of tears. "I want your presence to be a flurry in my peripheral, a shadow in the night and the day, and if your hand so much as threatens my face again, I will throw myself off a roof and end this bizarre matchmaking scheme for everyone."

His body tensed as his chest puffed, but he didn't say another word before disappearing into the veil of bushes surrounding the reflecting pool. I, on the other hand, relaxed and flopped to the edge of the pool so my tears could fall unnoticed into the water.

Thrust to the Wall

I dated. Oh, how I dated. So many young stupid boys wanted to be the ones to help bring medical cures to humanity through perfect-DNA babies. I wasn't even sure that was really the goal, but in the end that was what the prophecy and the scientists were toting, so if you weren't on board, it meant you didn't want to cure disease.

My sycophant boyfriends arrived at my door early to bring me coffee and pastries. They arrived midday to walk with me in the gardens. After dinner, I watched the sunset with them. They even showed up in the middle of the night, bravely sneaking into my room to kiss me goodnight.

To my surprise, Terrin did not interfere with my interactions with my male companions. Once he had approved them all as worthy DNA subjects—except for poor Jeffrey—he didn't seem to care what happened. Unlike a true chaperone, he was supportive of me getting pregnant, regardless of my marital status.

It was on one such night that his resolution to his duty became a problem.

Lex, one of the oldest suitors, was sensing his attentions were not being received well. I hadn't meant to exclude him, but he was simply not my type. I hadn't been aware I had a type, but apparently lanky and hairy was not my preference. That, and his breath smelled like food all the time.

I had slipped into bed when there was a knock on my door. Reluctantly, I got up to accept the now choreographed goodnight kiss that several of the men had scheduled with me. I wasn't sure how they agreed on what nights, but they never deviated. It took some of the romance out of it, but it was better than kissing three different men in the same night.

It hadn't occurred to me that this was no one's designated night until I opened the door to find Lex standing there. He pushed in before I could question his arrival. He shoved the door closed and pulled me into a heated kiss. Heated on his side, at least.

I pushed him away. "Lex, what the hell? This is my bedroom. You need to come back tomorrow."

"No, don't you see? It's the prophecy."

"Yeah, yeah, that's why we are all in this stupid dating game." I glanced around, looking for Terrin's shadow, but he blended in so well, I rarely noticed him during the day, let alone night. I often wondered how he could sleep standing up, but apparently it wasn't a problem for him.

"Dating is unnecessary, only conception."

"Technically, neither is necessary." I moved to open the door, but he blocked my path.

"I am the one to fulfill this prophecy. I will be the father of the perfect child."

"Perfect child? Geez, what are they spewing out there? Look, Lex, I understand you want to be a part of something great, but I don't like you that way. I've just started dating and I know 16 is old enough to make a baby, but I don't want one right now."

"The prophecy demands a child."

"I don't love you, Lex."

"The prophecy does not demand love." His features shifted incrementally, but I could see it and I knew enough to fear it. "Whether you accept me as your lover tonight, I will be a part of the future."

I froze, unprepared to handle the decision facing me. Choose him or be raped by him. What a lovely story to share with our children and grandchildren!

He moved forward, and I bolted around the center table in my room, which served no other purpose than to hold flowers. I darted toward the shadow on the far wall that looked like a gattaw standing between the columns. Before I made it to the sanctuary of inhuman strength, Lex yanked me back by my long coral locks.

I yelped as I hit the floor. He muffled my shriek with an enthusiastic kiss. I bit him and he pulled away. Rather than beat me for the indiscretion, he did what he had come for.

I expected him to drag me to the oversized bed, but he didn't. He didn't even try to smother my screams for help. He simply undid his pants and ripped away the thin panties from under my nightgown. I kicked at him, but he seemed oblivious to the pain I caused him. Then he was on top of me, shifting to find entrance.

It was happening too fast.

I needed time to think. To strategize. To find an exit strategy.

I pushed and shoved against my attacker, but such was the difference in strength between men and women. When it was clear I had no options beyond being a damsel in distress, I screamed, "Terrin!" The outcry nearly shattered my voice box, but my hero did not come. "PLEASE!"

"I cannot interfere with the natural way," he explained from the shadows.

"This is NOT the natural way!" He didn't answer, so I screamed and bit Lex. Something I did finally affected him and he hissed in pain before continuing with his task. "I hate you!" I said, not identifying who should have the honor. "I hate all of you!" I fell back crying against the floor. There was no one to save me. Everyone wanted a piece of me from the day I was born; why should this moment be any different?

I gave in and waited for the event to be over. I had no more control over it than any other in my life. I might as well make everyone happy and get pregnant.

Lex fumbled quickly to get himself into me while I was still yielding. I closed my eyes and prepared for my defilement, but he halted. I heard a solemn yelp from him and the sound of glass shattering. I opened my eyes and saw Terrin looming over me, breathing hard like a bull ready to charge. Lex was on the floor to my left, along with the remnants of my full-length mirror.

When he rose, he looked at Terrin, somehow hurt by his reaction. "I am the prophecy!" he demanded, shaking his fists like a spoiled child. His still exposed flopping member did nothing to diminish the imagery.

"No, you're not. You're just a horny little boy with no honor. You are no longer welcome here. Leave now or I will crush your skull in as many pieces as that mirror." Terrin poised his body to attack, but the boy remained still as Terrin's threat broke his resolve.

"I just wanted to help my people." Lex looked down at me, forlorn, seeking forgiveness, but I had none to offer him. He was a brainwashed idiot, and I understood how he had come to this conclusion, but I didn't understand how he could think his abuse was justified.

Terrin escorted the boy out with a firm grip on the nape of his neck. He watched at the door for a minute before shutting it and locking it. He waited at the door for another moment before he returned to me. I was still lying on the floor, trying not to pity myself. He extended his hand, and I let him pull me up.

Somewhere in between my instincts of self-preservation and my desire to have some control of my life, I found the nerve to slap him. Gattaw were not a gentle people, nor were they tolerant of physical authority, especially from humans, but he didn't slap me back.

When it was clear my hand had not wounded his face as deeply as he had my heart, I slapped him again. I cried at seeing that he still had nothing to say to me. No apologies for standing by as a man attacked me.

I slapped him again and again.

I was still expecting him to throw me across the room for my audacity, but he didn't. He took my abuse with stoic resolve. When it was clear he had no intention of defending himself, I leaned my head against his chest and wept.

A moment later, I felt him take in a deep inhalation. His arms reached around me, holding me. I sunk into the embrace further, clasping my hands around his back. He pressed my head to against him and stroked my hair.

After that night, an unspoken truce had been reached. I accepted his oppressive presence willingly, and he started treating me like a person instead of a duty.

Back and Forth and Back

"Can I ask you something?" I posed after three days of reading, trivia games, and inflight movies.

Terrin looked up from his reading pad. He perked his hairless brow. "It's not about the gattaw reproductive cycle again, is it?"

"No." I chuckled. "God no. I could have gone another year without that explanation."

"What is it then?" He put down his book to listen.

"Are they pressuring you to get me pregnant?"

He looked down momentarily. "You don't need to worry about that, Mallory. I'm not going to rush you."

"But they are, aren't they?"

He shrugged. "They just hate waiting. You're seventeen now. A reasonable age by most standards to bear a child. You are further ahead in your education than the average human of your age. And it's not as if you need to supply an income. You could focus on motherhood."

"What about love?"

Terrin frowned, but he quickly covered it with a smile. "I'm sure you will find someone who can provide you with both love and a family."

I shook my head. "I'm a princess with superior DNA. As if money wasn't enough of an issue, I have to find a man who wants me for me and not my biological potential. Whatever happened to a good old-fashioned player, who just wants you for your body?"

"I know this isn't easy, but it is important. You know that, right? You know that a being with perfect DNA could provide a map doctors could use to cure diseases—and not just humans. There are countless species that could benefit from this. They could even unlock traits that have been dormant in humans since the dawn of time."

"They have you pretty brainwashed, don't they?"

Terrin narrowed his eyes at this suggestion. "I agree with the goal, that's all. Beyond that, this is—"

"Just a job?"

"That's not how I meant it. I think you know by now my efforts to remain indifferent to your charms are futile."

"Are you saying I'm charming?"

"You are tolerable most days. Today notwithstanding." He winked and lifted his pad again.

"How much money am I worth?"

He licked his lips and dropped his book again. "Pardon?"

"You heard me." I puckered my lips in thought. "How much money could the government make off of my baby's DNA? Give or take a few billion."

Terrin stared at me introspectively. "I really don't know the answer to that, Mallory. I would love to tell you that I am not being paid extremely well for my duties, but I am. You are a project that requires time and funding." His brow deepened sympathetically. "To answer your previous question more accurately, the more time you take to *fall in love,* the more money they have to spend. So, yes, they will become increasingly more impatient, and eventually I will have to encourage you to find someone, or lose my position. And I don't want anyone else handling this."

"Neither do I."

"I know. That is why I am going to do my best to help you find love, or at least a lover. You have your whole life to find love."

The Dead Guy

And so, we come to my most epic moment. The moment I single-handedly shamed my best friend, abandoned my parents, retreated from my duties, and achieved my dreams.

It was the stars; you see. I couldn't resist them. They were my first and truest love. For three days each year, I found sanctuary in them. They never left my thoughts, not during the brightness of the day, and certainly not when my eyes closed at night. It was all I wanted. All I had *ever* wanted.

I stepped out of the taxi ship with Terrin gently corralling me forward. He was sick, as usual. Landings seemed to be worse than take offs for him. I moved forward and let him pass. He paused at the end of the ramp, scarcely containing his meal.

"Terrin are you—"

He held up a hand waving me away.

"I'm gonna take a walk. You collect yourself and then we'll head home."

He waved an objection and then pinched his fingers together.

"I'll stay close." I rubbed his back, which seemed to cause more lurching, so I stopped.

I walked around the bustling space dock. The ships arriving wafted hot wind into the area, making my long navy-blue hair tangle. I pulled it to the side and wrapped it in a tight knot before proceeding further into the port. I glanced back to see if Terrin was missing me, but he was gone, no doubt giving in to using a public restroom.

After weaving through push carts and small vehicles dragging fuel barrels, I found an empty aisle and wandered down it. The further I got, the more dilapidated the ships looked. The area served as long-term parking; however, some ships looked like they had been there for years.

I found a small crowd of men near an outmoded ship. There was some bidding going on and the men were frantically one-upping each other. By the severity of the endeavor, I might have assumed they were bidding on valuable art, but as it was, the bid wasn't even high enough to pay for a lightyear of fuel. The excitement seemed to be in the deal they were going to get on the rust-bucket before them.

"What is this?" I asked a young man in the back row who was taking measurements of the ship with a laser pointer. He looked at me with peculiar distrust, and then his eyes widened.

"Should you be here?" He looked around for my security. "Alone?" he added.

"My bodyguard's indisposed. What's going on here?"

"We're bidding on a freezer lock."

"What's a freezer lock?" I asked.

He seemed a little annoyed, but since he recognized me, he must have decided I was important enough to bother with. "These are all freezer locks." He motioned to all the ships in the section. "They're ships that have been found floating in space because their captains either didn't wake up from hypersleep or died en route."

"These ships have been confiscated? Can you do that? What if the captains wake up?"

He shook his head. "Not a chance. We give them four years from the initial freeze date. After that, they are legally dead and we sell the ship and donate the body."

"So, this ship's captain has been asleep for four years?"

"Four years and thirteen minutes." He tapped his tablet.

"What happens to the body?"

"Cadaver."

I grimaced at the thought, since it meant it would technically be a live cadaver. Surgical practice and whatnot. "And there is no chance they can wake up?"

"The probability of waking up after two years is pretty small. After three years, it's classified as a miracle, and after four, well, that's just a myth."

"Sold!" the auctioneer announced.

"Excellent." The man smiled at me.

"You won? I didn't even know you were bidding."

"I always win." He winked at me and moved forward to collect his prize. The other men cleared out, and I moved forward to observe the transaction.

"Here is your key card, Mr. Davis."

"Thank you." He smirked and held up the card to me. "Want to go for a spin?"

I smiled and shook my head. "No, my chaperone would have a fit. Why do you need a key card? Isn't this new enough to have a laser-scan ID?"

"Oh, yeah, but it's a pain in the ass to get it switched over, so they make a key card to bypass the scan so I can get it started and get it the hell out of here as soon as possible."

"It actually runs?" I asked.

"Yeah, you missed the test run. It's actually a pretty nice boat. Too bad I have to scrap it."

"Why do you have to scrap it?"

"It's too old. No one will buy it. I can get more with the parts than the ship." Mr. Davis twirled the key around his finger. "You sure you don't want to go for a ride?"

I glanced over to see if Terrin was waiting for me. "I really don't have time, but maybe you could give me a tour."

"Sure thing." He waved me to follow him and we slipped up the ramp into the belly of the cargo bay. Toward the bow, we passed several storage rooms. Davis explained the ship's capacity, but it didn't register with me since I didn't ship products.

We climbed a flight of stairs to the passenger cabins. They were small but adequate, and enough to hold three dozen people, which surprised me since the ship was relatively small.

"With luxury comes size," Davis explained.

We climbed up another stairwell and he pointed out the mechanics of the ship: the engine room, which took up the whole aft upper and middle decks. There was extensive plumbing and duct work accessible through the floor of the upper level. Most of the workstations were on this level in semi-transparent cubicles.

"This is where the crew would monitor the ship's systems and adjust environmental controls."

"How many do you need to crew this ship?"

"Originally four or five, but this one was upgraded to a pretty expansive autopilot, so just one or two, depending on what kind of workload one wants to take on. The cockpit is pretty archaic, but it has a modern J2 operating system. Anyone with a degree in astro-aviation could fly it."

I nodded. "Been there, done that."

"You're a pilot?"

"Much to my parents' dismay. Wasted degree, they said."

"You're young for a pilot's license."

"I'm young for a lot of things, but I don't have the luxury to take advantage of it." I cleared my throat. "Can I see it?"

"The cockpit? Sure!"

"No." I paused. "The hypersleep pod," I said carefully.

"Morbid curiosity, huh? I understand. Can't blame you. Come on, I'll show you."

Davis led me toward the cockpit, but we veered off to the right to a door with the ship's insignia plastered on it.

He pushed open the door and revealed a twin bed that may as well have been a king compared to the passenger cots. Someone neatly tucked gray-blue sheets onto the bed, demonstrating military precision. The shelves over the bed were full of various medals and trophies.

"What are the awards for?" I asked.

Davis glanced over the shelves and moved to investigate. "I don't know."

I bypassed the closet and went straight for the elephant in the room: a sleep pod, not unlike a sun bed, sat at the back of the room in an alcove. The surrounding screens and steady beeps from the mechanisms all conveyed one thing to me: life. This man was alive, but forever trapped. It was a toss-up of who was crueler: Davis for wanting to dispose of the body, or me for wanting to keep it in this perpetual state.

I lifted the lid of the pod, which was really only a low-level radiation chamber, offering Vitamin D. Inside, the lined bed rippled at designated increments, massaging the tissues so the pilot didn't get bed sores while he slept. The nose tubes provided oxygen and a slow drip of nutrients to the stomach. Very important not to get those mixed up. His muscles twitched sporadically as the electrodes glued to his skin allocated electrical pulses, preventing atrophy. Other than a few heart and oxygen monitors trailing from the body, the captain was naked.

To make matters worse, he was glorious. He was tall, broad, and muscular. His toned arms looked strong, even in their relaxation. His cream skin looked healthy and silky to the touch, though I didn't dare touch him. I ignored his lower nudity, since I didn't know what to appreciate about it in this relaxed state. His short auburn hair sat tightly on his scalp—despite the years that had passed, the stasis had only allowed his hair to grow enough to curl around his ears. His eyes were closed, but I suspected they would be brown, maybe with a tinge of red, like Terrin's.

He was beautiful, and it was a crime he couldn't wake up, but Davis was right. He was dead. He was Snow White on a cosmic level.

Unfortunately, I was quite certain my kiss would not wake him from his living death. Nothing short of the will of God could do that, and I wasn't much for prayer.

"Looks like he's a jack of all trades. Some competitive driving, archery, marksmanship, boxing, and—huh, a pie-eating contest. Well, the man at least had a fulfilling life and a sense of humor."

"I'll take it," I said without turning to look at him. I couldn't take my eyes off the captain.

"Ahhh, no, I don't think you understand. There are strict rules for body recovery. I can either donate him as organs, or leave him hooked up, but that's it."

I blinked away my confusion and turned to Davis. "No, the ship. I'll take it. I'll buy it."

"I just bought it." He shrugged.

"You said yourself you're going to scrap it."

"At a significant profit," he said, recoiling from my perceived presumption.

"And you still will."

"Yeah right, you're kidding."

"Listen Davis, I need a ship, and I need it now. You know who I am, and how much my credit stamp is worth, so shoot me a number."

Stoney Limits

"How long before the transfer goes through?" I murmured as I headed toward Terrin. He looked unhappy that I had slipped away. He had long since stopped monitoring my movements with a magnifying glass, but it didn't mean he wasn't doing it with a telescope. I waved at him.

"About five minutes." Davis poked at his computer pad, finishing up the last of my paperwork. "After that, the ship can be taken out of the dock, once the clearance from the tower is given."

"And how long does that take?" I asked.

"There isn't a lot of traffic from that section, so maybe a minute and a half after the request is submitted."

"You might get in trouble for this," I warned.

Davis snickered. "Yeah right. *I* was never here." He veered off before I could ask what he meant.

"Who was that?" Terrin asked, looking over Davis suspiciously.

"Another in a long line of *not interested* men." I huffed an exhale and hooked my hand into Terrin's arm. "Feeling better?"

"Much. Where were you?"

"I told you." I nodded to Davis.

"You didn't spend twenty minutes flirting. Where were you?" He stared me down.

I tipped my head back and sighed. "I was star-gazing. What else? Junior Megabucks over there thought he could impress me with his ample portfolio. It took him ten minutes of hard flirting to realize he was vaunting to a princess who was set to inherit a quarter of the freaking galaxy. Then suddenly he was only interested in my portfolio, and that isn't a metaphor."

"Perhaps you should seek a man who isn't interested in money or power."

"Oh, that's genius. Have you met one of those lately?" I checked my wrist com for the time and started walking. "Even you can't claim to be above monetary compensation."

"It's not unheard of for people to require incomes." He walked with me, allowing my arm to remain hooked in his as I counted our steps. "Gattaw and human alike, we all have to eat."

"Yes, I understand that."

"I'm not sure you do. You've led a rather sheltered and privileged life in the last seventeen years. Do you really think you understand what it's like outside of the bosom of your family?"

"You think my dreams of space travel are an ignorant fantasy, don't you?"

"I think your dreams of space travel are based on pretty stars and magnanimous planets. It's one thing to hop from planet to planet, but to actually travel outside of our system is dangerous and lonely."

"Lonelier than being stifled by my parents?" I stopped at the door to the transport. The door to the boxcar slid open, allowing us entrance, and we stepped aboard.

"Careful, Mallory, you're starting to sound spoiled."

"Starting? I thought I landed that part on my twelfth birthday when I was screaming at my father for getting me a pony instead of a unicorn."

Terrin smirked at my quip and touched my cheek with his stubby, black-clawed hand. I always expected his touch to be cool, but it was hot. "I imagine you have grown some since then. And for the record, although you may be lonely, you are not alone."

My heart ached at his sentiment. Why did he have to be so damn sympathetic now? Before I could stop myself or second-guess my reasoning, I kissed him. Fueled by broken remnants of my childish crush, my impassioned kiss also contained guilty torment.

I stepped away from him as the doors sounded to shut. His eyes were instinctively closed, so he didn't see me step off the tram and back onto the space dock. I didn't wait to see his befuddlement when he opened his eyes. I sprinted down the long central lane we had come up through.

People leaped frantically out of my way, fearful I might run them over or collide with them. I must have looked like a fugitive, because I had security radioing in from every transport I passed.

I turned into the nearly vacant freezer lock section and slipped on something wet—hopefully grease. I righted myself and saw a green head bobbing through the crowd after me. He was quick. He was always quick.

I pushed on, not willing to stop now. I had the means. I had the opportunity. And despite what Terrin believed, I had the courage. Naivety was certainly a birthright for me, but I combated it every second of my life with a hard-earned education. Even Terrin had no idea what I was capable of.

I saw the ship ahead, and I made my lungs burn to get there faster. My feet clanked up the metal ramp, and I slammed my hand on the door close button.

I climbed the emergency ladder that went directly to the cockpit, buying me vital seconds. I pushed through the metal hatch and jumped into the captain's chair.

I shoved the key card into the slot, and the buttons and screens popped to life. I started the engine and put on my headphones. The tower clicked on as soon as I saw Terrin come into view through my windshield, surrounded by security guards. Everyone was radioing into the tower, trying to stop me.

"Tower this is—" I yanked up my arm and read off the numbers to my ship. "I'm requesting immediate flight."

"That's a negative. Freeze lock 8-6-9 is not cleared," the tower supervisor announced in a mechanical voice.

"The clearance is coming through now. I am requesting an immediate medical evacuation."

"8-6-9, we are receiving a contradictory request from someone outside of your ship. Explain your current condition and purpose."

"I bet you are," I mumbled. "The man outside of the ship is an impostor. He has just attempted to assassinate President Kit's daughter. I need him detained for questioning, but in the meantime, I need to get her to a medical facility."

"I can't authorize that, ma'am."

"No, but I can. Executive order Richard Kit 3-8-9-1-6-5, alpha, theta, bravo."

There was a brief pause on the other end. "Executive order cleared; you may proceed through bay twelve to your immediate left."

I heard the clamps release, and I engaged the lift thrusters. I felt the beast shimmy as it lifted, but it rose. I dipped the nose and angled myself port-side.

I could see Terrin on the tarmac, successfully wrestling away from six men. He saw me through the glass and halted. He bared his teeth in a snarl I had never witnessed. He mouthed, or perhaps he was yelling, "*I will find you.*"

I knew he was right, but the question was... when.

I ignored his fury, as well as my guilt. The bay doors opened, and I maneuvered the ship into the pressure lock. The doors closed behind me, and in an instant, the expulsion of atmosphere propelled the ship into space.

Adding to the momentum, I turned on the thrusters. The ship bucked forward with impressive speed and I sat back in my seat to watch the stars at a cruising speed that would keep me free.

Tℏe Boy Toy

Two years later.

I stepped out of the bank with my cash in hand. I had been using cash during my long-term stays to keep the bounty hunters off my trail. I knew they were following me, but in the last few months, they seemed to have disappeared from my wake. This naturally made me even more paranoid.

Every day, I expected Terrin to step into my path, but I was always two steps ahead of him. I supposed in some ways I wanted him to find me, but only because life in space was as lonely as he said it would be.

Since I had a cargo ship, it was easy to find work. There were always people to transfer, packages to drop, and assorted don't-ask-don't-tell cargo to be delivered. It took me a while to get the hang of whom to trust and not to trust, but even that changed from day to day.

I pulled up the hood of my brown jacket and pushed through the crowded foggy streets of the planet Pallo. I couldn't tell you what city I was in. I barely kept track of the solar system, let alone the planet or port.

This planet, however, had an interesting story that made it memorable. It once had a system of vast oceans, not dissimilar to old Earth. However, a few hundred years ago, a passing asteroid, with a massive gravitational pull, decompressed the planet's atmosphere and dragged away every bit of breathable air.

The planet might have died, but the sudden shift in pressure cold-boiled the oceans, sending an immense amount of moisture into the atmosphere. That water converted into oxygen and hydrogen. The oxygen replaced the breathable air in the troposphere, while the hydrogen rose to the mesosphere, immediately rebuilding the atmosphere from the ground up.

The death toll for the population was still catastrophic, but eventually, things balanced out and the people learned to live without the oceans. The perpetual monsoon forecast gave them an endless supply of rainwater. However, when it wasn't raining, it was blindingly foggy.

There was no asking for directions. There were no scenic tours. There wasn't even the luxury of strolling casually to your destination. The only mode of transportation was a bumper car game through a deluge of people just as blinded by the misty veil as you.

I pressed on, ignoring my instincts to apologize for my missteps. The flashing lights that pierced the fog gave me an inkling of which direction I was going. My tracking device was coming in handy since I now needed my ship to find me, instead of the other way around.

I kept my money firmly in my hand since pick-pocketing was a career field here. The prostitution, however, was something I had not expected. There was apparently a great demand for public fornication in the area. I had gotten propositioned—or should I say groped—more during my brief visit than in my entire endless year of dating back home.

My elation at finding my ship turned to alarm as someone pushed me against the hull and pinned me there. I reached for my weapon, but a hand pressed firmly against mine. "Wait," a man whispered in my ear. "I'm not going to hurt you."

"Yeah right." I gripped the handle.

"I can help you."

"I'm not interested in a quickie, but thank you," I grumbled and tried to move.

"I'm not offering a quickie," he said, pressing his body closer to mine. His hand slipped around to my backside, cupping my ass. I immediately thought of my key card—even though I had already stuffed it in my bra—and followed with my hand to safeguard it. "I can be yours," he murmured softly.

"My what?" I shifted to see his face. Even through the fog, I could see his beautiful pale brown eyes and thick, dark hair. He noted my appraisal and smirked. He was no doubt accustomed to women's approval.

"Anything you want," he drawled and moved back to my ear. "I will be your slave in all things." His voice was silky with the promise of proficiency. "Your lover." He kissed my neck and his lips made the same promise. The tantalizing offer sent shivers down my body, and for a moment, I forgot about tricks and traps. "Your everything." He brushed his lips across my cheek. "Just get me the hell off this planet." He kissed my lips before I could ask him to translate his request.

His experienced and wanton kiss contained a neediness and urgency that ruined the moment for me. Not that I stopped him—it was still a damn good kiss, and as I said, the galaxy was a lonely place. I heard a *thunk* behind us. I opened my eyes amid my increasingly tangible attentions to determine the threat. A loud pop sounded, coinciding with a forceful expulsion of air. The fog before me bloomed away in a negative mushroom cloud, revealing a small metal ball on the ground.

The clearing allowed me to see an approaching gang of thugs. The four-armed human and humanoid men arrived in rain gear not unlike my jacket—although perhaps a little less stylish. They also had the addition of micro-fans on their shoulders, which likely allowed them better vision in the fog.

I pulled my gun, but kept it low in a universal symbol of "hey look, I have a gun, but I'd rather walk away."

They each successively removed their goggles to inspect the scene before them, which was—contrary to my usual privacy level—quite provocative.

"Easy, cowgirl. We'll let you finish your ride," the leading thug said. He was either an ugly human, or a humanoid species I was not familiar with. In the end, it didn't matter so long as you knew which end talked and which end didn't. "You going somewhere, Ayil?"

"I'm working." He continued to nuzzle my neck, but I was no longer lonely enough to play this game. I pushed him away and immediately noticed the ageless face before me. He was younger than I suspected, possibly even late-teens young. I wasn't far from his age, but he seemed so much younger than me.

"The lady and I were discussing a price." Ayil's bedroom eyes and dulcet voice vanished. He stared at me, silently begging me for help. He wanted to escape from these men and seduction was his best hope of achieving that goal. Was I the only ship he could invite himself onto? Perhaps I was the only semi-attractive female captain. If that even mattered.

"Is that right?" the ugly man asked and turned to me. He was drooling now. I wasn't sure if it was a normal function of his mouth or a result of his mood.

I raised my handful of money.

He nodded and pinched his mouth shut in thought. "Well then, pay the man. He's not for lease."

"Is he your slave?" I asked.

"So, what if he is?" Ugly asked defensively.

"I'm looking to add to my crew. He looks strong." I glanced at Ayil, who did indeed look strong. Stronger than me, at least. "Can't hurt to have a man on board."

Ugly laughed and his crew joined in. "You can't pay me enough for him. That there is my golden boy. Everybody wants him."

I glanced down at my wad of money. "Not enough, huh?"

"Nope." He shook his head.

"Give me a ballpark." He laughed again. "Come on, everybody has a price."

He thought about it. "How about you?"

"How's that?" I asked.

He smirked and moved closer to me. "You look pretty tasty. I bet you would make up the difference."

"Easy, pimp." I raised my gun. "I'm not for sale."

"Everybody has their price," Ugly mocked. His men laughed and spread out, disappearing into the fog to block my escape. "Besides, I didn't pay for this one." He moved over to the boy and hugged his shoulder tightly. "I caught him and broke him." Ugly kissed him hard. I could see Ayil's hands scrunch in frustration, but he didn't fight the man. I couldn't imagine how long it took him to learn that level of submission.

Ugly released him and looked at me. "Just like I'm gonna do with you." He pulled his gun and tipped his head, proud of his dominating position. Before he could go on, my wrist chirped.

"Oh, excuse me." I waved apologetically to the toad before me and activated the coms device. "Kit here."

"Should I do it now?" a woman's questioning voice came on.

"Yes, Aresties, that would be fine."

Ayil and Ugly looked at me strangely as I hung up. "I apologize. Where were you? Oh yes, you were going to tell me how *I have nowhere to run* and *fighting is futile*. Then I was going to offer you one last chance to save yourselves, and then you were going to laugh maniacally. That about sum it up?" I asked, searching for the men who were sneaking up on me from the slowly encroaching fog.

"You really think your slow shooter is going to save you?"

I glanced at my pulse gun. It wasn't enough to kill, but it was enough to subdue. The only problem was it took a beat between shots to charge, making self-defense against multiple offenders difficult. "No, this won't save me. Starla will, though."

"Who is Starla?" Ugly asked.

I tapped the belly-heavy metal ship behind me. "She's Starla."

The man examined the ship carefully, searching for the source of my threat. When he didn't find any, he smirked at me. He thought I was bluffing, and had I intended to use the ship's weaponry, he would have been right. I'd been through the ship's operating manuals more than a dozen times, and I still couldn't run the system to save my life.

However, I wasn't intending to fight him.

A blaring siren pierced our eardrums. Four bright rotating yellow lights lining my ship temporarily blinded my potential captors. I grabbed Ayil and dragged him closer to my ship, tucking us both under the curve of the hull.

Before Ugly could recover, all four load ramps dropped open, slamming against the concrete. One ramp landed on the head of one man. I heard several guns cocking and the charging hum from a few others.

I could see Ugly looking over the dozen armed men and women standing on the edge of my cargo bay glaring down at him. He was debating his options. Despite being outmanned and outgunned, he was still considering a fight.

"Throw down your weapon and run like a scared little boy!" I heard Aresties yell in the tiniest voice a woman could have. It was far from threatening, but one doesn't really need a booming voice when you are holding a harpoon gun.

Ugly grumbled. "Come on, boys." He caught sight of me between the ramps. "Don't ever come back to Pallo, or I'll kill you."

"Don't ever leave Pallo or I'll kill *you*," I countered.

He paused, considering my threat, but he walked away rather than continue the back and forth.

LONELY

"**D**id we do good?" Aresties asked as I squirmed myself out from under the ramp. Ayil followed, scanning the fog for his owners.

"You did very good. Thanks everyone." I waved at my bus of misfit travelers and planet-hoppers. They mumbled some reciprocal appreciation and moved back to stow their prop weapons. Most of my antique arsenal didn't work, and some weren't even technically weapons, thus the harpoon gun Aresties was haphazardly waving in my face. "Aresties, sweetheart, there is no safety on that device."

Despite her tiny voice, Aresties was not a small woman. Her voluptuous features front and back drew the attention of many men. Men who preferred more to grab in the bedroom. She was cute as a button, with tight curls that made her long copper-blond hair appear short when it cinched close to her face. Had she been a tad smarter, I was certain she could rule half the universe in less than a year, but as it was, she was barely useful enough to be called my copilot.

She looked me over with a small smile that told me she didn't know what I was trying to communicate to her. I pinched back the bulk of my smile and took the harpoon from her hand. "I'll put this away for you."

She looked down at the weapon absentmindedly and released it to me. She looked over at Ayil—our damsel in distress—and mouthed, "*Yummy.*" That was her answer for everything she liked, be it men or something on her dinner plate.

I turned to the young man behind me, who was taking in the ship from the edge of the ramp. I felt embarrassed that only a few minutes ago I was making out with this complete stranger. I never did grasp what the appropriate pace with men was. I either threw myself at them or prudishly avoided them. In the back of my mind, I believed I was waiting for Mr. Right. Unfortunately, there had only been two men in my life I ever felt dizzyingly attracted to. One was a gattaw and for reasons of obvious pain and mutilation, I could not be his lover. The other was a coma victim and for reasons involving my disgust with necrophilia, I was also not going down that road. Ayil should have been a perfect fit, but something told me he wasn't really interested in a grown-up relationship so much as just a ride.

"In or out?" I asked and pushed several buttons on the wall of the hull, activating the hydraulics to lift the ramps back into place. I held my hand over the last button and waited for his response. He looked over the hustle of people on the back wall. Someone was arguing about the previous position of their firearm. "I don't have any promises for you, but I have a ship. I can get you off the planet, but after that, you'll have to figure out what you want to do."

"I thought you said you needed a crewman," he pointed out.

"I do, but it's not like I have anything to pay you."

"Food, water..." He paused and stepped closer to me. He was taller than me, but that wasn't exactly an achievement where I was concerned. "...and a bed." He pushed my finger into the button and the ramp groaned back into position, recreating the wall and closing up the ship.

I let his hand rest on mine momentarily as I assessed his demeanor. Ayil was even more attractive in the light. The temptation to pick up where we had left off was overwhelming, but I knew this was an act. It was the only thing that had worked for him so far. If for no other reason than to be difficult, I wanted him to know he didn't have to seduce me to get what he wanted.

He could just beg like normal people.

"Alright, but for the record, the food sucks, the water isn't filtered, and the beds are hard as rocks."

He smiled and opened his mouth to respond, but two men came to my side, asking about the schedule and if we were going to be on our way soon. They were both very concerned about their cargo. Cargo I didn't ask questions about. My only rule was no human trafficking, but after that, well, let's just say space doesn't offer the luxury of being a good guy all the time.

A woman joined the inquisition and complained she wasn't told she had volunteered to be security for my ship. I ignored her and motioned to Ayil to follow, and he did so, following along with my entourage.

Another question came from a fourth humanoid. He was concerned his cargo was getting too hot. He wanted to use my freezer. I answered all the questions with the standard responses. *We will get there as soon as we can. If you want commercial luxuries, then fly commercial ships.* And last but not least, *NO!*

Most of my clientele were poor, secretive, or plotting revenge against someone. I didn't inquire about the specifics when they boarded, but I also didn't offer my ship as a buffet for their uses. Cargo stayed in the bay, people stayed in their designated quarters, and no one went onto the upper level unless they worked for me.

I paused at the tight, steep staircase leading to the upper level. I looked back at everyone with a stern resolve. They immediately stopped speaking and wandered away, back to their minimalist barracks. Ayil watched everyone go, apparently impressed by my clout. I didn't have much, but as the owner of the ship, that was enough.

"Follow me. I need to get this beast going, and then I'll give you a tour." I climbed the steps and Ayil followed with a nimble grace that told me he was still showing off.

I arrived in the corridor I called the ship's heart. From this point, I could reach my cockpit and my quarters, and in the opposite direction, every manner of pipe, conduit, piston, blast furnace, and wire that made the old bird fly.

I moved on to the cockpit and settled into one of the two chairs in the room. Ayil paused, unsure of his place, but after a moment of me clicking buttons and turning dials, he sat down like he owned the place. The act continued. I knew he was terrified, but he wouldn't reveal that to me.

I shoved my card into the designated slot, trying not to make it obvious that the ship didn't run by finger scan. Fortunately, none of my guests knew that or they might mutiny. I glanced to see what he thought of that, but he was staring out into the fog. I peeked over my panel, hoping to see what he had seen, but it was gone.

I pulled my headset on and started my take-off speech. "Everyone secure your crap. We're going up. And don't ask me to hurry. Our options are jet-propelled rise or ignite the upper atmosphere with our boosters and kill the entire planet. I think we can all agree patience is a virtue in this case."

I heard the click of the aero-station and a grumpy old woman came over my com. "H-class ship, designation Starla. You are requesting access to leave the planet."

"That is correct." I sighed and shook my head.

"Are you aware of the hydrogen gas content of our air?"

"Yes, ma'am, I sure am. I've actually been to this planet eight times this year alone."

"Are you aware of the flammable nature of hydrogen gas?"

I turned to Ayil and crossed my eyes. "Yes, ma'am, I am. That's why I am using my jets instead of my boosters."

"In order to exit the atmosphere, you will need to keep your thrusters off. Only air-propelled movements are allowed."

I leaned back in my chair and politely agreed. I had tried getting angry on previous trips, which only made it worse. After ten minutes of listed mandates, we were on our way up, slowly but nevertheless mobile.

"That should hold steady," I said, flipping on the autopilot. "I'll show you around the ship." I led the way out and realized my jacket was going to be too warm for the boiler room. "Hang on a second." I veered off into my quarters, unzipped my jacket, and removed it. I rubbed my hands through my short spikes of blue-tipped black hair.

"Who's the guy?" Ayil asked from inside the room.

I whipped around, momentarily very aware of the bed behind me. I looked over at my sleeping beauty and searched my mind for an explanation that didn't sound self-serving or naïve.

"Husband?" Ayil asked and looked me over, pausing at my freshly exposed frill, which made him smirk.

"What? No, never met him. He's freeze-locked. I just don't have the heart to yank him—the plug."

"Good. I mean that he's not your husband." Ayil stepped closer, and I was about to move away, but he grabbed me around the waist and lifted me. I shrieked, unprepared for my loss of footing.

Somewhere between my balance being upset and grabbing on for dear life, we were on the bed, with me on top. It was a strange maneuver, I thought, since he had to lean up to kiss me, but I imagined this was a control thing. If I had the control, perhaps I was less likely to object as strongly.

Despite the advantage of the position, I was still being manipulated like a doll. He pulled on my neck, bringing my lips to his for another tantalizing kiss to match the earlier one. My legs were straddling him already, but he lifted his pelvis, pressing against me. My hands battled, trying to push away from him, but he pulled my hand away and directed it lower.

"Ayil." I finally freed my lips long enough to speak his name, but it wasn't so much an objection as a bookmark at the moment. He was beautiful, sexy, and everything a woman could want.

Everything I would want.

Before I realized what I was doing, the pistol was off my hip and into his temple. He immediately released me, lips and all. I leaned back to stare at him in stupefied terror. "Who sent you?" I asked.

It was ridiculous, but so was a man this beautiful, conveniently coming to me for his rescue. If he was smart, he would have found a faster ship, with a stronger, better-equipped captain. This was why no one was looking for me anymore. They were setting traps. Sexy, young, six-pack-abs traps.

"What the hell?" Ayil's eyes widened on my face as he took in what two years alone in space had done to my paranoia.

"Who sent you?"

"Who sent me where? I just got here."

"Did someone hire you to have sex with me?"

"What? What is that supposed to mean?"

"Why are you seducing me?"

"Because you're cute. If I had known you were crack-ass crazy, I would have skipped the meet and greet."

"Do you know who I am?" I asked, pressing my muzzle against his temple.

His eyes glanced at the weapon, and he gulped. "I know you are a beautiful and frightened woman." He whispered. "I know you don't want to pull that trigger any more than I want to be on the other side of it." He raised his hand slowly and touched my arm. "I don't know what your trouble is, but you've helped me out of mine. If I can do the same for you, I will. I swear." He moved his hand to his face, kissed two of his fingers, and raised it to the sky.

I took a breath and lowered my threat. I rolled off him and he quickly, albeit cautiously, moved off the bed. He skirted around the room until he reached the door. I looked up at him from under my brow. There was an apology due, but for reasons even I didn't understand, I had trouble with those.

"I'll ask someone to find me a room. We can do the tour tomorrow." I nodded, and he slipped out of the room, escaping the crazy lady it held.

After he was gone, I flopped back on the bed and tried to remember when my life had truly gotten screwed up. Was it directly after birth? Or was it when I had tried to fix it?

I turned and looked at my strong, silent, kind-of-dead boyfriend. Then I curled myself around a pillow and went to sleep with my gun still in hand.

True as Steel

"Hey!" I griped at Ayil for throwing another chocolate wrapper at me from the second seat in the cockpit. "Are you even going to try to learn how to fly this ship?"

"Tell me," He demanded as he shoved yet another candy in his mouth. He was lounging in my copilot seat with his feet on my controls. That, combined with food on the flight deck, was enough to make me consider kicking him off my ship. However, he had invariably become useful, as most men do from time to time.

"No, it's too embarrassing."

"Did you or did you not put a gun to my head the first day I stepped on this ship?"

"I did."

"And you don't think six weeks later I deserve to know why?" I didn't answer. I stared at my dials, which had become as hypnotic to me as the stars outside the window. "Come on, Kit, I know you have a past. We *all* have a past."

"Yeah, but yours is petty theft and prostitution."

"Prostitution is not in my past," he said with a high-pitched voice that made me question his preference for women. I often wondered how his obligations affected his perceptions of real-life relationships. Not that I was anyone to judge, since I was in an emotional stalemate with a coma victim. "Come on, I'm not going to quit asking. You already know how annoying I can be." He tossed another wrapper at me.

I sighed, and he leaned forward, anticipating my surrender with barely contained drool. "I'm a princess."

Ayil chuckled. "No, no, tell the truth. I want the sick, twisted past you've been hiding."

"That is the truth. My mother is an empiric queen, my father is—or was, last time I saw him—the leader of his planet. I am a semi-engineered genetic gold mine, and everybody wants a piece of me. My body, my babies, my freedom." I glanced at him to see what he thought of that, but his expression told me he was still absorbing what I had said.

"So..." He slipped onto the arm of the chair and leaned over his knees. "You can make super babies?"

"Sort of, with the right guy. Maybe. It's all theoretical rhetoric."

"Hmm, and what do these super babies do?"

I chuckled and shook my head. "They aren't superheroes, they're just babies. Babies with perfect DNA."

"And that's good?"

"I guess. It's mostly myth. They haven't actually been able to recreate it. They tried test-tube babies, but that didn't come close. A few hundred years ago, they returned to the original doctrines discussing it and began trying to create it naturally. They've been close for a while, but each time they get the almost perfect combination, the candidate turns out to be sterile. I am as close to a fully viable and readable DNA strand as they have ever gotten. They think with the right man, I could create a child with absolutely perfect DNA."

"Is that even possible?"

"It shouldn't be. That's why they stopped relying on science to make it happen. They are basically hoping for a miracle."

Ayil absorbed my confession and then a question registered on his face. "What would a human with perfect DNA be like?"

"I don't know. I'm pretty sure it would be a girl, though." I winked at him, and he smiled.

"No arguments here, but isn't DNA like on or off? Who decides what perfection is? An obsession with blue eyes and blond hair has already gotten humans into trouble once."

"I don't think it's about features. I think it's about health. They want to cure the human race of all diseases."

"Bullshit," Ayil snapped. "They've been *curing* us for centuries. It hasn't helped yet."

"Maybe they want to find the fountain of youth. Maybe they're chasing the hope of an idea. I don't know. All I know is, I'm not going to be a lab rat, or a... mail-order bride. I certainly am not going to let them poke and prod my offspring just to find the cure for the common cold."

"I see why you left that all behind. Are they still hunting you?"

I shrugged. "I thought they would never stop."

"You sound sad saying that."

"I am, I guess. I was so damn important and then about a year ago... It seems like they gave up. I keep waiting for him to pop out of nowhere."

"Him?"

"Them."

"You said *him*."

"My father hired a bodyguard to watch over me. We became close."

"How close?" Ayil perked a curious brow.

"He's a gattaw."

Ayil hissed. "Tell me that didn't happen."

"Nothing happened. I don't have a death wish. We just... We were friends."

"And you miss him?"

"Yeah, well, that's a requirement of friendship, isn't it?"

Ayil stood and stretched his legs across the cockpit. I had considered the conversation over, but he soon peeked over my chair. "Do you wanna try it?"

I gave him a sidelong glance. "Try what?"

"Making a super baby," he said with undue enthusiasm. I laughed. "What? You can't tell me we wouldn't make a beautiful little girl together."

"You don't care about super babies; you just want to have sex."

"And what is wrong with that?" he objected, somewhat insulted. I shook my head at him. "I'm really good," he said, using in his favorite voice of seduction.

I smirked at him. "Of that, Ayil, I have no doubts. However, I think you and I should stick to what we are good at."

"What's that?"

I paused, glancing at him again. "Wallowing in the opposing spectra of propriety, so we can avoid real human connections."

I could feel his eyes all over me, absorbing what I was saying and determining if I was insulting him or not. "What does that mean?" he asked serenely.

"Nothing, forget I said anything." My chair spun at shocking speed and I was facing him. He still wasn't sure if he should be mad, but he was.

"You don't know what I've been through," he grumbled in a low tone that made me think he was repressing his volume... or his tears. "You might have had every man this side of the galaxy vying for your uterus, but you had a bodyguard. I've had a line of men and women outside my door for the last three years. So don't you dare judge me for teaching myself to enjoy it. I wouldn't have survived if I hadn't." I could see the tears in his eyes and I opened my mouth to defend my hurtful words, but he ripped himself from my chair and left the room.

I waited a few seconds before running after him. I had to run to catch him at the stairwell. "Ayil, wait!"

He paused on the first step down, putting us face to face. I opened my mouth to speak the apology he deserved, but it caught on my tongue. Why was that so hard for me to say?

Instead, I touched his cheek. It was clammy, with freshly wiped tears. He didn't back away, so I brought up my other hand and embraced his face, wiping away a couple of fresh tears. I leaned in and pressed my lips to his forehead. I peppered his face with gentle kisses the way my mother used to when I was a very little girl. I kissed him the way any adult should have kissed him three years ago, without intent.

I pulled him into a tight hug and he raised his arms, limply hooking them around my waist. "You're a free man, Ayil. Do what you want. I won't judge you."

He pulled away and looked at my face. "All I know is sex, Kit. I don't know how to be close to anyone without that."

I nodded. "I had a massive crush on Terrin—my bodyguard. Still do, I suppose. Then he explained that sex with him would kill me." Ayil's lip curved, but then it fell when he realized I was revealing a legitimately sour memory. "Once sex is off the table, all that's left is the pillow talk. In the end, that's what really defines a relationship, anyway. So, pretend you and I have just made love, and we're lying next to each other... talking."

"They usually leave right after," he said bitterly.

I pinched his chin, raising his head enough to get his eyes back on me. "I'm not leaving, Ayil. Although I think in another few weeks, you are going to wish you had left."

He grabbed my hand and kissed it. "Alright, teach me how to fly this rust bucket."

Ship Wreck

Two years after that.

"Son of a bitch!" Ayil yelled as he twisted the wrench that was half his size. I was doing my best to pull as well, but the ship was roasting like an oven, and my hands were sweating like the rest of me.

With a roar of frustration, Ayil jumped away from the wrench. Milliseconds after I removed my hands, he kicked it, futilely demanding its compliance with the man's version of a hissy fit. His dark hair was curling into sweaty ringlets from the rising humidity. He had also taken to wearing no shirt while he worked in the engine room, since every shirt that entered the oily room came out stained, no matter how careful the wearer was.

My hair had fallen flat, leaving only the memory of its usual buoyancy. The long layers of pale apricot clung to my cheeks and neck. I combed it back and twisted it into a haphazard bun while Ayil finished his tantrum.

He had matured a great deal in the last couple of years, but he was still prone to boyish behavior. However, I wasn't sure whether to categorize this display as mannish or childish.

"We need to fix this," I droned over his long string of unintelligible curses. "Ayil!"

"I know!" he yelled back at me, kicking the wrench once more.

"What then? What do you need?"

"I need you to be fifty pounds heavier and a man." He paced back and forth. "This ship is designed to be run by a crew of eight."

"The computer system—"

"The computer system is buggy as hell! We either need a new computer system, which we can't afford, or a crew of eight, including two beefy men. That's what I need to get this open. You are too scrawny to do me any good."

"I think you mean petite."

"Whatever, Kit. Your arms are too small to help me! Who's on the manifest?"

"A couple of women and their children and an older man, but he doesn't look healthy."

"Find Aresties then. Maybe she can straddle this thing and push it down."

"If we don't get this humidity under control, it's going to kill the air filters."

"I know, so go find Aresties!"

"I'm going! Geez, you're bitchy." I scowled at him.

"It's 104 degrees in here, Kit!"

"And I'm right here with you!"

I weaved my way through the greasy pipes, adding streaks to my already stained clothes. I expelled myself from the engine room through a door that no longer opened over ten inches. I looked back at the opening and wondered how Aresties was going to fit.

"Kit!" Alana, one of my passengers, approached me in the corridor. "We need more water."

Although the corridor was significantly cooler, my sluggish mind failed to register the peculiarity of her arrival before the pixie-haired blonde reached me. "What the hell are you doing on my flight deck?"

"We... need... more... water," Alana said as she fanned herself with a plastic plate.

"What... the hell... are you doing... on my flight deck?" I repeated patronizingly.

"It's blazing hot in here."

"Get back downstairs!"

"We need water!" she insisted.

"There is none! The ship is exhausting everything into the atmosphere. It's not regulating temperature, so unless we can fix it, we are going to cook to death. Now get the hell off this floor before I launch you into space!"

"Bitch!" she seethed.

"There's only one goddamn rule: stay off the flight deck. How the hell can't you remember that?"

"Oh, what, are you scared I'll find out about your sick little fetish?"

Since the insult barely registered before I opened my mouth to respond, I was able to hide my shock. "No, I'm afraid you will annoy the crap out of me, so I need space." She opened her mouth to retort, so I drew my gun and raised it. "I swear to God I will shoot you just to not hear you speak again."

She backed off immediately. Perturbed or otherwise, she was not willing to take on my gun for the last word in the argument.

"Geez, Kit, is there anyone in the galaxy you do get along with?" Ayil said as he squirmed out of the engine room.

"Shut up. That door is too small for her."

"I know. I'm going to torch it open," he said, no longer distraught about the situation. We were good at taking turns being irrational.

"I'll go find her," I said.

I continued downstairs and found my first co-pilot in the ship's storage, organizing the shelves of miscellaneous non-perishables. She had a bad case of OCD, which made her helpful and annoying at the same time.

"Hey, girl, we need your help," I said as I leaned on the shelf she was organizing.

"Sure." She turned and smiled. She didn't bother to ask me what I needed help with. I could have asked her to launch out of a cannon and she would have.

She followed me back to the doorless engine room. With some effort, she made it through the piping to the notorious wrench. Ayil smiled as she arrived and she smiled back. I knew they had something on the side. Truth be told, I was likely the only woman on the ship who didn't have something on the side with Ayil. He rarely denied any woman the pleasure of his company. Nor did he deny himself theirs.

"Hey there, big beauty," he said, making *big* sound complimentary. "I need you to straddle this wrench for me." He winked.

"Why?" She glanced back at me. I was loath to admit to her we required her body weight to move the wrench.

Ayil, however, had a way of making everything sound sexy. He moved close to her and whispered in her ear. I could only imagine what he was saying, but she giggled. When he stepped back, he offered his hand, guiding her around the wrench so she was astride it.

"Okay baby, give us a little bounce," he said. She giggled again, and he grabbed the wrench and prompted her again. "Come on, Aresties, ride my wrench."

She smiled and bit her lip. She gave a little bounce, and Ayil pressed down as she did. I covered my mouth to hide my smile as she repeated the movement.

"That's good, baby, harder," Ayil purred with his bedroom voice, which I had become immune to. I preferred his bickering voice. It felt more honest to me. The wrench shifted, letting out a horrific screech that jump-started my heart. "Give me more!" Ayil hollered at Aresties and she bounced harder. I clasped my hands as the wrench squawked again.

"We're almost there! More, baby!" Ayil groaned with a carnal undertone. Aresties jumped up and let her full weight land on the wrench. It fell to the floor and the air circulation immediately activated, flooding the room with a fresh breeze. "Good girl!"

Ayil caught her before she could topple over and pushed her back into the wall. They started kissing and groping, with no concern for my presence. I opened my mouth to thank Aresties, but I saw Ayil unzip his pants and I opted for a quick escape instead. What he was about to do to her would be thanks enough for both of us.

The Mall

Two more years after that.

"This is a bad idea," I said, opening the ramp for our exit. "I can't even take my gun off the ship."

"I'm not going to listen to your arguments anymore." Ayil leaped down the ramp into the gleaming sunlight. The buildings ahead of us were bright white, and the streets were clean. I had never been to the small commerce "planet," but so far, it looked exciting. The vivid store signs and colorful tents were enough to make me consider a peek into the frivolous world of shopping.

"Come on, Kit, face it. No one is looking for you." He cupped his mouth to broadcast the announcement to me.

After six years, the hunt was undeniably over. I was sixteen solar systems and about eighty planets away from where I had started. Surely that was enough. I could spend the day on the most visited rock in the galaxy. I could use my credit without immediately jumping into my ship. Clearly, I had overestimated my value.

No one was looking for me.

No one at all.

My face must have shown my trauma at being forgotten because Ayil frowned and returned to the top of the ramp. He kissed my forehead and nicked his nose on mine. "Come on, Kit. It's time to give up the ghost... and the zombie." He nodded upward to my quarters. He pushed back my turquoise bangs, tucking them behind my ear where they would stay for at least five seconds. "Rejoin the human race. And for the love of all things pretty, buy some new clothes, cause girl, you are wretchedly out of style."

I looked down at my baggy clothes, which could have taken me from factory work to dinner in a sports bar with the simple removal of a hairnet. "I can't afford new clothes."

"You can't tell me mommy and daddy cut you off. You withdraw cash on every planet we stop at."

I shrugged, not willing to explain the specifics of my income. I took in the smell of caramelized onion fritters and roasted nut balls, not to mention the hot dogs being sold less than thirty feet from my ship.

"There she is." Ayil squeezed my shoulders. "There's the little girl who wants to get out of this crazy lady's body." I smiled at him. "Do you hear that?" I listened to the bustle of the people. "That music." I strained to hear it, but the jingling sound was too far away for my ears. "That's ice cream." He shook me. "Ice cream, Kit. Not freeze-dried, just add cold water and stir, but *real* ice cream."

"Are you going to be okay, or do you need a moment alone?"

"I may need a moment alone." He closed his eyes for effect and I chuckled. "Come on, you're my sugar momma today. Buy me shit I don't need and won't even want five minutes after I get it." He wrapped his arm around me and somewhat forcibly dragged me from my ship.

WHERE WERE WE?

After Ayil had leaped across a few more roof gaps with me on his back, he descended to the low road. We—He climbed down the fire escape to another alley and somehow found the energy to jog across the piazza toward the parking section.

"They're closing in on us," I said as I watched the crowd part for several bobbing green heads. Terrin's cohorts were not as tall as him. The trait of height seemed to be linked to their intelligence, but I had never figured out how that worked.

"Do you want to take over running?" Ayil asked over his panting breaths.

"You should have left me."

"I'm not leaving you! Shut the hell up and tell me if I need to duck."

"Duck!" I yelled as a blast of magnetic radiation barreled at us thanks to one of Terrin's underlings. Ayil veered to the side, easily avoiding the inaccurate shot.

"The ship is ahead. We just need to get inside. Aresties can get us separated."

"What if they tail us?" I asked.

"One panic attack at a time, Kit."

"Duck!" I yelled, but it was too late. The impact hit us on the side, rolling us. Magnetism took hold, dragging us the remaining few feet to our ramp where we beached ourselves.

Ayil growled and flopped around, trying to get free with brute strength, but with four magnetic strikes, strength was no longer an asset.

We were trapped.

I watched the six gattaw crowd around me, holding me in check with threat alone. Terrin caught up to the pack and emerged from between his men without urgency.

His face held little to no emotion. He looked over my predicament without a hint of guilt for breaking my heart—or perhaps I had already broken his, so there was no empathy left for him to offer.

His mouth opened to speak, but an ear-shattering, pulsing alarm broke the silence for him. A voice came over an intercom close to us. "Cease and desist all violent activity," a computerized voice said. "This ship's protection mode has been activated."

I looked up at the speakers now protruding from my ship's hull. Muzzles followed shortly after, re-situating and aiming at the nearest standing bodies with weapons in hand.

"Evacuate the area or you will be neutralized," the ship commanded.

"What the hell is that?" Ayil whispered to me, hiding his surprise at the development.

"Aresties must have started the ship's defense system," I whispered back.

"I thought you said it was broken."

"No, just very confusing."

"Ten... nine" The ship started a countdown.

"Drop your weapons!" Terrin ordered and the men immediately laid down their arms. Terrin removed his gun and the countdown stopped. He turned to me, finally showing the fury I knew he had been feeling for six long years. "Mallory!" he seethed. "Come with me now, before—"

The ramp activated, and we rose with it. I looked back for my hero and saw Aresties hiding around the corner. I was more pleased than ever that her intellect hovered on the right side of commonsense.

Terrin shifted to keep me in sight. "This place is crawling with bounty hunters. If you leave the planet, you're done for." The ramp clanked shut, cutting off my view of Terrin and silencing his words.

His *very accurate* words.

Welcome Back

Ayil struggled behind me as we hung upside down against the hull of the cargo bay. "That was fun," I said. "On the upside, you got your pants."

"Totally worth it," he huffed.

"We're not out of the woods yet. Terrin is right; these yahoos are going to follow us off this planet. Once we're out of the atmosphere, they can shoot us down."

"What's the plan, then?" Ayil asked, but only silence followed. "Kit." I could feel him turn to look at me. "Come on, Kit, we always get away. We always figure it out."

"I don't know. Maybe Aresties can help."

"Help what?" Aresties asked as she returned to the cargo bay with a demagnetizing gun in hand.

"Help us run the weapons systems so we can escape the bounty hunters," I clarified.

"I thought the weapons system was broken." She scrunched her nose and shot at us.

Our connection broke, and we fell to the floor, along with the metal grate, which clanged loudly on the floor. Ayil groaned in relief and moved away from me. I stood and dusted myself off.

"Didn't you activate the defense system?" I asked.

"No." She shrugged, indifferent to the concern in my voice. "I didn't even know you were in trouble until I heard the alarms."

"If you didn't start it—" The ship's engine rumbled to life, freezing us all in our tracks. I looked at Ayil, who was gaping back at me. Aresties finally sensed something wasn't right, though I doubt she knew what it was precisely.

"Who the hell is up there? You have the key, don't you?" Ayil asked.

I pulled it from my back pocket, dangling it in front of me as if it were a possessed toy.

"The engine won't start without that," Aresties declared the obvious and pointed at my card.

Ayil jumped into a sprint and I followed right after him.

"You don't think someone cut off his hand?" I hollered behind him, struggling to keep up with him.

"I don't know what to hope for, Kit," he called back to me.

I knew what I hoped for. I had fantasized about it for six years, but it was impossible.

My heart raced from more than my exertion. My ears went foggy and my vision blurred as I ran across the flight deck. I passed my quarters, seeing the door slightly ajar, but I couldn't see beyond my bed.

I pushed into the cockpit seconds after Ayil. He was at a standstill, staring at our new guest, or old guest, or perhaps *we* were *his* guests.

I stared at the familiar face and newly clothed body. For the first time, his eyes were open. Beautiful gray-green eyes stared vacantly back at us. Not the brown I had once suspected. He looked tired, if that was possible, after sleeping for ten years.

"Captain?" I stepped forward.

"Don't move, Kit!" Ayil threw out his arm, and I stopped. I looked at him for an explanation and I saw a glowing red dot on his forehead. I gasped at the threat against him. "Yeah, you too." He nodded upward.

Two tiny muzzles had dropped from the ceiling and aimed their laser trackers at us. The captain shifted back to his console and within a few keystrokes the thrusters were raising us up.

"No, wait!" I stepped forward, and the weapon beeped its preemptive threat. I stepped back again, and the sound stopped. "Captain Rayne, please."

"How do you know my name?" he asked with a hoarse voice, but I got the impression it was usually a deep throaty tone, anyway.

"It's all over the logs, and your uniforms, and your medals."

"Who are you? Why were those gattaw after you?"

"It's a long story." I evaded the question, since we didn't have time for a backstory.

"Are you criminals?"

"Not exactly. I'm wanted for reasons of political and financial interest."

"What about you?" The captain turned to look at Ayil.

"I'm a prostitute. Everybody wants me." Ayil pushed his tongue into his cheek and winked at him.

"Ayil," I whispered disapprovingly, but the man hardly reacted to his dissension. "The bounty hunters are after me." I waited for him to ask another question, but he seemed to be slowly taking in everything. "Can Starla's defenses protect us against multiple ships?"

"Starla?" He turned to me, his face crumpled in confusion.

"It was carved in the console. I assumed it was the ship's name."

He looked over the controls and found the word etched into the metal between buttons. He touched the name, but he still seemed confused by its presence. Temporary or partial amnesia was common after an elongated hypersleep. I wondered how much ten years of sleep had cost him, and for how long. He was lucky not to be a vegetable, let alone to know what a vegetable was.

"Captain, I'm sure you're very confused. I don't know what you remember, but we need to focus on the moment. You are leaving the atmosphere of a protected planet. Once we are back in common space, we are going to be attacked by several...

probably M-class ships. We are currently on an H-class ship, with an upgraded J-class operating system. Do you remember if the weapons system was upgraded too?"

"No," he answered succinctly.

I pinched my lips and hissed an exhale. "I'm sorry; no, you don't know, or no, it wasn't upgraded?"

"Sit down," he commanded.

"Still being targeted, Cap." Ayil pointed to the tiny muzzles aiming at each of us.

"You can move now. They won't follow you."

Ayil took the first step. When nothing beeped and his head didn't explode, he nodded for me to follow. He took the copilot chair, and I stood behind him.

"Sit," the captain insisted again. Ayil scooted over, leaving me enough room to sit next to him in the chair. "Seat belts."

Ayil glanced at me and rolled his eyes before drawing the four belts across us into the central buckle. It automatically tightened, pulling us tightly to the seat and against each other.

"What about Aresties? She is still downstairs."

"Attention all crew," Rayne announced over the intercom. "Buckle in. We are about to lose environmental gravity." He continued to push buttons and a muffled siren filtered in from the lower levels.

Rayne strapped himself in and shifted the steering column into place for manual driving. It wasn't something I used often, since the ship wasn't capable of quick maneuvers like modern ships.

The siren stopped as the glaze of atmosphere left our view. I felt the gravity switch off, and my hair lifted, floating into Ayil's face. He pushed it out of the way and grabbed my hand. I glanced at him, unsure of what emotion he was exuding with the interaction, but he wouldn't look at me.

"They won't take you, Ayil. They only want me."

He shook his head dismissively.

"What?" I asked.

He shook his head again.

I wanted to ask more, but the ship rocked with the impact of multiple laser strikes. The disturbed deflection field caused the hull to vibrate. I looked at Rayne, but he was unfazed by his ship being almost ripped apart by the first few shots from a superior ship.

"Rayne, these weapons are far more advanced than yours. The deflector can't disperse that much energy. Not to mention there are" I could only see three ships through the front window, but the sensor panel showed otherwise. "...six ships, geez." The ship shuddered again with another hit. I rested my head back, looking away from the monitor so I didn't have to see, in glowing red, how outnumbered we were.

"I'm not deflecting the energy." Rayne glanced at me as another attack came. "I'm absorbing it."

I looked at Ayil, but he was already leaning forward to look at Rayne. "That's not possible."

"It's not possible for them. It's very possible for me."

"Are you sure you are remembering right? You've been asleep for a while," I stated gingerly, not wanting to insult the crazy man beside us. I doubted he knew how long he had been under. Even if he saw the atomic clock on the console, he may not have noticed the additional turn of the one number second-to-last.

"I am very sure," he said and pushed a button on the station. A large pulse expelled from the ship's gunner—a gunner I had never fired in the entire six years I had been aboard the ship.

A yellowish pulse of energy hit one of the attacking ships. The energy saturated its deflector field, breaking it apart. Completely exposed, the ship veered off, willingly surrendering.

"How the hell did you do that?" Ayil asked. "You took out their deflector with one shot."

"Not technically one shot. I absorbed... what was that, five shots?" Rayne clicked a few more buttons as the other ships maximized their fire.

I cussed as sparks came out of the console. The lights in the room went out. "Rayne, they are ripping you to shreds. Even if you can do what you are saying, they are going to kill us before you can get off another shot."

Despite the alarms going off, he seemed ignorant of the danger.

"If you aren't going to save us, put us into an escape pod!" Ayil yelled at him.

Rayne ignored us and continued to monitor his energy levels. When they reached maximum capacity, he flipped up a toggle switch. A bright blue button bleated its objection to being awoken. He hovered his hand over the button and looked over at us. "You might want to watch this. It will be easier for you to believe later." He pushed the button.

The ship vibrated with the hum of rising energy. I afforded a glance to Ayil before craning my neck to get a better view of the other ships. I felt the power peak and the whiplash release that jolted us against our restraints.

A sphere of yellow bloomed from the ship's weapons. It expanded as it grew, netting the attacking ships with the impact. The effect of the hit disintegrated their deflectors. An invisible aftershock knocked them back. As they struggled to get control of their ballast, they each turned away, forfeiting the battle.

"Holy shit!" Ayil gasped and laughed. "Where the hell did you get this technology?"

"I invented it." Rayne shut down the weapon and returned power to the environmental systems, including gravity.

Ayil unlatched our belt and stood up. "You invented this? Why aren't you shitting gold?"

"Ayil."

"If you sold this—"

"Ayil!" I scolded, and he looked at me acridly. "Captain Rayne has just woken up. I'm sure he has other concerns." Ayil's face dawned with understanding as he recalled how many years Rayne had been under. Whether he intended to sell it was irrelevant. "Maybe we should take a moment to—"

The hull echoed with a new impact and we all exchanged looks.

"Shit, someone brought a suckerfish." Ayil bounded past me before I could even take my first step.

"What's a suckerfish?" Rayne asked, following behind me.

"It's a small ship that attaches to the hull of other ships in order to board them," I explained.

"How will they get in? I've locked all the ports."

"Laser torch," I answered.

He grabbed me and turned me to face him. "Someone is cutting a hole in my ship?"

"Yeah."

Uninvited

Rayne didn't bother asking any more questions. He ran ahead of me to defend his ship. By the time I reached the cargo bay, Aresties was screaming and writhing against her newly arrived bald, tattooed captor. Ayil was beating some poor man senseless and Rayne was training a harpoon on a third overly inked man.

"Let me go!" Aresties yelled.

"Let her go!" Rayne brandished his weapon.

"Not until you give us the girl," the third man conditioned.

"The girl isn't going anywhere with you," I announced when I entered the room.

An arm reached around me from behind, ruining my sarcastic you'll-never-take-me-alive speech. Hot breath hit my cheek. "And who is going to stop us, princess?"

Rayne glanced back at my predicament, but he could hardly lower his defenses against his potential attacker. Ayil left his nearly unconscious man and charged head first to my rescue. My captor pulled me tighter and shoved a knife in my face. I flinched, and Ayil stopped his approach.

"You got to be alive, but nobody said anything 'bout being pretty," he hissed in my ear. Ayil panted and bared his teeth at the man behind me. I shook my head slightly, begging him not to do something stupid. "Listen to your bitch, boy. She's smarter than all three of you put together."

"And yet I'm still at knife-point," I murmured.

"You are smart enough to know when to give up. Isn't that right?"

I took a deep breath. "Will you leave the others alone?"

"He's not taking you off this ship!" Ayil yelled.

"No one else has to get hurt," the bounty hunter said as he trailed his mouth along my neck.

"Don't you fucking touch her! You're not good enough to lick her shoes," Ayil frothed.

The bounty hunter chuckled and moved back to my ear. "He thinks I want to lick your feet."

Ayil took another step forward, but I put up my hand to stop him. "He's just taunting you, Ayil. I know the rules of my bounty specifically demand no sexual assault. He won't touch me. If he does, he'll lose his bounty. And if my parents have any say about it, the trespassing appendage will be abdicated as well. Am I right?"

He whipped me around to face him. I had seen the tattoos on his arm, similar to the other men, but I didn't realize they only covered half his body. His head was half-shaved and tattooed, but the other side was untouched, coiffed, brown hair and a handsome smile. "That's right, princess, but it's a long trip back. You might get a craving before we get back, and who am I to deny a royal decree?"

I shook my head. "I don't just *play* hard to get, Two-Face. I've got an entire planetary alliance hunting for what's between my legs, so I would be careful how close you get. You wouldn't want to get caught in the crossfire."

The bounty hunter bit his lip and looked me over. "You get your men to back off and walk into that ship, or I will kill every last one of them." He nodded to the oval circle at the back end of the cargo hold.

"Let Aresties go first. She's harmless. I don't like him handling her like that." I glared at Aresties's attacker, but he was indifferent to my complaint, since he was still struggling to hold the ample woman in the first place.

The bounty hunter thought about the condition for a moment, but nodded to his partner to let her go. He did and Aresties skirted the wall, sniffling and whimpering. "Kit?" She frowned as she passed me.

"It's okay. Go lock yourself in your room until they're gone." She scurried off, and I turned to Ayil. He was already shaking his head, but I shrugged. "I'm out of ideas."

"You can't give up," he snarled.

"I'm not giving up, but I'm also not going to endanger you."

"Go." Two-Face bumped me forward. I moved forward with him pinned to my back. Ayil shifted as we passed and Two-Face rammed the point of his knife into my neck, making me yelp in pain. "You be careful, boy. I don't make idle threats."

I could see Rayne as we passed. He seemed to calculate the knife at my neck, and the harpoon in his hand. He must have determined it was too much of a risk, because he lowered it slowly.

As we reached the opening, Two-Face turned his back to monitor the men as his crew slipped back into the suckerfish. Ayil petitioned me once again with his angry disappointment. Rayne was still calculating his options, few as they were.

Two-Face shifted to back through the opening. He tugged me along, but I elbowed him and twisted out of his grip. Before I could run to safety, an explosion threw me forward.

This Sucks

The suckerfish exploded, sending me, my captor, and a blast wave of hungry fire across the cargo bay. I landed beneath Two-Face, but the suction of vacuous space immediately pulled us back.

I pawed at the floor, trying to get a grip before the suction dragged me out of the ship. Two-Face latched onto me, no doubt hoping if I achieved my goal, I would save us both. I flailed, feeling nothing but knobby metal floor and slick rails.

Seconds from almost certain death, I felt someone catch my hand. I looked up at my savior and found Captain Rayne. He stared back at me as we hung in midair, tethered between the draw of space and the leather strap he had lassoed to his other hand. He strained under the pressure of the two bodies he was holding, but he looked determined not to let go.

"Hang on!" he mouthed more than yelled, since the wind carried his words away like the rest of the unbolted cargo.

Alarms sounded, and yellow *danger* lights tinted the gray walls a sickly green. I frantically searched for Ayil. I found him crawling along the side of a plastic crate. His hands were bleeding from the metal straps he was gripping. If his hands got too wet, he would slip.

Two-Face shifted, nearly losing his grip on my waist, because he was still hanging on to his blasted knife. I shifted my position, clasping him between my legs as best I could. Had I wanted to, I could have kicked him off and sent him hurtling into space, but I didn't.

I felt the air getting thin—the windstorm was depleting the ship's atmosphere, and soon it wouldn't be able to keep up oxygen production. I looked at Rayne, but he had closed his eyes to concentrate on holding us both. If it came down to it, I would have to let go so I could save them. There was a chance I could survive. A very tiny chance.

I heard something clanking, and I found Ayil slamming his fists into the rail clamps that kept the heavy cargo secured to the floor. Once released, one could move the box down the ramp. However, given the current situation, the vacuum would suck it toward the hole, taking Ayil with it.

"Ayil! No!" I yelled.

The first clamp released, and he maneuvered to the second one. He looked at me, not necessarily because he had heard me, but because he was on the same altruistic train of thought I was and he wanted to say goodbye.

I shook my head vehemently, and he smiled and nodded. He rammed his fist into the clamp and it released. The blue plastic box tumbled toward the ship's hemorrhaging hole, with Ayil in tow behind. If it landed wrong, Ayil would either be crushed or sucked out into space.

I winced as the bin landed against the hull with a thunderous *thunk*. The vacuum died down, leaving only a quiet balloon squeal from minor air leaks. I flopped to the floor with my bounty hunter still attached to me.

I had lost track of Ayil, but I didn't have time to find him before Two-Face started climbing up my legs. With his knife still in hand, he prepared to continue right where he had left off. Rayne kicked him in the face, and I scrambled away.

The environmental alarm stopped, replaced by the emergency alarm. Gravity gave way and my crawling turned to a floating swim, but I was only as fast as my initial propulsion allowed.

I grabbed a strap on a passing crate and turned myself around. Two-Face was right behind me in an equally slow pursuit. I rocketed myself off the crate to the other side of the bay.

Rayne tried to reach him before he could pursue me, but the weightless battle left everyone floundering. I hit the wall. With nothing to hang onto, I pushed off before I lost the opportunity to make a substantial move. My angle was all wrong, and I directed myself on a path right past my pursuer.

I tucked my arms and legs in and glided past him as he thrashed inches out of reach. Rayne followed behind him. He reached out and pushed me, throwing me off my path, and hopefully out of danger. Consequently, he moved in the opposite direction, losing his chance to catch Two-Face.

I didn't have enough momentum to get to the cargo straps again, so I continued to float to another wall. Just as Two-Face ricocheted off the wall, Ayil popped up from behind the crate I thought had crushed him.

"Kit!" He threw something at me.

I skipped the *thank God you're alive* emotional rhetoric and leaped for the baton he had thrown at me. I grabbed the metal rod and Two-Face grabbed my neck. He brandished his knife at me.

"You cost me a ship and my crew. You aren't getting away from me that easily."

"You call this easy?" I gasped. "I'm exhausted."

I activated the object that could have been mistaken for a light saber in its original blueprints. The magnetism dragged me downward out of Two-Face's grip. Taking me to the nearest metal surface, the handle adhered to the floor.

I shut off the device and bounced back up. I came at Two-Face from below and took a much-deserved crotch shot to get the party started. He swung his fist at me, but I was already gone, dragged away by the best little invention for lifting cumbersome cargo.

Before Two-Face could get his bearings, Ayil reached him and punched him in the face. Two-Face slashed at him with his knife, ripping his shirt and bloodying his chest. Ayil activated the other handle to our pair and escaped before more damage could be done.

Two-Face glowered at me as he wiped the blood from his lip. Apparently, he didn't like me anymore. I was more trouble than I was worth.

He reached behind his back and pulled a gun. I couldn't outrun a bullet. Ayil was now too far away to stop him.

He raised it at me and I froze. I heard it fire, but it didn't sound like a gunshot. Two-Face's hand jolted back as a harpoon stabbed into his wrist. He lost his grip on the gun, and it floated away. I followed the spear's leash of wire back to Rayne. He had retrieved the second harpoon gun from the utility case. He stared sourly at my would-be murderer.

Two-Face groaned in pain as he tried to remove the spurred arrowhead from his bleeding wrist. The alarm sounded again, and I shifted down the wall to get to the floor before gravity reset. Ayil and Rayne did the same, but Two-Face dropped like a rock when it came back on.

Two-Face continued to cuss and lunged at Rayne when he approached him. Rather than defend himself, he activated the reel on the gun, and the wire snapped the spear taught against Two-Face's fresh wound.

"I will kill—"

Rayne stifled his verbal torrent with one punch. He sank down to the floor, unconscious.

I glanced at Ayil to see if I was the only one impressed by this. He was dead yesterday, now he was a bad-ass. He had apparently earned his trophies.

Ayil circled around the men to me and touched my arm. "You okay?" he asked.

I didn't answer nor ask the appropriate return query. I just hugged him. He hugged me back.

"Why did you save him?" Rayne asked as Ayil and I parted. My brow knitted at his question. "You could have kicked him off, but you actually held onto him."

I shrugged. "I'm not a murderer."

"He just tried to kill you," he pointed out.

"I didn't say I'd do it again," I grumbled, and Rayne's lip tipped slightly.

We had won the battle, but three successive explosions outside the ship indicated that the war was far from over.

Old School

R ayne, Ayil, and I ran back up to the cockpit. Blinking lights and bleeps on the console were announcing the danger afoot. Environmental controls were having a fit about the semi-plugged hole in the ship. Until we could graft a patch to it, we would continue to lose vital, difficult-to-replenish oxygen.

But, of course, that was the least of our worries. The massive ship circling us was dropping remote detonated explosives right on us. Rayne's defensive screen could not absorb the antiquated artillery. Even if they continued to *only* threaten us with premature explosions, the shrapnel was liable to mar the ship's hull enough to cause another leak. Thankfully, Rayne's hunk of junk was an old-school design with a thick hull.

Otherwise, we would have already been torn to pieces.

I sat down in the copilot's spot and started reporting the facts and figures as Rayne tried to reroute power to the deflectors. Since oxygen was still the primary concern, the ship wouldn't allow him to do much.

Ayil pointed to a flicker on the screen above the window. "They're calling to threaten us verbally, too."

I sighed and pushed the button to put them through. I put on my smack talk face and looked up to the screen. Every thought in my head vanished when I saw Terrin on the screen.

Of course, it had to be him.

He paused a moment, taking in my face, but as soon as the sentiment he was feeling was gone, he was all business. "Your ship is failing, Mallory. You can't take her into space leaking like a sieve. You can either land on the planet and surrender to me, or you can dock with me... and surrender to me."

"She isn't leaving this ship without a fight," Ayil announced firmly.

Terrin looked Ayil over, determining a few things just from his physique. He looked back at me, asking a slew of questions with his eyes that his mouth didn't have time for. "The fight is over. Be thankful I saved you from the suckerfish, or it would have been over sooner."

"Saved us?" I balked. "I nearly got sucked out into space, Terrin!"

"You know this *gat*?" Rayne asked with notable disdain for the species.

Terrin looked at him, taking his measurements as well, but he didn't acknowledge the prejudice in the statement. "You were never in danger. I had divers ready to retrieve you if it came to that."

"And what if I was already on the suckerfish when it exploded?"

"I knew where you were." He paused, letting a small smile play across his lips before he continued. "I have always known where you were."

I searched his face for the meaning of that, but the only answer I got was more subdued amusement. "I don't want to go back, Terrin."

"Then you shouldn't have gone shopping today," he answered. "There's nothing more to be done. There are three more ships waiting on the perimeter. If I walk away now, they'll take you instead."

"We'll take our chances with them," Ayil interjected. He only had two solutions to every problem: punch it, or sleep with it.

"I won't," Terrin snapped at him. "Mallory, you're coming with me. I'm not leaving until you do. If that means waiting for your oxygen to fail and carrying you out unconscious, then so be it."

I glanced at the dials and confirmed that the oxygen was incrementally dropping. The explosion depleted the emergency reserves, and the leak in the hull prevented the scrubbers from keeping up with production.

"It's over," Terrin said softly. "Let me take you home."

I closed my eyes and took in the precious oxygen while I could. "Will you fix the Starla so Captain Rayne can be on his way?"

Terrin inspected Rayne again. "I will give him whatever he requires, so long as you swear not to escape from my ship."

I could see Terrin was not taking any chances this time. He was already a step ahead of me, ready to block my tactics.

"I'm not gattaw. What's holding me to such a promise?"

"Love." He stared me down, daring me to deny it.

"What the hell is this?" Rayne whispered, looking to Ayil for some answers. Ayil shook his head and scoffed.

"Fine," I caved.

"Fine, what?" Terrin leaned in. "Say it."

"I promise I will not escape from your ship."

"And you will return home," Terrin amended.

"You get one promise from me, Terrin. That's it. I don't owe you more than that."

His eyes narrowed on me. "You have no idea how much you owe me." The screen clicked off and he was gone.

"Kit!" Ayil yelled.

I whipped around to face him. "What? What do you want me to do? We are bleeding air in the slowest fucking ship in the galaxy. The only option left is to save you and Aresties before I hurl myself on a pyre."

His mouth twisted, and he shook his head, still defying the defeat. "I don't trust him," he added, as if it was an afterthought to make me listen to reason.

"I do," I admitted. "I trust him with my life."

"He's kidnapping you," he argued.

"No, he's retrieving me. I'm a runaway, remember?"

Surrender

I gathered my clothes and packed them in an oversized duffel bag. I tried not to think about life as a breeder. I tried not to think about the countless men I would have to endure. Perhaps they would skip that part and impregnate me in vitro. No, that would go against the so-called natural order of things.

"Are you and that gattaw together?" Rayne asked from the door.

I jumped and turned to see his face crumpled with disgust. I rolled my eyes and shook my head. "Not that it's any of your business, but he is my friend."

"I think we've skipped the personal boundaries portion of the day, or are you not picking your underwear up off my floor?"

I looked around the room. Nothing had changed since I took it over. His medals, trophies, and personal items were still sitting on the shelf over the bed. I should have mentioned that I had been dusting them for six years, but I wasn't ready to destroy his life.

He was a miracle by any standard of human resiliency. I wasn't entirely sure a sudden shock wouldn't do him in.

"Last time I checked, it was still illegal to pirate a man's ship while he was still aboard."

"Captain, I don't have time to explain everything, but rest assured, I am not a pirate."

"Pirate, stowaway, it doesn't much matter. What does matter is that your *friend* fixes my ship and gets me on my way. I've played hero long enough for today. Your friends are going to have to catch a ride on his boat."

"No, they aren't," I said firmly, and turned to face him. "You are going to keep them on as your crew."

"I don't need a crew."

"You have no idea what you need, Rayne. Your ship is in severe disrepair, and except for your weapons system, which is oddly advanced, you need an upgrade."

"What the hell did you do to my ship over the last six months?"

I stared him down, debating my options. "Six..." I bit back the words. "You are a smart man, Captain. I know this because everything about this ship says you are. Nontraditional, yes, but very smart." I took a step toward him. "I'm not a pirate. This is my ship."

"This is not your ship!" His nostrils flared with each breath.

"Check the clock, Captain. Ayil and Aresties are staying on, or I will have Terrin tow *my* ship back to my home planet."

"That gat is not touching *my* ship."

I took another step forward. "That gattaw is my friend, and if you want to keep Starla, you will stifle your prejudice until I am gone."

His brow dipped, and he shook his head. "The ship isn't named Starla."

"Then why is it carved into your control panel?"

"I don't remember."

"How much do you remember?"

"I..." He shook his head. "...never mind all that. Why do you think my ship is yours?"

"Because I bought it. I'm the legal owner."

"How the hell did you weasel a ship out from under a sleeping man?"

"You're not sleeping, Captain. You're dead." I waited for him to glean my meaning, but his eyes were still searching the room for signs of change. "Check the clock, Rayne." I nodded to the sleep pod. "I've been sleeping next to you for six years." His eyes widened. "By the way, it's nice to meet you, finally." I pushed past him, not wanting to endure the next few minutes with him.

Emotional summits and mental breakdowns were best experienced in private.

The Ex...ish

"Stop!" I pushed Ayil back for the third time. He was still trying to play his tough guy against Terrin's stoic superiority. To his credit, Terrin was taking his pomposity in stride. However, I knew if Ayil broke past me, Terrin would not hesitate to give him a lesson on gattaw muscle structure.

We had hardly made it off the ship before the argument began. I didn't prefer standing in the vacu-tube between my ship and Terrin's during a testosterone overload, but I couldn't avoid it.

"You call yourself her friend and yet you are going to take her back to that hell!"

"Which hell are you referring to, young one?" Terrin's eyes dimmed with boredom. "The palace or the mansion? Dreadful places, both of them."

"You know what I mean," Ayil said.

"No, I don't. She is liable to be subjected to an arranged marriage, but I hardly consider that hell."

"It's captivity one way or another." Ayil butted up against me, but this time it wasn't to get by me. He wrapped his arm around me, over my chest, and hugged me to him. "She has a right to choose the men she loves."

Terrin's jaw worked as he stared at the contact. "We need to speak alone, Mallory."

"Her name is Kit, you green bastard."

Terrin's hands knitted into tight fists, but he took a soothing breath before he acted on his instincts. "Enough of this, Mallory. Call him off or my civility will wane."

I tapped Ayil's hand, and he released me. I turned to him and covered his mouth before he could speak. "Stop. I am in no danger. Do you hear me? I meant what I said before." His eyes dimmed in defeat and he stomped off.

Making her way down the corrugated passageway, Aresties paused at my side. Rayne stopped by her, observing the situation with interest. "Everything okay, Kit?" She gave Terrin a once over, trying to determine if I was safe. And if I wasn't mistaken, she even glared at him.

"I'm fine, really. You can go inside. Terrin and I just need to talk."

Reluctantly, Aresties continued down the tube. Rayne gave Terrin a feral stare before following her.

Terrin waited for them to be out of earshot before speaking again.

"What did you say to him?" Terrin asked.

"Who?" I asked.

"You told the boy you meant what you said."

"I said I trusted you with my life." Terrin looked me over, searching for the knife I might stick in his back, but I didn't have one. "What did you mean by always knowing where I am?"

He smiled. "You have a tracker between your shoulder blades."

"What?"

"I implanted it shortly after—" I slapped him, or at least I tried. He intercepted my hand and kept talking, indifferent to the intended violence. "It doesn't work over long distances, but rest assured, I could have found you. I did several times, but..."

"But what?" I relaxed my arm in his grip.

"As I said before, you have no idea how much you owe me." He pulled my hand down and repositioned to cup my palm in his as he walked me to his ship. It was almost like holding hands, or at the very least, a gentlemanly leash. "Tell me about these men."

"What do you mean?"

He scowled at me. "You know what I mean. Are you sleeping with them?"

"Geez, are you giving me credit for maintaining two men at once? I am talented, aren't I?"

"I know you want to make jokes, and any other time I would at least humor you—"

"I doubt that," I mumbled.

"—but..." He stopped and pulled me to face him. "You know how devoted your father's people are to preserving your DNA for themselves. If you have a child by either of these men, I need to know."

I scoffed. "I haven't slept with either of them. Not that I haven't tried with Rayne, but nocturnal hard-ons don't last long in hypersleep." I smiled at my joke and waited for Terrin to give me a hint that he was still the man I once knew. He didn't. He was all business, and he would be until he wasn't. So, I guess he *was* the man I once knew. "I have never given birth to a child," I answered carefully. "I haven't even..." I swallowed hard, feeling the embarrassment of my admission even before saying it. "I don't date much," I said, sidestepping the entire subject.

Terrin's eyes flickered over my face. "I'll get your ship fixed up. Are you sure you don't want to keep it?"

"No, it technically belongs to Rayne; he's just been dead for the last decade, so he couldn't contest my ownership. Besides, Aresties and Ayil don't deserve to lose their home because I was stupid enough to get caught."

"Once it is fixed, you can say goodbye to your friends, and we will leave them behind. I suggest you take the time you need to speak to them now, but remember your promise. I will hold you to it." He released my hand and continued down the corridor.

"Why love?" I asked. He stopped, but didn't turn back. "Why did you think I would keep my promise for love?" He still didn't turn around. I chuckled. "You think I love you enough to be bound by a promise to you? Apparently, you forgot about my first disappearing act."

He turned and pinned me with scolding eyes. "I didn't think you would keep the promise because you loved me. I thought you would keep the promise because I love you." He turned away and walked off, leaving me with the complicated feelings of a friendship that was almost something more.

Indigestion

"How long do we have?" Ayil asked quietly from across the table.

We were in a small waiting area with snack machines and uncomfortable seating. Aresties had grabbed a few nibbles to share with Rayne. He looked over the prepackaged food, which had transformed over the last decade. They had replaced the traditional freeze-dried crap with a variety of MRE-style packs with an instant heat catalyst.

"It won't take them more than an hour to fix the ship. Terrin will make sure of that. They'll patch-weld the hole, and refill the oxygen reserves, but that's it. You'll have to fix the micro-fractures en route."

Aresties showed Rayne how to pop the bubble that rapidly heated the mini meal. The edge popped open, releasing the excess steam. He poked at the food and took a few bites. I wondered if eating was a little weird after ten years of semi-hibernated bowels.

"En route to where?" Ayil asked. "Where do you think I'm going?"

"You're just being stubborn now, Ayil. I know you want to save me, but I don't think there is any point in risking your life for this."

Rayne dove into his food as if his stomach had finally registered the ten-year famine.

"They won't kill me," Ayil said.

"Terrin won't kill you, but my people will if they think you are a threat to my DNA potential."

Rayne burped loudly. He looked mildly embarrassed, but I smiled at him. He had earned the right to be a little uncouth with his mealtime.

"Why did they pop back up after so many years?"

"I don't think they ever stopped looking. My wanted picture might be old, but so long as the price tag is still viable, those bounty hunters would have come after me no matter what."

Rayne dove into more of Aresties's shared food, but a few bites into the second one, he leaped from his chair and ran to the nearest trash bin. Several hard heaves later, he was back to square one.

I gave him a sympathetic look as he sat back down at the table. "Give it some time, Captain."

"Is that a joke?" he snarled.

My eyes widened, and I glanced at Ayil to see if I had indeed been insensitive. He rolled his eyes and shook his head. "She means quit wolfing down your food. You were a freaking vegetable a few hours ago."

"Ayil," I quietly scolded.

"What?" he squawked. "He doesn't need to be talking to you like that. Not after what you did for him."

I afforded a glance to Rayne to see what he thought about that, but he was back to staring off into space. I couldn't imagine what he was feeling. There was no description for a decade's worth of displacement. I wished I could help him, but fate, it seemed, had prevented Captain Rayne and me from getting acquainted.

Sweet Sorrow

Aresties hugged me so tightly I thought I might need to get an oxygen mask when she was through. We were saying goodbye in Terrin's enormous cargo bay instead of the corridor. For some reason, he didn't want me getting close to my ship.

Strange.

Aresties was crying, and it was making me weepy. I had always expected my little crew might leave me someday, but I never thought I would leave them. "Maybe we can visit you." She pulled me back, suddenly bright-eyed with her ingenious idea.

I smiled and nodded. "I would like that very much, but Starla has a new captain and my home is very far away." I glanced at Rayne. He looked white as a sheet from his rerun meal. Since Ayil had scolded him, he hadn't said a word. He was just going through the motions until he figured out what to do. It was probably a good thing Ayil and Aresties were staying on board with him. Whether or not he knew it, he was going to need some help to adjust to his new life.

Ayil pushed between us and hugged me against him. "Tell me the truth," he murmured in my ear. "Is this what you want?"

"No, but it's pointless to draw guns so I can avoid a mail-order husband."

He pulled me back. "You should have had my babies."

"If I had, they would have ended up being lab rats or killed."

He frowned as he took in my words. "They really are serious about this DNA thing."

"I'm the next big thing in gene therapy. If I can give them a baby, they'll probably be testing it before they cut the cord."

"And that's what you want me to let you go back to?"

"No, that's what I don't want you dragged into. Just go on with your life, and be happy."

"You won't be happy, will you?"

"I will be taken care of. I will be safe." I motioned to Terrin, who was standing guard over my exchanges. He nodded to Ayil, confirming my declaration.

Ayil hugged me again. "Don't give up, Kit." He backed away before I could object to his endless endurance.

I looked at the next in line to say goodbye. I stared at Rayne as he passed. Neither one of us knew what to say or do. He was as much a stranger to me as the green men lumbering through the bay, and yet I had slept next to him for six years. I had stared at his frozen face when I was lonely. He was my fantasy come to life, and as beautiful as he was in motion, he was not the man I dreamed about.

"Good luck." He offered his hand to shake, and I took it. It was warm, strong, and slightly rough, despite years of disuse.

"Thank you. I'm sorry you had to wake up to all of this." I rolled my head, gesturing to everything.

He nodded. "I guess I should be happy to have woken up."

"You will be," I assured him. "After the anger and the pain wear off, you'll find the strength to enjoy it."

He didn't have a response for that, so he squeezed my hand again and let it drop. I watched them all walk away down the stretched corridor to my ship. I waited there to watch the vessel to float away. When the boosters were only a memory, I burst into tears. I hadn't expected the ache in my heart at having to watch my friends leave me behind.

After my hiccups lessened to sniffles, Terrin put his hand on my shoulder and ushered me away. They were gone, but I wasn't alone.

Broken Promises

I sat across from Terrin and pushed the food around on my plate. He had invited me to his quarters for dinner, but I suspected it was for part two of his interrogation. The plush, dark interior of his cabin was not what I expected. My ship was vastly outdated compared to his, and the captain's den was proof of it. A cozy apartment setting had replaced the cold nautical theme one usually saw on commercial ships. I almost forgot I was on a space vessel.

When he hadn't asked me a single question by the end of the meal, I suspected he was waiting for me to begin the conversation. "Terrin," I started softly.

"Don't," he grumbled, staring at me from his relaxed position across the table. "Don't apologize. I know you aren't sorry you left."

"You're right, I'm not." I dropped my fork on the plate. "And if I had been given the chance to do it today, I would have again." He narrowed his eyes at me. "Promises aside, I mean."

"Yes, those pesky promises. They do burden one, don't they?" His demeanor was still relaxed, but I could hear the acrid sarcasm in his voice. "Like the one I promised to your father and mother."

I looked away, but it wouldn't save me. I had mistaken his invitation for an interrogation. This was, in actuality, my belated ass-ripping, and I was going to have to hear every word if I wanted to earn his respect. Love may have been a given, but trust wasn't.

"Do you have any idea how much shame I endured at losing track of one girl?"

I shook my head.

"I was fired!" He leaned forward, finally reflecting the anger in his body. "I took on a ship and hunted the galaxy for you. Just two steps behind you for months. You were clever and careful; I'll give you that." His jaw twisted as he remembered the frustration of the hunt.

"Why did you continue to look for me if you were fired?"

"Because I made a promise!" His hand slammed against the table, cracking the decorative wood veneer. "It may mean nothing to you, but to me, to my kind, it still means something."

"Freedom still means something to my kind."

"Don't throw that word in my face, like I don't understand sacrifice. Hard labor is the birthright of every gattaw. Only a few of us ever make it into respectable positions. So, no, Mallory, you do not get to complain about fine linens and aged wine."

"It's a prison, whether it's beautiful or not!"

"It's a home. It's two homes, with loving parents."

"I am a science experiment to them!"

"No, you aren't!" Terrin stood and leaned over the table. "Your father was devastated when you left. You were the only real thing in his whole damn life. Your mother hid her sorrows better, but I still bear the scar from her ring." He motioned to a line of discoloration on his cheek. "She wanted me dead for letting you run away, and she nearly got her wish."

I shook my head, even though I knew he wasn't lying. I did miss them. They were shit parents, but they were still mine. If I was a normal girl, I wouldn't have had to go so far away from them. I could have visited.

"I let you go, Mallory." Terrin lowered his head and sighed. "I had you so many times, but I chose to let you go. I stayed close. Just in case you were stupid enough to stay too long on a high traffic planet." He shook his head, rebuking me for my stupidity. "We have no choice. You can't keep running and I can't keep letting you conveniently slip through my fingers." I pinched my lips, not wanting to admit anything. "I've done right by our friendship, Mallory. You can't say I haven't. Now, I need to do right by my duty. And so do you."

I sucked in a breath, trying to swallow the hardest word of them all: duty.

δuty

I sat in the back of the limo, nervously running my headscarf through my fingers. Terrin sat across from me, vigilantly watching me. He was naturally the picture of calm as he accompanied me to my doom. "I like your hair," he commented. I instinctively touched the freshly colored avocado locks.

"You've never commented on my hair before."

"You've never gone green before," he smirked.

I couldn't help but smile at him. "It's shorter than when I left," I said.

"I noticed. Not as short as it was right after you left, though." His eyes dimmed slyly. "The blue was cute, but not quite you."

"And the green?" I asked. "Does it suit me?"

"Green is definitely your color," he said with a smile.

I smiled and sighed. "My parents will hate it." I lifted the hot pink scarf and wrapped it around my head, hiding almost every inch of green.

"They aren't going to care about your hair, Mallory. They are going to be ecstatic that you are home again."

I scoffed. "They must be eager to see me if you managed to get my mother to come to my father's house for this meeting."

"It was logical. His planet is the closest, and you know she wasn't going to let him see you first."

I laughed. "True. This will probably be the first time my parents have been in the same room since I was conceived."

Terrin frowned and looked out the window.

"What was that?" I asked.

"Nothing; we don't have time to discuss it now. We're here."

"Is it too late to fake my death?" I asked.

"Much too late," he answered as he opened the car door and stepped out. He reached back, beckoning me out with gentlemanly assistance. When I didn't take it, he resorted to flailing his fingers, demanding I come out.

I clasped his hand, unsympathetic to the fact that I was squeezing too hard. He had gotten me into this mess; he could suffer a few pinched fingers. Before I could think of an excuse to delay, he yanked me out of the vehicle and dragged me toward my father's house.

The estate hadn't changed as much as I had expected it to. It was still the gorgeous vision my father's gardener had in mind when he took the job. We climbed the steps to the columned front door. "Don't leave me," I mumbled to Terrin.

"Your mother and I do not get along. It would be wise for me to let you do this on your own."

"Please."

"Mallory, they are your parents, not criminals," he scolded my childishness.

The front door opened before we could knock. The butler was new. He gave Terrin a hard gaze before clearing a path for us. Not slowing down, we continued through the foyer and the conservatory. I felt my stomach clench as I saw my mother's bodyguards standing at the patio doors. They stepped together, blocking our passage.

"The queen has declined your admittance, gattaw," one of them condescended. I had already had quite enough of people's prejudice for my friend.

Before Terrin could respond, I jumped in. "Then the queen has declined *my* admittance. Terrin is my bodyguard. He has been protecting me since I was fifteen, and if you think I am going to ask him to step aside for a couple of lackeys that were probably hired last week, you are sorely mistaken."

"The queen said—" the man objected again.

"And I said no!" I snapped.

"Yeah, she said no!" a little girlish voice said behind me. My face twisted with confusion as I turned to Terrin and then back to the source of the voice.

I looked down at the little girl in perfect blond curls and a pretty pink dress. She crossed her arms and scrunched her face, a perfect performance of defiance. I grinned at her and glanced at Terrin to see if he found as much amusement in her as I did. However, he wasn't looking at her. He was watching me—or evaluating me.

"Let my sister through!" the little girl screeched at the men and they reluctantly stood to one side.

I laughed at her forcefulness until I realized what she had just said. I looked at her pretty little face with a different perspective. My brow dipped in shock, but this revelation didn't surprise Terrin at all.

"Sister?" I asked him and he nodded. "This is my little sister?"

In one heart-shattering moment, anger and grief flooded my mind. I had a sister, and no one told me. My face must have shown my accusation of betrayal, because Terrin stiffened, ready for a fight.

"I'm Elizandra," the girl said and shoved out her hand to me.

Trembling and on the verge of tears, I shook her hand. "I'm Mallory—or Kit, whatever you prefer."

"I like Kit."

"Okay, I'll be Kit to you then. How old are you, sweetheart?"

"I'm almost five."

"Five." I chuckled and wiped away an errant tear. I kneeled down to look at her more closely. "That's a pretty dress; did your mommy give you this dress?"

"Nope, Daddy did. He said my sister was coming home today, and I should dress up real pretty so she would like me." Her mouth twisted. "Do you like me?"

I smiled and nodded. "Oh, yes, Elizandra. I like you very much, but you know what?"

"What?"

"I would have liked you even if you were covered in mud."

"No!" Elizandra giggled and threw her head back. "Not mud. That's gross!"

"Mud is fun." I smiled. "I'll show you how fun mud can be."

"Mommy won't let me."

I pinched back my lips and nodded. "She never let me play in the mud either, but I know Daddy will let us."

"Let's go ask him!" She jumped up and down exuberantly.

"Okay. You go ahead; I'll be right out."

Elizandra ran out to the courtyard to find my father—*our* father. I stood and faced Terrin, ready to lay my charges of betrayal at his feet.

"Would you have come back?" he asked, interrupting my attack. "If I had told you about her, would you have come back?" I stared at him, refusing to open my mouth and let loose a truth I didn't want my ears to hear. "Contrary to what you might believe, Mallory, your parents' lives do not solely revolve around you."

I felt a triple pronged sting of rejection with that declaration and the realization that followed. "That's why they stopped looking for me." My lip quivered. "They had a replacement, so they didn't need me?"

Terrin closed the space between us. He cupped my chin, forcing my gaze up to him. "They never stopped looking for you. No one could ever replace you." The sternness in his tone reminded of the man who spouted his rules to me like I was a dog, but the way he was looking at me... the way his thumb was stroking my jaw... I felt like I was fifteen again. All he had to do was tell me I was a *good girl* and I would roll over and let him rub my belly.

And that's not even a metaphor.

As if recognizing the stupefaction of a horny teenager, Terrin abruptly released me and drew away. "We can discuss this later. We need to go see your parents. Dry your tears," he ordered.

I cleared my throat and blinked away my remaining tears. I turned to the door and took Terrin's hand in mine. He glanced down at the contact. "Is this really how you want to be reintroduced to your parents after six years?"

I frowned at him. "You're right." I released his hand and ripped off the headscarf I had so carefully used to cover my green hair. I flipped my head upside down and rustled about a thousand snarls into my hair for the proper volume I needed. When I returned topside, I grabbed Terrin's hand again. "Okay, now I'm ready."

He tried to scold me with his gaze, but the delight in his eyes told me he liked my audacity. With no further objections, he led me out to meet with my parents.

The Green Girl

I approached the paved patio, my green hair waving in the wind, and my green friend at my side. I was ready for anything my parents had to dish out.

"Mallory!" my father wailed and came running at me. He embraced me and six years of anxiety melted away. "My sweet, sweet girl." He pulled back and looked at me. Nothing in his eyes suggested anything but love for me, albeit a little sadness that I was six years older.

Richard turned to Terrin and nodded. "Thank you." He looked back at me. "I can't tell you how much this means to me."

"Hi, Daddy." I smiled at him.

"Move aside, Richard," Susan said from behind him. He grimaced and moved away.

Terrin retracted his hand, but I tugged on it, demanding to keep my security blanket for this reunion.

"Mommy," Elizandra exclaimed at her side, "she matches the green man."

Susan glanced down at her before setting her eyes on my hair. She turned her attention to Terrin next. "I thought we had an understanding."

"I want him here, Mother," I said.

Susan examined my face, searching for any hint of weakness, but I was determined to get what I wanted. Since she recognized the fortitude from her own reflection, she could hardly argue. "And what do you expect from me, Kit?"

"What do you mean?"

"I mean, you ran away. Left us for six years, without any hint of your condition. Am I to rush into your arms like your father and forgive you instantly for your selfishness?"

"No, I would expect you to stand there and lecture me while you look at me with haughty disdain." Susan's eyes lit with anger. Anger that had the backing of an entire galaxy. Terrin squeezed my hand, begging, or perhaps demanding, that I not press my luck. There was, after all, no guarantee she wouldn't have me imprisoned for life. Especially since she had a replacement daughter lined up.

"It's been a very long trip, Your Majesty," Terrin interjected. "Your daughter isn't thinking straight."

"Don't speak to me," she snapped back at him.

"Don't talk to him like that," I snapped right back.

Susan shook her head at me. "I should have expected you to behave like this. Six years on your own couldn't have improved your attitude. I won't make the same mistakes with Elizandra."

"You already are," I said.

"Mommy, Kit said we can play in the mud," Elizandra announced, adding to the frown on my mother's face. I smiled at her.

"Princesses don't play in the mud," Susan corrected.

"The cool ones do," I countered, and winked at my sister.

"Go sit with your father, Elizandra." Susan practically pushed her away. "Before things get too out of hand here, Kit, I need you to know that your absence has been a constant source of sorrow for me, and as much as I want to be mad at you right now, I am glad you're back."

"I missed you too, Mom," I said, losing some of my scowl.

"That being said, you need to know that nothing has changed. You still have obligations."

I nodded. "I know."

"Good, because we don't have time to play these childish games anymore. In one week, you will marry the man I have selected for you. You will have an *appropriate* marital relationship with him." She glanced at my hand gripping Terrin's as she said appropriate. "You will provide us with an heir and if you fail to do so in three months, we will find you a different husband. So forth and so on, until you have an offspring."

My stomach clenched as I tried to comprehend this new dating process, more akin to a breeding program. If there wasn't such a focus on the religious prophecy, I might have been able to bathe in semen until I got pregnant, but that wasn't what they wanted. They wanted the chosen one. The natural result of a man and a woman, and their overbearing parents.

Righteous Kiss

After the tensest meal ever, I arrived in my old childhood bedroom and dove into my private bathroom to puke out the feelings I had been hiding for most of the day. I wasn't surprised that my mother was raising the stakes, but I was surprised she was starting so soon. I supposed I should be grateful I didn't arrive home to my wedding in progress.

"What happened?" Terrin asked from my bed where he had been waiting out the dinner. My mother had been tolerant of his presence, but asking her to share a meal with him might have caused a planetary war. "Are you alright?" His voice sounded closer to me.

"No, don't come in here. It's just emotional indigestion." I was sure he would hold my hair back like a proper gentleman, but I didn't want him to see me at my worst. Not that hearing it left much to the imagination. "I'm okay now," I said, flushing my last meal. I moved to the sink and washed up. "I just needed to get that out of my system. Bad news is always better on an empty stomach."

"On the topic of bad news? You didn't say much on the veranda when your mother was done with you." I heard the bed squeak as he sat again. "I don't presume dinner went any better." He sighed. "Mallory, talk to me. What are you feeling right now?"

I stared at the woman in the mirror, trying to figure out what exactly I was feeling. I had lost my two best friends, my fantasy lover, and to top it off, in a week I was going to marry a man I didn't love and attempt to conceive a child with him.

I stepped out of the bathroom and found Terrin leaning over his knees on my bed. He looked up at me with a subdued concern I only saw when we were alone. "Make love to me," I whispered to him.

"Excuse me?" he asked, looking uncomfortable for the first time ever.

I nodded. "Let's do it."

"Mallory, you know we can't." He furrowed his brow at me.

"No, it's okay." I moved to him and straddled him.

His mouth gaped as he stared up at me. "Oh, Mallory, please tell me you're joking."

"It will be a fabulous Romeo and Juliet story, only painful and very bloody. But at least I'll get to be with the one man I want before I die."

"Ma—" he objected, but I smothered his lips with a hard kiss, leaving no room for friendship in its meaning.

I could feel him tense, prepared to push me off, but I pushed myself against him, demanding his full attention and destroying any images he might still have of me as a child. He grunted at the stimulation and wrapped his arms tightly around me, pulling me closer.

He gripped my head and pressed his tongue between my lips. I whimpered as my body erupted in tingles of anticipation. I barely felt him move before I was under him. He pressed against me and started biting kisses down my neck. I lamented loudly, and he shushed me.

He continued to slide down my body and I gasped, preparing myself for more. He slipped off me, and I waited for him to return unclothed, but he didn't. I propped myself up to find the cause of the delay.

I found him sitting in a chair in the corner of my room. He was leaning over his knees again, slightly out of breath, watching me. He looked almost mad.

I sat up, still ready to raze my body for one night with him. "Please don't stop, Terrin. It could be worth it, couldn't it?"

He frowned. "Worth it to die for, maybe." His jaw clenched as he shook his head. "Worth it to kill you for, no." He huffed and rubbed his face. "I know you're scared right now and I would give anything to be the right man for you, but I'm not. I have never been the right man, biologically or otherwise."

"You have to be. I love you." I stood and moved to him again.

"Stop!" he barked and held out a hand to stop my approach. "We are not doing this. I shouldn't have let it go this far, but I…" He glanced at the bed. "I love you too, Mallory, and that is why I will *never* make love to you."

I fell to my knees in front of him. "Terrin, no!" I tried to caress his face, but he collected my hand and held it hostage. Realizing he would make good on his declaration, I groaned and flopped back to the floor. Still holding my hand, he tried to ease my fall. "Why can't life make sense?" I growled.

"Because if it did, you would be bored. Then you would complain about that." He dropped my hand.

"Stop mocking me. I'm at a vomit level of distress right now."

"Mallory, in one week you are going to marry and do your duty, much like your mother did."

"Yeah, see how that turned out."

"You will make babies, and you will live a semi-normal life," he continued. "This is no more than an arranged marriage and it is hardly worth Shakespearean suicide to avoid."

"Nope, no good. I don't feel better."

He groaned and pulled me upright again. "Listen to me, Mallory. I am trying to empathize with you, but I am about done with this behavior."

"Do you realize I have only had three friends in my entire life—four if you count my zombie nightlight? Ayil and Aresties are halfway across the galaxy. All I have left is you, and when I marry, you will leave me." I reached to touch his face, and this time he let me. "I don't want to lose you, Terrin."

He pulled my hand away, giving it a kiss before letting it drop again. "You have to think about the bigger picture. Your DNA has the potential to save a lot of lives. Doesn't that mean anything to you?"

"Oh, geez, don't worry about the DNA. It's fine."

"What do you mean? You said you haven't had children."

"I haven't. Crap, Terrin, I'm a virgin." I laughed and moved to stand, but he pulled me back down.

"You're not telling me something." He scanned my face, reading my lies as if they were written there. "What is it?"

"It's fate, Terrin. Whatever happens is supposed to happen? Haven't you read the prophecy?"

He frowned. "What have you done?"

I smiled and pulled my hands from his. "Nothing." I stood, and he joined me, still begging for the answer to his question. "Since you refuse to kill me with great sex, I should probably get some sleep. I have a wedding to plan." I feigned excitement.

"You don't fool me for a second. You know that, right?"

"Goodnight." I leaned forward and kissed him chastely on the lips. I smiled and backed away from him.

"Goodnight." He narrowed his eyes at me before leaving me to sleep.

Star-Crossed

I flaunted the next dress with a spin and a booty shake. My mother did not find the performance amusing, but my little sister, Elizandra, giggled to no end. "Must you make a mockery of this?"

I smiled at my sister. I was probably supposed to resent that she was my replacement, but the walking, talking doll of a girl had won me over with her very first pouty command. She was destined to be spoiled, and with my help, she would be a brat too.

Just like her big sister.

"Yes, I must, Mother." I continued to smile to hide my annoyance from Elizandra. "Because if I don't, I will rip this dress to shreds," I said cheerfully, making my sister laugh purely from the charm of my voice.

"I'll make you a deal," Susan said, playing with Elizandra's bouncy curls. "I'll let you choose the dress."

"Any dress?" I asked, more intrigued.

Susan smiled. "Any *white* dress that isn't inappropriate." I chuckled and rolled my eyes at her. Naturally, she interpreted all female rebellion as potentially provocative. "In exchange, you will dye that green out of your hair."

I frowned and fiddled with the bow on my corset. "You want the boring blonde back?" I asked.

"I don't care what color you choose, as long as it isn't green." Contempt seeped into her voice.

I looked up at her. "Speaking of green, where is he? I haven't seen him in two days."

"He's being kept away."

"I want him at the wedding, Mother."

"Elizandra." Susan pouted to her daughter with sad lips. "Mommy is so thirsty. Would you bring Mommy a drink?"

"I want to see the dresses," Elizandra complained.

"I will wait until you come back to try another one," I told her. "I'm thirsty too. Do you think you could carry two waters, or do you need help?"

"No! I can do it!" She jumped off her chair and ran off to flaunt her independence, as I knew she would.

"She's so beautiful," I murmured.

"As you were. Still are, minus that hair, of course." Susan smiled at me and I reciprocated the civility with a small smile of my own. "Kit, that gattaw—"

"Terrin, Mom. His name is Terrin. I will not continue to have this conversation unless you can offer him that small respect."

"Fine." She raised her hand in surrender. "Terrin. He is a dutiful man and I am thankful your father hired him to watch over you. I was disappointed by his failure to secure you after you ran away. However, I also know you are a clever girl, and only your father and I can be blamed for that."

"Yes, I know how much you hoped for a stupid child," I teased.

"I'm grateful to him for finally returning you."

"But?" I offered her the transition.

Susan frowned, revealing concern more than anger. "You know this... infatuation is unhealthy—for both of you."

"I'm well aware of the anatomical complications, if that's what you're saying."

"That's not what I'm saying, Kit. This man was at your side for a good portion of your transitioning adolescence. Now you're back, and I can see you are just as enamored with him as you were at sixteen."

"We are friends." I shrugged, delivering my stock line.

"Terrin is a grown man, and I know he will eventually make the right choice and leave you to live your life. Unfortunately, I don't think he is ready to do that just yet and I don't want him making a fool of you before he does."

"What do you mean?"

"I mean, I don't want you standing at the altar next to your husband-to-be, making doe eyes at the gat in the back of the church," she snapped.

I shook my head. "I need him, Mother."

"For how long? I'll ask you the same question: do you realize how unhealthy this relationship is for *both* of you? You say you need him, but what does that mean for him?" Susan shifted to the edge of her seat and glanced around. "I hate to be the bearer of bad news, my dear, but with no paycheck from your father and no hope of sex with you, he is not going to stay by your side."

I looked around, trying to hold it together while I futilely tried to stitch my heart back together. It was selfish and ignorant of me to assume Terrin would stay by my side like a damned dog. My mother was right. Terrin was right, too. I was being a spoiled brat. I needed to face this with maturity.

"I'll dye my hair and wear whatever dress you want, but I need him at the wedding."

"Have you heard nothing I've said?" She threw her hands up, exasperated.

"I've heard every word. That's why I need him there. I need to at least say goodbye."

"Fine, as long as you go down that aisle with a fertile human man, then I will let him attend." Susan glanced over at Elizandra as she arrived, carefully balancing two full-to-the-brim cups of water. She shook her head, but smiled at the incorrigible girl. "Good job, Elizandra," she said, taking the waters from her hands. "Now we need to finish helping your sister choose a dress, and then we will help her choose a new color for her hair."

Elizandra gasped. "No more green?" she asked sadly.

"Nope, no more green," my mother said and glanced at me for confirmation.

I smiled, disguising the tears in my eyes as a sparkle.

Dumb-Dumb-Dee-Dumb

Three women ran around me, desperate to get my gunmetal gray hair to lie just right. A few loose tendrils here and there and silver embellishments to add a little sparkle to the otherwise boring color, and I was looking like a proper cake topper.

When no one was looking, I added another layer of black eyeliner to balance the pink lipstick they insisted looked good on me. A cloud of hair spray later and I was ready to be shoved into my dress with the help of three human shoehorns.

After ten more minutes of being groped, I felt like I was truly ready to walk down the aisle, if for no other reason than to get away from my attendants.

My mother arrived to check on my progress and I looked up at her with expectant eyes. "Is he here?"

Her awestruck eyes shifted into a glare. "Of course your groom is here." She smiled with threat as she looked over our three-woman audience. "But you can't see him before the wedding."

"Why not?" I smiled back.

"Because tradition demands that you don't see him before your vows are complete."

"Oh, crap." I frowned, realizing our sub-textual conversation was true. "I really can't see this douchebag before I'm married to him."

"Sweetheart." Susan laughed for a moment before snarling at me. "Language. This is your husband-to-be."

"Maybe just a peek?" I suggested. "I'm sure you have a photo, Mother. That doesn't count."

"Oh, for Pete's sake, here." As I suspected, Mother had packed a wedding disaster plan in her bra. She pulled out a folded picture and handed it to me.

"Oh," I said as I looked down at the handsome face with reddish brown hair. "He's kind of cute." I shrugged.

"Yes, he is," my mother announced. "I certainly wasn't going to have ugly grandchildren. He's also very polite, articulate, and from what I can tell, he's... not lacking in any physical features."

I smirked at my mother's thoroughness.

"He's a kind man, Kit. And even if he wasn't, your father and I have imposed our great expectations on him. He will be a good husband. And provided that you two cooperate, you may not have to go through this again."

"You do realize no matter what you say, all I can think about is how much you and Dad hate each other."

Susan nodded and took the picture back from me. "I had that in mind when I chose this man for you. Your father and I... well... we tried, but the only thing we were ever good at was making babies. As evidenced by you and your sister." She winked at me.

"Is it worth it?" I asked her. "I mean, I know you love us, but if you could have had a normal marriage, maybe slightly different kids... would you?"

Susan took a breath. "I know you want to hear something that will make you not fear the future, but the truth is, dear, all we ever have is right here, right now. You can't make decisions for yesterday or tomorrow. You can only do today what feels right today."

"How can you say that when every decision ever made for me has been based on the possibility of a prophesied future?"

"Yes, and those are the decisions your father and I made for you. It's our job as parents to help you get to the best possible outcome, but you are an adult now. It's time to start choosing for yourself."

"Does that mean I can go home?" I pointed to the door.

My mother took a breath and opened the door to my makeshift dressing room. "The doors aren't locked," she said and left.

"No, they're just battened down with a mountain of guilt," I grumbled.

Iron Henry

After receiving the last of my instructions, my bevy of beauticians clamored out the door. I had ten more minutes before surrendering to my new future. It was time to drink.

Against the advisement of a few commandments, I picked the lock on the cabinet holding the sacramental wine and chugged down half the bottle. The door clicked shut behind me and I struggled to get the bottle off my mouth without dripping on my perfectly white gown.

Bent over and holding my booze at arm's length, I looked over to see how much trouble I was in. Terrin stood inside the door in a black tux. A smile crept onto his face as he looked me over.

I laughed as I imagined what I looked like. "Hi."

"Hi." He smirked at me and came around to grab the dangerous red liquid from me. "Hasn't anyone ever told you not to eat or drink after you get the dress on?"

"I'm just glad it was you. If those old biddies saw me, they'd probably postpone the wedding to touch up my lipstick."

Terrin's eyes moved to my pink lips, after which they dragged down my body to take in my dress. The strapless bell gown was fairly traditional, but it was simple and terribly comfortable. "You look beautiful."

I tried to smile. "Last chance, Frog Prince, pucker up."

He chuckled. "I don't think another kiss is going to change this frog."

"We could try." I shrugged. After a moment for the levity to clear, I spoke again. "Listen, I know you have a life beyond me. Actually, I didn't know that. I was informed yesterday that I might not be the center of your universe and... wow..." I gesticulated my mind being blown. "I'm still trying to figure out how that's possible." Terrin smirked at my comedic relief. "So, anyway, upon the advice of my mother—uck—I am going to relieve you of any obligations to me." I rubbed my face. "Geez, that sounds condescending."

"Don't rub your makeup away." He pulled my hands from my face. "Your mother also spoke to me." I scoffed. "No, Mallory, I agree with what she's saying. I've always known how you feel about me, and, to the extent that it was permissible, I did return those feelings. But now you're an adult, and I'm finding it difficult to think of you as a little girl with a crush."

I wanted to reach out and touch him, but I already knew where this conversation was heading.

"I wish things were different, but they aren't. Perhaps having a proper lover will do you some good. I also think a little distance would put some perspective on our... feelings."

"So, I go my way and you go yours?" I asked, looking at my feet.

"This isn't goodbye, Mallory." He tipped up my chin.

"You aren't staying for the wedding, are you?"

His face dimmed. "You are far too beautiful right now for me to watch you walk away." He leaned in and pulled my chin to open my mouth. His eyes never left mine as he gave me a gentle, painfully slow kiss.

When he backed away, I was panting. "Do you want me to throw you up against the wall just to be sure?" I asked.

He laughed and shook his head. "I'm sorry, Mallory, this isn't a spell we can break." He grazed his finger along my cheek and left without an official goodbye.

I stared down at my stolen bottle of wine, and dove right back in.

I Guess I Do

Despite the noble efforts to make my hair and makeup perfect, I had to cover it up with a head veil. The heavy white fabric disguised my face from my future husband. However, it also masked most of my view.

I barely made it down the aisle without tripping. When I veered into a pew, an attending guest had to redirect. That time, however, might have been due more to my excess blood alcohol level. The audience politely giggled, and I continued down to my father.

The priest asked for the names of my former captors and my father offered his name and my mother's name. He lifted my veil just enough to kiss my cheek. My belated pucker missed his, but my veil was down already.

I turned to make the final approach to my betrothed and completely biffed on the single step I hadn't noticed. Down I went to my knees. I tried to play it off as a genuflect, but I wasn't fooling anyone.

A hand slipped under my elbow, assisting my rise. I looked in the general direction of my savior, but all I could see was a black tux. I tipped my head back, trying to angle the open weave closer to my eyes, but it was no use—my groom was wearing the same damn veil, only in black. There was something ironic about a bride arriving in white and a groom in black.

While the priest performed a lovely ceremony, I amused myself by making faces at my husband-to-be. Drunk or not, I found this to be immensely entertaining. When I almost lost control of a fitful giggle attack, I heard my mother clear her throat from the front row.

The priest asked for the exchange of rings and my husband-to-be slipped mine on my finger. I couldn't help but peek at it under my veil. Judging by the audience's chuckle, I was not as surreptitious with the movement as I thought.

I slipped his on his finger, but it got stuck on his knuckle. I grimaced and tried to push it on, but he pulled away and adjusted it himself. Whoever was in charge of rings obviously dropped the ball. When our hands rejoined, the priest asked for the final I do's. I gave mine, and he paused.

I stood frozen before him, wondering if he was having as many doubts about this marriage as me. Once again, I was so caught up in my perspective that I hadn't even realized this poor sap was going through the same thing, just from the opposite side.

"I do," he finally mumbled.

The priest announced our marriage and gave us permission to kiss. As instructed, we each lifted our veils halfway and met our lips. The perfunctory kiss was as I expected it to be. Two strangers doing as they are told.

The audience cheered for our union. Then our chaperones whisked us away for our wedding night, while our guests overindulged in wine and food in our honor.

Lovers' Perjuries

The hotel was less than a mile from the church. My mother wasn't taking any chances. The driver stopped and allowed me, my husband, and our four chaperones to exit the limousine. In most cases, the chaperones were there to make sure couples didn't start their honeymoons early, but in this case, I presumed they were there to keep me from escaping.

Ignoring propriety, I hoisted up my skirt to make it up the concrete steps to the hotel door. My ladies slapped my hands, but I shooed them away. Once inside the hotel, they collected our keys and all six of us stepped inside of an elevator together.

I glanced over at my husband and his two male chaperones. I still couldn't see crap through the veil. What I could see, however, was that he was not the least bit curious about me. He was stock still, as if he were about ready for a battle. I lifted the edge of my veil and peeked at the strength my mother had referred to earlier. His shoulders were a little broader than the photo showed. His ring remained jammed just past his knuckle.

A chaperon swatted my hand for peeking, and I resisted the urge to scold her. She was just doing her job.

While the elevator took its time to arrive, I enjoyed the pop music and my happiness-harboring buzz. My little jig finally caught my husband's attention, but I couldn't tell if my silliness amused or disgusted him.

He could have been silently screaming for all I knew.

Exiting the elevator, we paraded down the long hallway to the honeymoon suite. We must have been quite the sight, chaperones in front and back, two idiots in between.

The chaperones reached the double doors, swiped the key card, and opened the door in one choreographed motion. We stepped inside behind them and followed them to the gargantuan bed that would be the scene of my deflowering.

I peeked under my veil again and cringed at the cheesy heart-shaped pillows. I felt one woman touching my back and then my zipper slid down. "Excuse me!" I whipped around to face them. "What do you think you are doing?"

"Undressing you, Majesty."

"I think we can manage that part on our own," I said, appalled by their lack of respect for the occasion.

"But Majesty—"

"Get out!" my husband yelled, startling the entire room.

The chaperones scurried away and closed the doors behind them. I stared at the double doors, wondering if the chaperones would lock them until morning. Or perhaps until I conceived. "Sorry about that. My mother is committed to getting a grandchild ASAP."

He mumbled some kind of response. I sat down on the bed and touched the silky bedspread. As terrified as I was of this future, I knew my mother was right. The here and now was the only thing I needed to worry about. When I had children, I could worry about their futures, but until then, I needed to focus on the moments in front of me.

I removed my veil, careful not to snag it on my hair. With clear vision, I looked over at my black-veiled man. He had removed his jacket and tossed it over a chair. He did the same with his bow tie. After undoing two buttons on his dress shirt, he noticed my uncovered face.

His hand froze at his collar as he stared over at me. Even with his face covered, I could feel his eyes looking me over. My breathing increased as I realized I was about to finish what I had started the other night. Granted, it was with a different man, but still.

"Just so you know, this is not what I normally look like." I motioned to my face. "I mean, this takes three highly trained beauticians."

He approached me, removing his cuff links and pocketing them. He paused before me and sat down on the bed next to me. I could see a hint of movement behind the cloth as his eyes flickered over me.

I reached forward and undid his remaining buttons. He looked down at my shaking hands with interest. With only a few more left to go, he took my hands in his, rubbing the back of them as he set them back on my lap.

"Don't you want to consummate?" I grimaced at the word. It didn't sound sexy, but I couldn't very well say *make love*. This wasn't love. It was a one-night stand we couldn't walk away from.

His head tipped as he looked me over. I sensed a smile, but I couldn't be sure. He scooted closer to me until our knees were touching. He inhaled sharply and reached for his veil. At the last second, I closed my eyes. I wasn't ready to see him. It didn't matter, anyway.

Within my created darkness, I panted, waiting for him to touch me. His first touch was his finger gently sliding down my cheek. It was so innocent, but my heart thrummed. I was ready.

I tipped my chin forward to receive his kiss. He waited for what seemed like an eternity as I licked my lips in preparation.

Finally, he shifted his hand to cup my face, and he kissed me. I nervously moved my lips, searching for a rhythm with his. As our gentle nibbles grew in fervor, he shifted, putting his arm around me. He found the opening in my zipper and slipped his hand under the material.

He pushed closer to me, opening his mouth for deeper kisses. I squeezed his thigh and slid my hand up. I could barely breathe and I was about to have a heart attack, but I wasn't thinking about yesterday or tomorrow. Just the moment.

"Damn Rayne, you don't have to play the part *that* well," Ayil's voice spoke from behind me.

I whipped around and looked for my friend. Ayil leaned in the bathroom door, smiling at me. "Ayil?" I gasped and ran to him. He caught me in a hug and lifted me off the floor. "What are you doing here?" I asked when he put me down.

"Rescuing you, stupid." He thumped my forehead, but all I could do was stare at him with a stupid grin. "We found out about the wedding and did a little switch-a-roo. If I had known you were going to be so appreciative, *I* would have worn the suit instead of Rayne." He popped his brow, teasing me.

It wasn't until he said the name the second time that I registered it. I looked back at the bed I had only recently come from. Captain Rayne was still sitting there, a slight glare on his face reserved for Ayil. When he caught me staring at him, he didn't look the least bit chagrined at taking advantage of my predicament.

I should have been mad, but the only thing running through my mind was the feel of his lips on mine, and his hand on my bare skin. "I need some air," I said and slipped into the bathroom.

Unveiled

Trying to avoid any confusion, I washed most of the makeup from my face and undid my hair. Thankfully, my overnight bag was already in place, so I changed into a pair of jeans and a white silk blouse. Unfortunately, I hadn't packed my tennis shoes, so I switched to a pair of red flats in case I needed to run.

I stepped out of the bathroom, feeling remotely in control of my life. "Alright, boys, let's run away."

"Hey, what happened to the dress?" Ayil complained over a mouthful of nuts from the gift basket on the entryway table. He was also downing a bottle of sparkling champagne meant for my honeymoon, but that didn't matter anymore. "The makeup too," he grumbled as I got closer.

I glanced at Rayne, who was patiently waiting by the minibar. He took in my change of clothes. "Better, you look more like you."

"Yes." I nodded. "We wouldn't want anyone to confuse *me* for someone else," I said tersely.

Ayil snickered. "I told you she'd be mad." He nodded to Rayne.

"I'm not mad. I'm just ready to get out of here. Let's go."

"No go. Your mother has two chaperones outside the door," Ayil said. "And eight security guards in the lobby watching the exits."

"Holy crap, that woman is determined to get me laid." I rubbed my face, ignoring the snort from Ayil. "Okay, where's my ship?"

"*My* ship is still in orbit," Rayne corrected. "They wouldn't even let us into the atmosphere. We had to take a pod."

"And where is that?"

"On the roof," Ayil said. I shrugged, still confused about why we had a problem. "Of a building about three blocks down."

"You're kidding. She locked down the roofs?"

"We're getting a shit deal on parking, too." Ayil popped another nut in his mouth. "I can't believe they made us pay upfront. Like they suspected, we might try to stiff them when we escaped the planet. Whatever."

Rayne gave him a sympathetic shrug.

"Your plan is what, to hop roofs?"

"No way. I'm not doing that again. I was kind of hoping you would have a plan."

"Seriously, what kind of rescue is this?"

"Here's the thing," Rayne interrupted. "We have about thirty minutes to get the hell off this planet, because your betrothed is going to wake up and probably mention that he got knocked out and missed the ceremony entirely. So, we need to do something quick."

I paused, thinking about our options. I looked around the room for options. I noticed the room had a balcony facing the street. "The chaperones in the hall. Male? Female?"

"One male, one female," Rayne answered.

"Perfect." I smiled at him. "Take your clothes off."

Escape

I tightened the knot on my female chaperone's hands as she whimpered at me, fearful of her fate. "I'm sorry, Princess. I didn't mean to slap your hand."

"Ready?" I asked Ayil, who was behind the male chaperone.

He popped up and leaned on the man's back. "This brings back so many memories," he said wistfully. "Sometimes I miss being a dominant."

"Okay, you two." I stood back on the balcony and looked at my terrified chaperones dressed in my wedding dress and Rayne's tuxedo. We had used the sheets from the honeymoon bed to tie them to the railing. "We need a good performance. Your motivation is *damsel in distress* and yours is *hero*. And... action."

Ayil lifted the poor girl up and tipped her over the edge of the railing. She screamed, no doubt fearing for her life, but the sheets easily held her weight. She dangled mere inches from the railing.

"Let's go." I slapped Ayil on the shoulder when it was clear no one was actually in danger.

We ran out of the room and into the elevators. On the way down, I wrapped my telltale hair in a colorful scarf and added another layer of red lipstick to my lips.

"You do realize if we get caught, Susan might actually put you in prison?" Ayil warned me.

I shushed him and looked around the empty elevator. "Don't say her name aloud. It gives her power."

As the doors opened on the main floor, we jumped into character. "All I'm saying is you could help with the dishes once in a while," I whined with a nasal voice as we stepped out of the elevator.

"Why? You're the one messing them up," Ayil argued in his best scumbag tone. "Two behind us," he murmured as we left the elevator area. Two men in black suits guarded the narrow hall, monitoring anyone coming down.

"Yeah, making *your* dinner." I waggled my head and glanced at the seating area across from us. "Two on the sofa." I spoke without moving my lips, before turning up the volume again to continue our faux argument. "Maybe you'll just have to stop eating?"

"Good, I hate your cooking!"

As we approached the door, I could see the other four were standing guard inside and outside of the front doors. There was no way I could get past all four of them without being recognized. "What?" I ripped Ayil's shoulder back. "You love my cooking! You always say that!"

"I lied!"

Before we needed to go off script, Rayne ran in from outside looking panicked. "Somebody call for a rescue unit," he yelled out to the front desk. "There's a woman hanging off the balcony upstairs. I think she's gonna fall." Rayne ran back outside with one of the security guards on his tail to evaluate the situation.

"Oh my gawd, that poor woman!" I covered my mouth. "Wait for it," I mumbled to Ayil. The guard came running back in, bringing the outside guards with him. "Now," I said.

"Baby, I'm so sorry," Ayil said and leaned in and kissed me as the guards ran past us. We pulled apart and walked outside, hand in hand. We met Rayne on the street and started walking at a good clip. When we were clear of the hotel, we jogged and then ran the remaining three blocks.

"This is a good day for you, Kit," Ayil said as we piled into the building's elevator.

"You mean because I'm escaping the clutches of my family for the second time? They really are going to be pissed."

"No, because you got to make out with the two hottest guys on this planet."

I chuckled until I caught Rayne's eyes. I still wasn't sure what to make of our make-out session. Why didn't he just tell me who he was after the chaperones left? Did he seriously take advantage of my vulnerability to cop a feel?

"Yeah, it's been an interesting week," I admitted, thinking about how quickly my prospects for men had changed.

Missed

Aresties squealed as I climbed out of the pod. She wrapped her arms around me and squeezed me until I couldn't breathe. "I missed you too." I begged for help over her shoulder.

"Come on, Aresties, don't suffocate her with those voluptuous breasts of yours." Ayil peeled her off me and kept her in a sideways embrace. "It was hard work, but we made it."

"Do you mind?" Rayne said from the small door on the pod. All three of us were blocking his exit.

"Sorry, Cap." Ayil pulled Aresties back, and I stepped out of his way. "You driving?"

"Yes," he said and headed up to the flight deck.

"He lets me drive." Ayil pointed after him.

"He doesn't let me drive," Aresties added with a frown. "Anymore."

"It's okay, baby." Ayil rubbed her back. "It did look like a drink holder."

I refrained from laughing at what must have been a troubling misunderstanding for her. "So, what did I miss? Are you guys all best buds now?"

"Yeah, well, as *best* or as *buds* as Rayne allows. He's super quiet and when he gets pissed, just duck, cause something is getting punched and you don't want it to be you."

"Really?" I glanced after the man and wondered if I hadn't made a mistake leaving my friends to him as casually as my ship.

"But he's super sweet, too." Aresties touched my arm. "After he yelled at me for messing up his new console, he bought me a no-spill cup. It's designed for anti-gravity."

"I take it you didn't go into hypersleep for the trip?"

"No." Ayil shook his head. "Rayne said he won't go back into that machine ever, and I don't blame him. So, for the last few months, we've been helping him upgrade the ship. I mean, it's still a hunk of junk, but he really knows his stuff. We haven't broken down once since we—hey, don't be mad." Ayil touched my shoulder.

"Oh, no, I'm not," I said, defending the frown that had slowly crept onto my face. "I'm happy for you guys, and the ship, and Rayne, but... I was just wondering when you decided to come rescue me."

Ayil tipped his head and touched my cheek. "I decided that the minute we stepped onto Terrin's ship. For Rayne, however, it took a few weeks of convincing."

"Weeks?"

"Yeah. Fortunately, the upgrades allowed us to catch up with that freighter Terrin calls a ship.

"Nice. What else can she do?"

Upgrades

"O h, holy hell, that is the sexiest thing I've ever seen." I gaped at the brand-new console and screens in the cockpit. Smooth-surfaced pressure pads replaced the mechanical dials and knobs. The slightest glide of a finger would be all it took to change direction and speed up.

I moved toward the console to touch something—anything—on it, but Rayne grabbed my hand. I nearly forgot he was there, since the nook of the driver's seat obscured him. "Don't touch. I have everything how I want it."

I glanced at my held wrist and he let me go. "Listen Rayne, I appreciate the rescue, but you and I are going to have to get a few things straight about this ship."

Rayne stood from his chair and faced off with me. The three inches he had on me in height didn't concern me nearly as much as the four inches in girth. "And what do we need to straighten out?"

"You upgraded her from port to stern, but she is still mine."

His eyes gleamed with irritation, but he didn't start punching yet. "We both know I could contest that and win."

"And we both know it would take years for the paperwork to go through. In the meantime, Starla would be mine."

He frowned. "Stop calling it that."

"What's her name then?"

"It doesn't have a name. It's a ship."

I gasped in shock and turned to Ayil. He looked between us, trying to remain neutral, but clearly, he wanted to laugh at my theatrics.

"That means you don't really love Starla."

"Stop saying that name!" Rayne yelled at me, forcing me to fall back.

Ayil grabbed me around the side as I stared at the maniac in front of me. My earlier concerns for my friends' safety reignited.

"Hey guys, it's okay," Ayil mediated in an almost mockingly calm tone. "Let's just get to the bottom of this. There is a lot of emotion in this room right now, so I think we should identify it."

"Asshole—there's an identifier," I contributed.

"Rich bitch is another," Rayne added.

I gasped at the insinuation I had worked years to separate myself from. "Do I look like I brought the sum total of my parents' wealth with me in these pants? The only thing I have to my name is this ship."

"The only thing I even *remember* is this ship!" Rayne snapped back. "If you think you are taking it away from me, you have another thing coming."

Ayil whistled and raised his hands as he stepped between us. "See, right there; that was a breakthrough. We're seeing motive now. Each of you has a reason to want this ship. Rayne has a problem with that particular name that was used earlier. And Kit, we all know you don't like to talk about the money situation, or the princess situation, or... anything in your past."

"Ayil, get to a point," I said.

"I was thinking." He looked at us. "Until we establish a long-term plan regarding this sexy ship, we could share her."

"We?" Rayne asked.

"Well, I of course don't have a claim on her, but while Kit holds the deed, you have invested in the upgrades, so kind of stock value situation. And while Rayne is the original captain,

Kit, you're like the second in command, the copilot. What do you say?"

I glanced at Rayne to see if this was working for him. He gave a curt nod. Ayil looked at me. I wasn't sure what I was really agreeing to, but I nodded. "If I'm going to be copilot, I need to know how to fly her."

Apologies

"Okay, now ease it up—not too fast." Rayne guided my hand along the console. "You gotta give the gravity a chance to compensate or the crew will be puking in their laps."

"This is amazing," I said, still in awe of his upgrades. "How is this hunk of junk capable of this?"

"Junk?" He shook his head. "This ship is a classic."

"Uh-huh. And that means old." I grimaced and gave him a small smile to show I was going for humor, not insult.

"We had to install new ballasts along the outer bulkheads. Thrusters were upgraded too. Ayil has helped me with the interior renovations."

I chuckled. "I bet he has," I mumbled, finishing up our full back-flip.

"He's an interesting young man; I'll give you that. Very capable, though."

"Yes, I'm sure." I tried to hide my smirk but failed miserably.

"If you're done mocking me, you can use that button there to activate the anchoring mechanisms."

"An anchor? Crap, Rayne, where did you get the money for this?"

"I have a few nest eggs."

"You remembered your banks?"

"I remember most everything until when I finished my weapons system. This ship was purchased specifically because the gauge of the metal could handle the excess stresses."

"Yeah, she's an iron bitch, that's for sure. Hey, that could be her new name—I mean name, period."

He glanced at me and activated the night mode. "I don't think it's wise to name your home and transportation *bitch*. I can't imagine what kind of asshole would call a woman that."

I caught his meaning, and noted the guilt in his expression, but rather than endure the discomfort of apologies, I kept us on the subject of the ship. "It's complimentary in this case. She's tough. How about the Iron Wench?"

"Could we..." He paused, getting control of his tone again. "...not name the ship tonight? You look exhausted, so why don't we call it a night?"

"What? No, I'm not even tired."

The corner of his mouth tipped up as he looked over my face. "Yes, you are. Your eyes are bloodshot."

"This is too much fun. You go to bed if you want. I'll just practice what you taught me."

He opened his mouth and shifted back to sit on the arm of the copilot chair. "You are clearly an excellent pilot and a very fast learner, but I would be much more comfortable if you would continue to learn with me."

I didn't like the control he was trying to exert over the situation, but no one wants their shiny new toys to be tarnished before their time. "Okay, I'll get started with the owner's manual."

"You want to read the owner's manual?" His brow dipped in disbelief.

"Yeah, of course."

"No one reads those things."

"Then how did you learn?"

"By poking buttons, like normal people."

"I led a very sheltered life in my adolescence. Everything I learned was from a book. Not really normal, but it's how I learn."

He sighed. "Fine. Will you promise not to... experiment?"

"I shouldn't start making promises to you. I never keep them. But yes, I will only read the manual tonight."

"Thank you." He shifted to leave, but returned to the arm. "Listen, I think I need to apologize for our earlier incident."

I looked back at him, and got caught up by the proximity of his beautiful eyes. I blanched at the thought of our kiss—the one that hours of tech talk had kept at bay, but the mere mention of it had my chest heaving like a damn asthma attack. My eyes fluttered over his. I wet my lips, and I waited for his statement.

The corner of his mouth tipped up slightly as he watched me. He shook his head. "No, not that incident. I'm not the least bit sorry for that."

My mouth gaped, but there weren't any words coming out. His lack of defense for his impertinence insulted me, but it relieved my heart to know he didn't regret our kiss. What I didn't know was if *I* did. Where was the manual for my hormones?

"I meant about blowing up on you. I shouldn't have yelled at you. That was against my nature, but... I guess it's a side effect of the long sleep, but there is no excuse for it. I don't always know what will set me off, but I promise—"

"Don't promise. Please. So much in life is beyond our control. Don't create expectations that karma will laugh at you for later."

"Okay. I will try not to be an asshole. If I fail, I will try to make it up to you."

"Thank you. I suppose I owe you one, too. Besides being a potential superior DNA carrier, and a princess, and a spoiled brat, I am also... scared to death of losing this ship. It isn't just my home and transportation. It's my savior. Without this ship, I would have never reached the stars. I would be stuck on Father's planet, living an intolerably safe, comfortable, and boring life." I shook my head. "I know this ship is yours, Rayne. I don't want to take it away from you. I always hoped you would wake up, but of course, in my fairytale version, you thanked me for not killing you and then vowed to show me the wonders of the universe."

Rayne blinked, trying to find an appropriate response.

"But this is good, too. We'll skip the honeymoon, go straight to the divorce, and draw a line down the center of the ship. Do you want shared custody of Ayil and Aresties?"

"We'll figure it out." He stood, indifferent to my jokes. "But I don't think we should skip the honeymoon." He paused to confirm I had caught his meaning. "Goodnight." He moved toward the door.

"Why did you kiss me?" I shifted to see him around my chair. He looked back at me. "You knew who I was. No reason to take the ruse that far."

He stared at me, and I waited for the prescribed response to my challenge. Some drivel about my beauty enchanting him. What more could you expect when three highly trained beauticians and an impeccably white satin dress tempted a man?

"You looked like you needed to be kissed," he answered, almost mournful. "Still do."

I gaped at his interpretation of my feelings. I could feel the tingling in my body threatening to warm my face. "Goodnight, Captain." I turned around before the moment could establish itself, and I heard the door close.

Rayne was right, of course. I had wanted that kiss. Never mind the identity of the man, or what the marriage certificate said. I just wanted to be kissed and held.

I had avoided it for so long, afraid of the consequences, but I was thinking I might never have it. As demeaning as an arranged marriage might have been to me, I was happy to have permission to let go. Permission to satisfy my desires without guilt.

I shook away the rest of my coquettish thoughts and returned to my studies. I may have needed a kiss, but I also needed to know the capabilities of my—*our* ship.

Fairy Tales

An hour later, my head nodded to the right, nearly unseating me before I woke to catch myself. I glanced around to see who might have seen my comical blunder, but no one was there. I shut down the tutorial I was laughably *watching* and headed off to bed.

I trudged down the short hallway to my quarters and slipped inside. The last few days of wedding plans had exhausted me more than anything I had encountered on my journeys in space. As I undressed, I wondered if my mother would send out a search party just to spite me. After all, she had Elizandra.

Poor Elizandra. She was the sweetest, dearest girl, and if I hadn't thought it would kill my parents, I might have been tempted to save her from them. Even if she would have the same fate as me, it would need to be her choice to leave. Maybe she would be happy. Maybe she wouldn't be as ungrateful as me.

Despite the guilt I felt for leaving my family again, I was happy to be back on my ship, in my room. I glanced over at the sleep pod that had once upon a time held my sleeping beauty. He was still a beauty, but he was also taciturn, bossy, and unpredictable.

Much too late, I realized, since he was no longer sleeping in the pod, he must have been sleeping elsewhere.

I turned around, hoping to land my eyes on closed lids, but Rayne's eyes were wide open, staring at me from the bed.

Staring at the naked me.

I gasped and grabbed my shirt from the floor to cover myself. It was long enough to cover my body, but nothing could cover my embarrassment. Even though the room was dark, there was enough light from the sleep pod to offer him a good view. Just as good a view as I had of his nude body, barely covered by a tangled sheet.

After a moment to catch my breath, I finally spoke. "What the hell, Rayne!"

Rayne propped himself on his elbows, still watching me with the interest of a predator. There was no point waiting for an apology on this front, either.

"Why didn't you say something?"

"I thought you'd come by to finish what we started."

"No!" I squawked. "I forgot you would be sleeping in here. I'll find an open bunk."

"You don't have to," he said, stopping my cumbersome exit. He nodded to the pod. "You must be used to sleeping next to me by now." I frowned and looked at the pod. "How did this part of your fantasy play out in your head?"

"Don't make fun." I glared.

"I'm not. I was flattered by what you said."

"This is the second time today you've taken advantage of my ignorance."

"A woman came into *my* room and started undressing. I thought you intended to take advantage of *me*."

"Alright, fine, let's put this down as an awkward encounter and move on."

"What shall we move on to?" he asked, holding his eyes steady on mine rather than looking at my body. "You still look like you want that kiss."

I wavered before him, searching for the right words. No? Yes? What the hell *did* I want? I must have stood there too long, because he shifted out of his sheet to the edge of the bed. He didn't seem to find the same humiliation in his nudity. Not that he should. His body was like carved stone. I had seen it up close many times, but he was far more impressive in motion. His sleeping self didn't do justice to his aroused self, either.

He raised his hand to me, baiting me like a fish. Since it was only my hand he wanted, I put it in his. He drew me forward with a gentle tug, and I was in front of him. My eyes floundered to find an appropriate target. I didn't want to look into his covetous eyes, but I also didn't want to openly gawk at his body.

He raised his hand again, trailing it along my cheek, down my throat, over my chest, along my stomach, and down my leg. The whole time he watched me; reading my reaction, testing my limits. I wasn't sure what he had learned, but he moved his hand upward, under the shirt I still clutched. His warm fingers grazed my inner thigh, and skirted dangerously close to somewhere of great importance to my people.

Without warning, my covering shirt was gone, ripped away like a tablecloth from beneath its banquet. I instinctively reached after it, but he raised his hand to stop me. His eyes challenged me to find fault with his actions. After all, he was already naked. Fair was fair.

He waited to touch me as my breathing hastened to a hyperventilation level. If I wasn't careful, I would pass out. A fitting end to yet another attempt to get laid.

Rayne looked me over curiously; his dangerous animal eyes had turned sympathetic. I was being pathetic, and it wasn't going unnoticed. I was a grown woman. There was nothing wrong with going to bed with a man. A normal man. Terrin had even said this would be good for me. I agreed. I really needed to get this part of my life figured out.

I steeled my resolve and took a tiny step forward. It wasn't the smoldering kiss and lunging carnal attack a more experience woman might have offered, but it was a huge accomplishment for me.

Rayne smiled slightly at my consent. He pressed his hands against my thighs, just under my butt, guiding me a little closer.

He held his hands against my hips while his lips explored my body.

Starting on my stomach, he kissed the flesh as if it were my lips. Pinching and demanding, I knew his vigor would leave me covered in pale bruises. As he moved up to my breasts, I winced at his fervor on my nipples. He pressed his fingers into my hips as if he needed to hold them prisoner there, lest he get too aggressive.

He tugged on my leg and I climbed into his lap, straddling him. Our bodies pressed together. Soft and hard. I stared at him, waiting for instruction. I had imagined it a thousand times, but in live action it felt so unromantic.

I leaned down and kissed him. He pulled me closer, and his tongue invaded my lips. I tried to pull back to soften the kiss, but he was already ensconcing me in his arms.

Before I could get back to my vision of the fantasy, he flipped me over and pressed me down against his mattress. I pushed against his shoulders and he drew back to look at me. "Did I hurt you?" he asked, looking me over for damage.

"I... just... couldn't breathe," I said, clearly breathless.

"Oh." He smirked. "Sorry." He released some of his upper body weight, but his lower body shifted to align himself with his goal.

I gasped at the addition of an internal pressure. As unnecessary to my pleasure as the pressure was, I knew I would never want for anything less ever again.

He continued to nibble on my lips as he rocked against me. My hands gripped his shoulders and back, pushing, pulling; demanding more. I wasn't sure what my role was, but I was understanding his part very well.

I sputtered a less-than-ideal proclamation before I tumbled over the edge of euphoria. Panting and shaking, I nearly cried from the relief and satisfaction. He groaned against my neck and collapsed on top of me. After a nibble on my ear and a compliment to the act, he rolled off and almost instantly fell asleep.

Tall Tales

Twenty minutes after the most epic transition of my life, I stared at my lover with bored fascination. I couldn't help but feel used as I listened to his purring breathing. I felt alone. More alone than I had felt before I was with him. How was that possible? How could I experience something so moving and yet feel so empty after?

Rather than question the psychological impact of my self-deprivation, I slipped out of his bed and grabbed my clothing. My one-night stand was over; I might as well move along.

I had over a dozen empty bunks to choose from, but I knocked on Ayil's door instead. After a scuffle inside, he opened the door a crack and peeked out. "Kit?" He opened the door all the way. "What's wrong?" His hair was in terrible disarray and the calm lighting in the hall was still enough to slit his eyes.

"Can I sleep in here tonight?"

"Yeah, of course." He ushered me in and shut the door. "Hang on," he said hoarsely, and I heard him move across the room. His bedside light turned on, illuminating the room with soft light.

"Are you just coming to bed now?" he asked, checking his clock before repositioning the blankets on his small bed. I would have had more room sleeping with Rayne, but I didn't want space.

"No, I forgot Rayne took his room back."

"Oh." Ayil looked me over. "What's wrong, Kit?"

"I can sleep somewhere else if you don't have room," I said.

"Shut up," he mumbled and waved me over. I slipped into his bed and he scooted in beside me. "Did you guys get into a fight or something?" he asked.

"We didn't fight." I shook my head, not wanting to admit the truth.

Ayil looked at my shy, shamed face. "You had sex with him, didn't you?"

I nodded.

"And?" he asked. I shrugged. "Did he hurt you?" His eyes narrowed.

"No. It was... good."

"Just good?"

"It all felt good, but afterward..."

"Yeah." Ayil frowned and brushed the hair from my face. "I know."

"Why does it feel so good, but yet so empty?"

"It just does sometimes. You two don't really know each other very well, so it's bound to be a little awkward at first."

"Is it ever like the stories say?" I asked.

Ayil smiled and pulled me against his chest. After a little repositioning, I found my niche and settled in. "This isn't a fairytale, Princess Kit. This is real life. And in real life, sex is a drug. It's addictive. I spent a lot of years trying to find a perfect connection that would make it feel like the fairytale. Do you know what I found instead?"

"What?"

"Shame, obsession, and low self-esteem."

"I can't imagine what your life was like before me."

"You don't want to." Ayil squeezed my shoulder. "I don't know how to get the fairytale, Kit, but I do know this: I've come closer to that perfect connection with you than with any person I've slept with."

I looked up at him, stunned by the compliment. "Really? I don't know what to say to that."

He kissed my forehead. "You don't have to say anything. Just remember, love and sex are two different things. If the sex is good, it's only the love part you need to work on." He reached over and shut off his light. The room went dark, and we cuddled a little closer before drifting off to sleep.

Blurts

"Coming, coming, hang on!" Ayil grouched as he slipped out of bed to answer the banging on the door. He opened the door a crack to peek out, which let in the glare of daytime lighting from the hall.

I glanced at the clock on his bedside table. It was nearly nine. My stomach told me I was long overdue for breakfast.

"What's up?" Ayil asked whoever was at the door.

"Have you seen Kit?" Rayne's voice filtered in. "I can't find her anywhere."

Ayil opened the door the rest of the way to reveal my presence. I sat up wiping the sleep from my eyes.

Rayne stepped in a little further, examining me on the bed. His concern seemed to fade away and a harsh judgment replaced it. He shared his glare with Ayil before storming off.

"Hey, Rayne," Ayil called after him. "Shit, he thinks we got something going on," he grumbled, throwing on a t-shirt and shoes.

"Let him." I shook my head. "We've got bigger issues to deal with before we can add jealousy to the plate."

Ayil ignored my suggestion and ran out after him.

To avoid the unfolding drama, I focused on a more pressing problem: my empty stomach. I took the liberty of switching out my fancy shirt for one of Ayil's t-shirts and headed downstairs to the mess hall.

To my surprise, there were three unfamiliar faces eating around a table. They each looked up at me with the same surprised look. We exchanged friendly smiles, and I headed to the communal fridge. I grabbed a prepackaged breakfast sandwich and tossed it in the microwave.

"Then what the hell was she doing in there?" I heard Rayne's voice coming even before I saw him.

"You gotta understand, Kit's a virgin—or was," Ayil blurted out behind Rayne as they entered the room.

I stared in shocked embarrassment at Rayne as he noticed me standing by the counter. The three strangers I had not even met yet were now privileged to the personal details of my sex life—as new as it was even to me.

"Ayil!" I hissed, and he looked over the occupied room of sniggering faces. His mouth curved into a silent "oh." For another few seconds, I stared between the two men searching for a smart-ass remark. Unfortunately, there was no hope of recovering any dignity. I left my breakfast behind and walked to the exit.

"Kit," Rayne said as I passed. He tried to catch my arm, but I dodged his reach.

"Kit!" Ayil redirected his panicked petition to me. He followed me down the hall. "I'm sorry. I was trying to explain why you sneaked out on him last night." He grabbed me and pulled me to face him.

"I didn't sneak out. Is that what he said?" I squawked.

"No, he just... you hurt his feelings," Ayil blurted out.

"Ayil!" Rayne's voice barked behind him.

Ayil grimaced and looked back at him as he approached. "Alright, look!" He stepped away from both of us and surrendered with his hands held high. "This is between you two. I'm obviously not helping by trying to help, so..." Ayil waved for the argument to commence and stalked off to the cafeteria, most likely to confiscate my uneaten breakfast.

Rayne watched him go before turning his attention to me. I stared at him, waiting for an explanation or an apology or something resembling human communication. He seemed to wait for the same from me.

After the awkwardness turned sour and I was on the verge of tears, I chuckled and walked away. "That's what I thought," I mumbled as I climbed the stairs.

"What was what you thought?" He finally spoke and ascended behind me.

"Look, Ayil shouldn't have told you what he did. My sex life, or lack thereof, is my business."

"I'm pretty sure it became my business last night," he said as he came in tight behind me on the final set of steps.

"I don't know what last night was." I sped up to get away from him.

"What did you want it to be?"

I turned to face him. He slowed his approach and eased uncomfortably close. I put my hand on his chest to stop him. "Just chill, okay?" I took a breath and stepped away. "I'm not playing a game, Rayne. I seriously have no idea what to do here. I know last night was my idea, or both our ideas, but I feel used." He frowned at the interpretation. "I don't know if that's normal, but I don't like it, so could you just back off a bit?"

"That's why you left last night?"

"I left last night because I had experienced intercourse for the first time, and there was no one there to talk to about it."

"You could have talked to me."

I frowned and shook my head. "I know you have to say that, but we both know it's not true. I don't want to make this any more complicated or emotionally pressured than it has to be, so give me some space."

"I understand." He nodded and stepped a little closer, despite my moratorium. He raised his hand to my cheek and caressed it. "Don't be too mad at Ayil. He didn't tell me anything I hadn't suspected. I'm sorry if I rushed you into something you weren't ready for. I'll back off... for now," he conditioned as he pulled his hand away. "Shall we get back to your lessons?"

Bit in the Ass

"Where are we going, anyway?" I asked Rayne as I punched in the coordinates he had given me. To my satisfaction and frustration, he had been ignoring me all week. My flying lessons were just as perfunctory as they were the first time. It was strange to me; I wanted him, and yet he unnerved me. It was a wonder men had any idea what the hell women wanted. *We* didn't even know what the hell we wanted.

"We are meeting an old friend of Ayil's."

I glanced back to confirm this with Ayil, but he wouldn't look at me. He sat in the jump seat on the back wall, staring out at the stars. "Who?" I asked anyone willing to answer.

"Gunder, I think he called himself," Rayne answered as he adjusted my settings to his satisfaction. "Is that right, Ayil?"

I shoved Rayne's hands away. "Stop it, they were fine."

"They are now." His arrogant smirk made me smile. "Have you told her all this, Ayil? Or am I putting my foot in my mouth?"

"All what?" I turned to Ayil for the explanation he still hadn't offered me. He looked uncomfortable. My mouth gaped as I saw a few tears drop from his chin. I ripped myself free of my safety restraints and moved back to him. When he still didn't speak, I looked at Rayne again.

"Do you want me to tell her?" Rayne asked him.

Ayil shook his head. "The guys you saved me from. They want me back."

"Yeah, so? They can suck it," I said.

Ayil vehemently fought his tears. "They took my son."

My heart sank. "You have a son?" I couldn't imagine Ayil with a child. He was barely an adult himself.

"No one was supposed to know about him. One of my clients. She got pregnant. She decided to keep the baby. I told her never to tell anyone who his father was."

"How old is he?"

"Six by now."

"Have they... done anything to him?"

"Gunder says no, but I know he won't wait long to train him."

"Holy shit," I whispered. "You've known about this a while, haven't you?"

"I knew before we went to the mall."

"Did you go there with the intention of turning yourself over?" I asked.

"I was supposed to meet him there. I planned to just... disappear."

"What, without saying goodbye? Without an explanation?" I asked, with disbelief at his cruelty. "Just gone?"

"I didn't know they were still looking for you, Kit." Ayil looked away from my pained expression. "I never would have endangered you," he pleaded.

"Endanger me?" I scowled and shook my head. "My problems are nothing compared to this. Why didn't you tell me? I could have helped."

"There's nothing you can do."

"The hell there isn't. Turn us back around," I ordered Rayne.

"What?" he balked.

"Take me back to my mother. I'll explain the situation. She'll be able to stop this. She can send her whole damn army. Blow up a few satellites or something." I moved to the panel.

"Holster your army, Princess." Rayne grabbed my hands, preventing me from changing the coordinates. When I refused to give in, he pushed me aside and locked the panel with his administrative code. "We are not going back."

"I can fix this."

"No, you can't. Your mother is not going to risk a galactic war for kidnappers. Besides, these people are too slimy for political plays."

"I'm not going to stand by—"

"Neither are we," Rayne interrupted. "We already have a way to get the boy back."

"You do?" I asked hopefully.

"We are going to make a trade for his son."

"No." I looked at Ayil, fearful of the degree of his heroic nature. "You are not trading yourself."

"He isn't. We're trading you," Rayne said without a hint of levity in his voice.

Value

"Excuse me?" I said after my dead stare hadn't kindled further discussion on the topic of my sale.

"We aren't actually going to give you to him," Ayil explained.

"But you are going to pretend, and I'm sure this little plan involves me being present for the exchange." I glared at Rayne. "Is that why you agreed to rescue me?"

"Ayil convinced me to help his son. Gunder wouldn't take my money, though. Only a lucrative trade. If Ayil wouldn't give himself up, then he wanted the sarcastic bitch who took him. His words, not mine," Rayne amended.

"And since the sarcastic bitch owes you for the rescue, she would naturally be on board to play bait," I snarled.

"It's not like that, Kit." Ayil stood and moved between us. "You don't have to do this."

"Of course I'll do it, but bombshells are not my favorite form of communication."

"You will?" Ayil asked. His eyes searched me for the truth, although I had just spoken it.

"Yes, I will." The words were barely out before he embraced me. "I can't believe that asshole even remembers me," I said as Ayil pulled away from me.

"He seemed to be very disappointed you outsmarted him," Rayne said.

"If we're sharing credit as blame, I would have to say Aresties was the one who outsmarted him."

Rayne chuckled. "Accidental genius," he mumbled as he moved to unlock the controls and fidget with my settings.

"Will you stop that?" I swatted his hand.

"You're a good pilot, Kit, but you read too many manuals," he explained smugly.

"Ayil, tell him..." I looked back for some support, but he was gone. I pursued him, but Rayne caught my wrist with one hand.

"Don't," he advised, without looking up from the screens.

"I want to talk to him."

"If he wanted to talk, he would have stayed in here." Rayne looked back at me. "He's scared, embarrassed, and guilt-ridden. Trust me, he doesn't want to talk."

"He's my friend." I yanked my hand free.

"Yes, but you have no idea what he is going through."

I looked at the door. I wanted to comfort Ayil, but Rayne was right. I had nothing to say to comfort him. We had very different lives. And since I had only recently discovered a world beyond my own problems, I was the last person skilled enough to understand his.

his

"Y ou wanted to talk to me?" I tapped on Rayne's open door. He was bent over his bed, inventorying his weapons. He glanced up at me from an intimidating knife collection. There were more than a few pistols, too. And one *very* dangerous bomb.

"I need to make sure you are ready for this," he said.

"We've been over the plan."

"I don't mean the bomb, I mean you. Gunder thinks I'm a slave trader. He thinks I'm providing him with human cattle. And I will play that part." He turned to evaluate me. He was still questioning my resolve to play bait.

"I will do anything to help Ayil."

"I'm not worried about your commitment to help. I'm worried about your tolerances. I will be manhandling you, groping you, and if necessary, I will hit you."

My brow dipped. I didn't know what to say to that. I had been fortunate in my travels to avoid the people who openly wanted to hurt me. Standing across from a man who was declaring his intentions to do so in the name of heroism was a strange twist.

"I need you to trust me."

I scoffed. "Trust that you won't hurt me."

"No, trust that I will. Ayil is a good man. I want to help him. I don't want you to make any assumptions about my gallantry because of what's happened between us. I won't risk Ayil's son to spare your feelings."

I swallowed hard. I wasn't sure I had ever swooned over Rayne's subtle flirtations, but I was definitely recovering from the affliction. I had to respect the man for his dedication to his endeavor, but that didn't change the ache in my heart.

"Gunder needs to believe I am giving you to him," Rayne added.

"I understand," I finally mumbled. "I'll keep my mouth in check so I don't blow our cover."

"Good." He looked down at his feet. "There's something else."

"More good news?" I tried to smile, but failed.

He looked me over and frowned. "You will need some old and new bruises. He won't believe you've been in captivity this long without abuse. A woman like you would have many."

"I don't even know what that means," I snarled defensively, even before determining if I should feel offended.

Rayne smirked and moved behind me to close the door. I turned to face him, prepared for an attack. What kind of attack was still in question. "It's a twofold compliment, actually." He looked me over, head to toe. "Firstly, you are strong-willed. I know if you were actually being contained, you would fight with every last ounce of strength. That would result in bruises." He stepped forward, and I stepped back. He shook his head. "You can inflict those bruises yourself. A belt strap should do it."

"You want me to bruise myself?"

"Yes. Concentrate on the arms and wrists. Most of the abuse would be from holding you down." I wavered, feeling a little sick at the idea of mimicking the bruises of multiple rapes. "You okay?" Rayne asked, seeing my discomfort.

"Yeah, I just... You said firstly. There's more."

"The second reason a woman like you would have lots of bruises is because there is no way a predatory man wouldn't take you at every opportunity." He stepped forward, corralling me toward the bed.

Before he could make his move, I shifted away from him. It didn't necessarily free me from his advance, but it took the bed out of the scenario. "What do you think you're doing?"

He shrugged. "The bruises. You're more than welcome to try inflicting your own hickies, but I'm not sure you're flexible enough. Unless you prefer Ayil make them. I'm sure he wouldn't mind." Despite the suggestion, he almost sounded insulted that I would choose Ayil over him for the task. He sat down on the bed, waiting for my answer. It was a trap. My obligatory duty was putting me in an indefensible situation. The only question was, did I want to be snared?

"Tell me something about yourself," I said.

"What?" He furrowed his brow.

"I'm not going to let you suck on my neck without at least knowing you better than the first time you did."

He looked me over, determining God knows what, but the shock wore away and he cleared his throat. "Um, I grew up on a farm with horses. I was on a saddle almost as soon as I could walk."

"You remember that?"

"Bits and pieces. I remember my mother staring up at me from the ground beside the horse."

"What else do you remember?"

He shifted and sighed. "Not much, Kit. I'm pretty scrambled still. I know me. I just don't know the specifics of how I got to *be* me."

I frowned. "I'm sorry. That must be difficult."

He stood and approached me. He wrapped his arm around my back and pulled me against him. "No more talking," he commanded and leaned into my neck.

His lips pressed, opening against my skin, sucking gently. He drew back and bit the skin lightly. I jumped at the minor pain, but didn't pull away. He pulled my shirt and bra strap aside and did the same to my shoulder, sucking hard to bruise it.

The sleep pod pressed into my back and I leaned against it for support. Without permission, he unsnapped my shirt and kissed around my breasts, drawing the tissue in tightly to make sure I would bruise.

I was vaguely aware of my bra cup being moved to the side before my nipple endured the same pleasurable suckling. I gasped and panted. "Rayne, I don't think he'll be looking that closely," I said breathlessly.

"Your tits are too fucking beautiful to resist," he hissed as he squeezed both my breasts. "Tell me to stop, and I will," he whispered. His hands moved to my pants, undoing the snap and zipper. He rose and brought his lips to my ear. "Did you hear me? You are in control of this, too."

I nodded, even though I didn't feel in control. I felt helpless, but he was right; all I had to do was speak up and he would respect my wishes.

I didn't, of course.

My pants fell and a wisp of cool air signaled that my panties were gone. Rayne was gone, and my knees nearly buckled as I felt his lips wrap around my sex. He pressed and suckled, drawing a gasp and a moan from me. I shook and bent over to grab his head.

I had meant to draw him away. It was too much. Too shocking. Too good.

Before I could pull him away, his tongue settled into a rhythm, dancing over me. The tantalizing tickle called to my body, eliciting an easy orgasm and drawing a mournful yowl of satisfaction from my throat.

My legs buckled, but Rayne was beside me again, lifting me in his arms. He carried me to the bed and removed the pants from my ankles. Still entranced by my euphoria, I missed the beautiful spectacle of his unveiling body.

He crawled into bed beside me and pulled my chin toward him. "I should have been gentler the first time. I'm sorry about that. I meant what I said. You have control of this, from the first kiss to the last—"

I kissed him hard. I was so appreciative that he was taking my ignorance and naivety into consideration this time, but I didn't want his words. As talented as his mouth was, I didn't want that either. I wanted the depth and pressure the feral part of my body craved.

I shoved him to his back and mounted him. I pushed myself onto him and groaned my appreciation for the fine instrument that felt expressly designed for me. He joined me in the lamentation and I rocked against him, calling for more of his desirous moans.

I watched as his face pinched in the same joyful agony as I imagined mine had only moments ago. I lacked the experience to understand my body, but I grasped the power it held over the man beneath me. Rayne was right. I had control of the act. What he hadn't admitted was that I had control of him. In that moment, I was everything to him. He was mine.

My lust for power and the cumulative friction in our bodies hastened me into a tumbling repetitive climax. When I finally fell from the apex along with Rayne, I landed against his chest, depleted of everything, movement and words included.

I listened to his heart racing. I felt his lips kiss the top of my head. His hand grazed the side of my arm, reminding me we weren't just a pile of exhausted bodies. He was holding me. As powerful as I had felt moments before, I now felt vulnerable. I felt exposed, naked beyond my clothes. The power had shifted, and I was now in danger of becoming his.

The Ugly Guy

I hadn't expected the handcuffs. Then again, I hadn't expected the girdle that shoved my chest into my throat and the high-slit skirt that revealed most of my left leg. I took it all in stride.

Or at least, I complained less than I wanted to.

"Stop walking like that," Rayne griped beside me as we stalked through the busy streets of Tahblak. The sun was still up, and the commercial foot-traffic in the city's center had shifted to the supper rush. Fewer business suits, and a lot more cleavage. At least I would blend in.

"How am I walking, master?" I sniped. I glanced at Ayil behind us before meeting the glare on Rayne's face.

"You're leading," he said. "You are supposed to be my prisoner. Walk like it."

"I'm afraid years of my mother's tutelage prevents me from walking like a slave." I perked an eyebrow at him. I felt his grip on my arm, and I came to an abrupt stop. His other hand grabbed my shoulder and forcefully twisted my body to face him. I was about to snap at him for the assault, but his hand grabbed my chin, pinching my cheeks. The fierce look on his face was as jarring as his grip.

"You remember what I said to you before," he whispered. I nodded in his grip. "I have to assume we are being watched. That means you have to assume the responsibility of your actions." He pulled my face close. "Do you understand?" I nodded again, but he didn't let go. "Say it... and mean it."

My eyes danced over him. He may have been playing a part, but he was damn good at it. Scary good. "Yes, master." I nearly gagged on the words, but I managed to say them with servile conviction.

He dropped his grip and took hold of my restraints. Guiding me like a leashed dog, he led the rest of the way to the designated meeting spot.

Plush chairs and leather couches decorated the lavish club. It wasn't as busy as I might have expected, but it was early. Not to mention the cover charge was enough to make me openly gawk at the wad of bills Rayne handed to the bouncer. The man leafed through the bills, finding no such amazement in its resulting number. Nor did he reveal any shock at my obvious state of captivity. Apparently, anonymity was part of the cover charge.

I started down the steps into the darkened, music-filled room, but stopped when I realized I was leading again. Rayne's hand slipped around my back and he nibbled my earlobe. "He's at the far end of the bar watching us," he whispered into my ear. I fought the instinct to look that way. "Please behave." He raised his hand and dragged a finger down my cheek, throat, and finally along my exposed, restricted breasts. Although he had touched them before, the public display and purpose angered me. I contained my rage, which in the end was probably the right mix of emotions to display.

Rayne pushed on my back and we descended into the party pit, where small short tables displayed half-naked dancers of every species, race, and sex. I was a universal traveler, but the variation between species, let alone the attraction to them, always impressed me. I supposed I was no exception. After all, it was only a matter of weeks ago that I was about to sacrifice my life to be with one such variant species.

Adding pain to my memories, I caught sight of a female gattaw performing on one of the tables. Her body was not much different from a human, save the horns, the spines on her back, and the green skin, of course. It was the internal differences that made her the only possible mate for a male gattaw.

We ascended the other side of the pit, where a pair of burly men greeted us. They were humans and twins, or clones—but there wasn't much difference anymore. They led the three of us deeper into the club. I looked at the bar where Gunder was sitting. He was still ugly, but he was in a suit and tie, so I could at least identify him as a human. He smiled at me and raised his glass of liquor to me.

Rayne must have caught my wandering eye, because he pinched my side. "Don't make him mad," he warned.

"What if he makes me mad?" I whispered.

"Then bite your tongue."

The bodyguards led us to a horseshoe booth containing two other *twins*. They instructed us to sit in the three individual chairs facing the table. Ayil sat on the left, Rayne took the center, and I moved to the right. Before I could sit down, Rayne dragged me onto his lap. I tried not to struggle as he freely groped my exposed thigh. His hand dipped deeper, tracing below my buttocks.

"Get comfortable, sweetheart," he grumbled. "You're still mine until I'm done with you."

Gunder interrupted my dithering reaction. "Don't worry, darling girl." He smiled, revealing age-yellowed teeth. "You'll be mine soon enough." As suggested, I bit my tongue. Gunder turned his attention over my shoulder to Ayil. "Well, well, well, all grown up."

I turned to see Ayil's expression. He was impassive. The light in his eyes was gone. I wanted to kill Gunder for that alone. I should have sent for my mother. I would have whored myself out to a thousand husbands for the privilege of watching her crush this man into oblivion.

"Now that I see you, I'm not sure I want to give you up."

"We had a deal, Gunder," Rayne drawled. "I didn't come all this way to look at your ugly face in person."

"Where's my son?" Ayil asked with barely contained urgency.

"Easy." Gunder waved his hand at him. "First things first." He slipped into the horseshoe booth and scooted to the back. The first two twins slid in behind him, flanking his other side. "We need to test the merchandise."

"No freebies, Gunder." Rayne smacked my butt. "You know what you're getting. I want to see what I'm getting."

"He's right over there." Gunder nodded toward the bar, but I couldn't see a child. "In the cage," he clarified.

I gasped and sat up as I saw the small cage over the bar. Inside, a naked little boy cried and tried to cover his nudity. One man appeared to be trying to coax him to dance in return for a chocolate bar. "You monster!" I screamed at Gunder.

Rayne slapped me and I nearly fell off his lap. "Shut up! Ayil, is that your brat or not?"

Rayne repositioned, pulling me back onto his lap. I glimpsed his irritated face, but I looked away. He had warned me about this part, but I found it hard to restrain myself. I apparently wasn't as good an actor as Rayne. At least, I *hoped* he was a good actor.

"Yes, that's him." Ayil looked over at his son longingly. I didn't want to believe Ayil knew what that cage felt like, but I sensed his life was so much harder than I ever even imagined.

"Let's get on with it." Rayne stood and shifted me to stand in front of him. "One boy, for one sarcastic bitch."

Gunder looked at Rayne carefully, then turned his gaze to me. "You don't like seeing that little boy caged, do you?"

I didn't answer. I couldn't imagine a set of eyes that wouldn't hate that sight. The ones that enjoyed it were so far out of my realm of understanding I had no choice but to classify them as subhuman.

"Yeah, I can see that. Those maternal instincts are in overdrive right now. Save the little boy." Gunder smiled. "You can save him, you know. I'll even let you save Ayil. They'll both walk out of here alive and well. I'll consider it a fair trade, but..." Gunder's smile grew.

"But what?" Rayne asked, annoyed.

Gunder didn't take his eyes off me. "But you have to get on your hands and knees, slip under this table, and suck my cock." I shifted, standing a little taller in the face of the frightening challenge. "When you're done licking me clean, you will then suck each of their cocks." He motioned to the men on either side of him.

"That wasn't the deal," Rayne objected. "I don't have time for this."

"Then *make* time!" Gunder slammed his fists on the table. "When we are all satisfied, we'll make the exchange. The boys will go free and you will spend the remainder of your life at my feet, drinking my cum like water. That is the deal!"

My fortitude failed, and I looked at the floor. I could tell Rayne was struggling to think of something to do or say. He had underestimated the depravity of this man. We couldn't do anything until we had Ayil's son at least nearby. It was too risky otherwise.

"That's what I thought," Gunder said.

I looked back at his smug face. "What's what you thought?" I asked.

"I can read you, girl. You don't like what I'm doing to that boy, and you would yell and scream at the monster doing it to him, but you aren't going to do anything to stop it. You're a coward."

I gaped and stepped forward. I didn't know if I actually had the gumption to crawl under the table, but I would have at least tried to strangle the man. That would be proof of my bravery.

Ayil jumped in front of me. "Let me." He bowed to his former master. "You'll have her the rest of your life. Let me express *my* gratitude for your generosity. Besides..." He glanced back at me. "She isn't very good yet. Consider my services a gift for a bargain well struck."

"Alright." Gunder nodded to him. "I'd be lying if I said I hadn't missed your skillful tongue."

Before I could think of something to uproot the scheme, Ayil ducked under the white tablecloth. There was a scuffle under the table, and Gunder shifted slightly. I stared in shock as the man's eyes rolled back in pleasure. When they opened again, his savage, carnal gaze was on me.

Rayne pulled me back, and he repositioned me on his lap again. I shifted uncomfortably, trying not to think of what Ayil was being forced to do for me. After Gunder finished with Ayil, he shifted back up in his seat and waved to a passing waitress.

The woman poured him a drink from one of the eight bottles securely mounted to her belt. She handed it to him and moved on to another table. "Tell me something, Rayne." Gunder swirled his drink, ignoring the mounting enjoyment of his neighbor. "Is she good?"

"When she stops crying," Rayne said with mild exasperation.

"I don't mind the tears," Gunder said. "I have to admit, I'm surprised you are willing to part with her."

The next twin slammed his hands against the table, prematurely succumbing to the alacrity of Ayil's skill. I frowned at the display and looked at Rayne's hand steadily encroaching on my extremely personal space.

"She has her uses." He pushed between my thighs, pressing inside of me. I grabbed for his wrist, but he gave me a scolding look, so I let him debase me to support his act. "I might even miss her." He withdrew his hand and licked his finger. Had I not been sitting, I might have fallen on the floor. I stared, in awe of his lewdness. Was this part of the act? "Yes, I'm sure she does. I have a feeling I might miss her too, when I'm through with her."

I could see Rayne's eyes widen slightly as he turned to Gunder. "Not going to keep her on as a laplicker?" he queried.

"Oh, I think I'll get a few nights out of her." Gunder glanced at the fourth member of their party to tumble into euphoria. One more to go. "After that, I'll sell the princess back to her people."

WANTED

I heard Ayil's head hit the underside of the table. Rayne and I remained unfazed by the announcement. Although, there was a fine line between dumbstruck and composed.

After a long silence, I laughed. Rayne didn't join in my amusement. Gunder did tip his head, curious to hear the reason for my levity. "That bounty is six years old. It's already been claimed."

Gunder puckered his lips. "I don't think so." He shook his head. "Finish up, Ayil." He knocked on the table, and the last member of the party shifted in slight discomfort as his experience got put on fast forward.

"I don't really care what you do with her." Rayne shoved me off to one knee, freeing his movement. "But what would you gain on a bounty you wouldn't earn tenfold by renting her out?"

"Oh, you can drop the act, Captain. I'm not as stupid as you think I am. I know you aren't a slave trader. I value your enthusiasm for heroism, but you are going to have to walk away from this rescue. All I want is the bounty on her."

"I told you, it's already been collected," I seethed.

"No, not this one. This is a new one." Gunder smiled, and I conversely frowned. He paused, giving me the opportunity to ask the obvious question, but I didn't bite. "I'm not surprised you haven't heard about it. It isn't technically a bounty. It's more like a job bid. And not the type of bid that comes out over common frequencies. I'm going to be a rich man as soon as I cut your head off and deliver it to your home planet."

I shook my head. My mother would never go this far. She would never hire someone to lob my head off. She would do it herself.

"Which planet?" I asked.

Gunder narrowed his eyes, not entirely understanding the duality of my origins. "Vagari," he clarified.

A shiver ran through my body as I considered the possibility of a dead or alive bounty on my head. For years, my parents had hunted me without much effort. The bounty for my retrieval was a reward for locating a missing child—funded and broadcasted by the crown.

If the Coalition was now the one hunting me...

What had changed? Why were they getting involved now?

I stood up slowly. Rayne followed. Ayil crawled out from under the table. The look on his face was what I had expected to see the first time. He had found his way back to anger. I couldn't say I had ever left it behind, but I was definitely beyond hiding it now.

"Did you accept the bid?" I asked.

"Clearly." Gunder nodded.

I chuckled again. "You idiot."

Gunder frowned. "Are you sure you want to insult the man who holds the date of your death certificate?"

"We may have underestimated you, but you have severely underestimated my people. If they want *me* dead, imagine what they will do to a piece of shit like you to cover up my murder."

"Listen here—"

"No, *you* listen! I will give you one chance to walk away from me and run like hell to the other side of the galaxy, because that's the only thing that can save you now."

"You are in no position to negotiate!" Gunder stood and leaned over the table. His goons shifted to stand.

Rather than stepping back, I stepped forward. I heard a muted objection from Rayne, but he didn't actually grab me. "I guarantee they are already here," I whispered.

"You're bluffing," Gunder challenged.

"I really wish I was," I confessed. Gunder's eyes looked over my shoulder, surveying the bar crowd with fresh eyes. "Ayil, get your son, now." I felt him wisp past me in pursuit of the boy. The men objected to the disruption in their entertainment, but didn't interfere. The boy latched onto Ayil the moment he was out of the cage and didn't let go. "We'll go out the front door. Once we're—"

"We will go out first," Gunder corrected.

I nodded and stepped back. Gunder and his men scooted back out of the booth. He paused next to me. His eyes shifted to Rayne behind me before returning to me. "If I find out you are lying, I won't need a bid to kill you."

"If I'm not lying, then you're wasting valuable escape time," I said.

Gunder's lip twitched before he broke away from me. I watched him and his men walk down through the pit and out the front door.

"That's a risky scam, Kit." Rayne surprised me with his proximity.

"It's not a scam," I whispered back to him. "We are about to die."

Dead

"Ayil?" I looked at the boy in his arms as we marched forward into the pit.

"I've got him," he said, keeping up with my brisk pace. "Better blind than a slave," he added, silencing my concerns.

We all knew the risks.

"Why are you still doing this?" Rayne asked quietly as he dragged on my arm.

"Keep moving," I hissed as we moved past the dancers in the pit and their attentive audience. Although, I noticed a few more glances our way this time around. "Be ready for anything."

"I don't understand," Rayne protested, releasing my arm.

"Just listen to her, Rayne," Ayil petitioned him.

I jogged up to the other side of the pit. Fourteen steps later, we were back at the main entrance, the bouncer only a few feet away. I ignored him and headed to the door. Six more steps to freedom and the double doors closed, blocking out the dusk light on the other side. It was no matter who had closed them, only that they were not likely to open them again without a code word or an extremely persuasive offer. With my father's planet fitting the bill for this execution, my bargaining chips were looking more like paint chips.

We all stopped just shy of freedom and turned to face the music—which coincidentally had stopped the minute the doors closed. The dancers, servers, and patrons had all turned their attentions to us.

"What the hell?" Rayne muttered.

More than one hand shifted. It made no difference that I had two and a half human shields blocking their bullets. They would shoot clean through, collect my body for evidence. Little did they know, all of them would be dead by morning. The Coalition didn't like loose ends.

I reached for the bulge in Rayne's side pocket. I ripped the cap off the cylinder with my teeth and shoved myself into his back.

"Ayil!" I screamed as I threw the slender can. I didn't know if he could hear me over the bullets that started the moment the canister appeared, but I prayed he was smart enough to duck for cover.

Milliseconds later, I toppled to the ground with Rayne. I pinched my eyes shut and buried my face against the floor.

A wave of searing hot followed the high-pitched blast and painfully bright white light. There was little you could do to defend your eyes from a radiant bomb. We wore protective contacts, which would save our retinas from being burned out, but even with that precaution, we were risking our vision being in the same room as the detonation.

The illumination dimmed to a tolerable brightness, and I looked up. Our adversaries were on the floor. The ones closest to the blast were unconscious and bleeding from their eyes. The farthest were moaning and rubbing at their eyes.

I rolled Rayne over and checked him. "I'm okay." He nodded to Ayil's huddled mass. He was crouched over his son, using his entire body to shield his son's eyes. Unfortunately, it left his own eyes without the additional protection of his arms or hands.

I moved to him, and he twisted to face me. His eyes were bloodshot and tearing up. "Are you—"

"It's blurry, but I'm not blind." He looked down at the boy. "What about Edric?"

"I want mommy," the boy whimpered, looking around at the chaos in the room, squinting at the remaining brightness.

"He's okay," I whispered to Ayil. "Come on. We still have to figure out how to get through those doors.

Even as I stood to assess our exit strategy, Rayne gave the heavy double doors a kick. The latch was hardly enough for the size of the doors, let alone the strength in his leg. The two men outside the door charged at him. A punch or two was all I saw before blood started pouring from their throats. They each fell to their knees, gargling and sputtering before slumping over dead.

Rayne turned back to us, panting and splattered in blood. I saw the knife gripped in his fist. He looked down at it and thrust it back into the holster hidden under his sleeve.

There wasn't much to be said about the death of two men who would have killed me without a second thought. However, the alacrity of the kills made me wonder how much I really knew about Rayne. This part wasn't just an act.

OR DEAD

Rayne unlocked my handcuffs, and I dropped them to the ground as we emerged from the club. We tried desperately to look nonchalant and not draw attention to ourselves, but with Rayne covered in blood, Ayil carrying his naked screaming son, and the oddly patterned sunburns we all had, there wasn't much hope of being inconspicuous. On the upside, however, the last vestiges of sunlight were disappearing, blanketing us in nature's best disguise: bar hoppers.

I experienced groping more than once while shuffling through the street party toward our ship. I wasn't sure if the trauma of Ayil's former boss had made me immune to the lesser deviants in life, or if I was just too scared to defend my propriety.

I glanced back to check on the others, but we had already gotten separated. I cursed and jumped up and down to see above the surrounding heads. My bouncing performance earned cheers, but I moved on after spilling someone's beer. Ayil and Rayne both knew where the ship was.

As I meandered through the crowd, I noticed a familiar face popping in and out of my field of vision. Not so much because I knew the man, but because he was staying with me on my arduous journey.

I wanted to be mistaken, but there was no room for questions. Instincts were all I needed. I had a price on my head, which meant every seedy bastard on this planet knew who I was and what I was worth. As happy as I was to disappear into the drunken crowd, I realized I was only helping to hide the identity of my murderer.

The man was on me before I could make any headway. He grabbed my arm, yanking me closer. The multicolored techno lighting glinted off the blade he thrust at my stomach.

I gasped and grabbed his wrists. I screamed and fought against him, but the music prevented anyone from hearing me, and a few more elbow pokes didn't alarm the inebriated crowd.

The man's head bobbed to one side, and his strength failed. I backed away as he fell to the ground, dead.

The tiny bullet hole in his head was the only evidence of the sniper shot. I ducked and looked around, but there was no hope of seeing the perpetrator. Worse, I didn't know whether the bullet was intended for the man it killed or for me.

I pushed through the sea of people, making my way to the coastline. Once I was free of sweat and smoke, I searched for Ayil and Rayne. I twisted and turned, trying to keep my wits about me.

"Kit!" Ayil's voice rose above the noise. I turned and saw him emerge from the party, with Rayne right behind him.

"Oh, thank—"

"Look out!" he finished the statement even as hands grabbed me.

Four strange hands lassoed my arms, chest, and waist. What minor struggle I could offer was futile. They dragged me back and lifted into the darkness of a van. Before the door shut, I saw Rayne sprinting toward me. The vehicle lurched forward, squealing its tires on the pavement. I screamed and writhed against my abductors, but my heroes were already too far away to help.

Gunshots pinged against the van, but it wasn't enough to slow it down. I panted in the darkness and stopped resisting. The hands holding me released me, letting me drop to the cold metal on the floor of the van.

I heard a scuffle and felt a waft of movement near my face. I whimpered and shrank down, waiting for a deadly blow to the head.

The dome light above me turned on, casting a harsh light on the three men and one woman surrounding me, all of them human. They perched against the walls, their rock steady faces all directed at me.

They were a military outfit, but not a well-paid one. The uniforms didn't match and their weapons were at least thirty years outdated. Granted, the bullets inside of them would still kill me.

I scrambled to stand and meet their threat with pride, but the truck's endless turns made it nearly impossible. Nearly a minute passed, and no one raised a weapon to shoot me. My fear diminished enough to speak. "What do you want?"

"You," the woman answered. Her short, dark hair and sharp features made me think of a witch. In another setting, I was sure she would be beautiful, but in the light of my imminent death, she was a crone to me.

"Where are you taking me?"

"To the lab," she answered.

I glanced at her partners, but they were stone cold. I was apparently lucky to be getting the verbose conversation I was.

"What will you do with me at the lab?"

"I'm not a scientist."

"What will the scientist do with me at the lab?" I voiced in a firmer tone.

"I don't know. I just deliver the lab rats," she snarled back.

"Who do you work for?" I asked.

"A competitor," she answered proudly.

"A competitor to my people?" I asked somewhat rhetorically. "Someone wants my DNA?"

"You got a death warrant out for you. If your government is willing to throw away spare parts, then we are willing to pick them out of the trash."

"You aren't going to kill me, are you?"

"Nope. Not until we get every last one of them juicy eggs out of you."

I frowned and looked down. I was familiar with the practice of human egg harvesting. They had perfected it over the last few decades. Artificial induction of egg production yielded several viable eggs for freezing. However, I sensed they weren't talking about that painless outpatient procedure.

They didn't want to go on an Easter egg hunt. They wanted the whole damn basket and when they were through, the Easter bunny was going to get her throat slit.

Lab Rats

"**G**et your hands off me, you traitorous bitch!" My flailing was uselessly against my harbingers of doom, but that didn't mean I couldn't cuss and scream the entire way to my grave.

"I have no loyalties to you," the brunette growled into my ear as she held me in a headlock. Her male compatriot unlocked the door to our back-alley destination.

"Of course not, cause you're a fucking *clitter* with no hope of ever having children," I yelled, trying to get a rise out of the woman and hopefully give myself an opening for an escape.

"Actually, I have three."

I gaped at her admission. "So, you know exactly what you're taking from me."

"It doesn't matter. You'll be dead before you can use those eggs, anyway. We just want to put them to good use." She shoved me through the door and her partner took over my right side. They dragged me down the stark white corridor with ease.

They took me through an airlock and into a large, brightly lit room. Despite the reference to a lab, it looked more like a clean room for a factory. There were several boxy stainless-steel machines, linked by rolling conveyors. On either end of the assembly line, thick plastic flaps covered the openings the products would pass through. The only thing remotely scientific about the location were the six surgically garbed men waiting for me around a stainless-steel table.

"No." I gripped the brunette's arm. "Don't do this," I pleaded. "Please, don't let them do this." I looked into her eyes, hoping for some female accord in my time of need.

"You got your shit to deal with, and I got mine. Three mouths to feed, remember?"

Once again, I was underestimating the burdens other people had to bear. Not that I was okay with those burdens being foisted on my plate.

I headbutted the woman and kicked the knee of the other man. Unfortunately, the *doctors* took over from there, dragging me toward the cold silver table.

"No!" I kicked at the approaching table, but I only ended up assisting their efforts to get me on top of it. "Stop!"

I screamed as loud as I could, but they ignored my appeals. Stripped of my shoes, pants, and underwear, they strapped me to a table with belts and rope. They spread my legs and handcuffed my ankles to the nearest machinery. Two or three tons of metal kept me open for operation. I bucked against the ropes, but I could barely wiggle the table beneath me.

I had never been so terrified in my life. These assholes were going to kill me and I was fresh out of white nights. Ayil and Rayne were certainly looking for me, but I had little hope of them bursting in to save me. Even if they could find me, my ovaries would be long gone, and I would still bleed to death from the aggressive surgery.

A clear plastic mask came at me and I twisted to keep my mouth free. "There are other eggs!" I screamed, desperate enough to reveal my secret. "You won't have the only ones!"

The urgent movement in the room stopped, and the goggled eyes surrounding me exchanged confused looks. The lead doctor revealed his face. "What do you mean?" he asked.

"I've been selling my eggs for years. I must have at least a hundred children by now."

"You're bluffing," he said.

"No." I trembled, feeling the metaphorical blade at my throat ease a bit. "I wanted the world to have my DNA. I just didn't want to be breeding stock for the offspring. I gave the little buggers a chance to spread. More eggs, more fathers, more babies, that's the best way to help the human race."

"How do you know you haven't wasted your DNA on half-breeds and weak genetic matches?"

"Then they'll just be babies! Normal, boring, uninteresting people!"

"You'll say anything to get away."

"You want your eggs? Take them, but leave my ovaries. I can tell you the location of one of my last egg banks. I'm sure for the right price you can get the spares. They reserve them in case the mother wants genetic siblings."

The doctors exchanged looks again.

"Hold her still," the lead doctor instructed as he approached me.

"No!"

"I'm going to examine you. With that many procedures, you should have scar tissue. Be still."

I did as instructed, wincing as the cold ultrasound wand entered me. The wand shifted around, searching for the scar tissue. I wasn't sure if there was or wasn't, but I assumed he was right. "You do appear to have some scarring. Wait a minute."

Despite my willingness to wait as many minutes as they wanted, the gunshots and subsequent blood spattering on my face and thighs caught me off guard. One doctor fell across my chest, dead, as the barrage continued. Another dropped beside the table. I could only assume by the silence following the gunfire that everyone was dead.

Everyone except the one firing the shots.

I panted under the weight of the doctor, unable to see the attacker. Was he a friend or foe? Was he going to save me or take off my head?

The slow-motion footsteps stopped just out of my view. A hand touched my thigh. I jumped, more aware than ever of my nudity. I prayed my new captor was only interested in my eggs.

A finger dipped inside my channel and swirled around before dragging out again. I cringed as I heard that finger being tasted, but then I relaxed. It was Rayne. That bastard was teasing me in my vulnerable state. I would *kill* him for that.

"Rayne! Just get me off this table!"

The body that was blocking my view flopped away, revealing an ugly grinning face, made uglier by his proximity to my body. "He's right. You are pretty tasty."

WORSE

"No!" I cursed loudly and fought my restraints with renewed urgency. "Get away from me!" I screamed at Gunder as he freely caressed my open legs. His clone men loomed behind him, eyeballing the advantageous opportunity before them.

"Now, I have to admit, I do prefer to hold you down myself, but it's been a long day. I think I'll enjoy the break."

"I'm surprised you can even get it up for me. Don't you prefer little boys?"

"Not especially. My tastes tend to veer toward breaking. And you, my dear, need to be broken."

I bucked one last time, but the futility of it was too much to deny. Slamming my head back against the table, I closed my eyes and snorted my breaths through flared nostrils. I pinched my lips over my clamped teeth and screeched at the feeling of cold, wet lubrication.

"So nice of those doctors to provide me with lube. You're going to need it. We're going to be here a while."

Gunder's hands pressed against me and I slammed my head into the table again, hoping to pass out before the defilement began. Shots fired again. Five consecutive bangs resulting in Gunder flopping against my stomach.

"Damn it," I muttered and shook my head. I didn't bother to open my eyes. Whatever fate lay before me could reveal itself as easily in the dark as the light.

A hand brushed against my forehead, taking the sweat-matted hair from my eyes. As tender as the movement was, I knew better than to believe it. If Rayne and Ayil had arrived to save me, they would have immediately released me. They wouldn't have stopped for pleasantries.

"Oh, just fuck me and get it over with, you bastard!" I seethed.

"We've already discussed that, Mallory."

My eyes opened, and I gasped at the handsome green face hovering over me. I strained against my confinement, trying to embrace him somehow. "Terrin!" I squawked and broke down into tears.

"Easy, let me undo these," he instructed.

I held still as he undid my belts and cut my ropes. He found a set of keys on one doctor and undid the handcuffs around my ankles.

I wept further at the relief of closing my legs. I tucked them against my body and curled into a ball on the table. Terrin brought me my clothes before checking the downed men for signs of life. With thirteen dead bodies in the room, there was hardly an inch of white between the pools of blood. I repositioned on the table and yanked my pants on. I looked around for my shoes, but I didn't see them.

"I can't find my shoes," I whispered. He returned to me, shifted his scoped rifle around to his back, and picked me up so I didn't have to step through the puddles of blood. "Terrin, what are you doing here?"

"I'm saving you."

"I know, but..." I touched his face as he carried me over the bodies. He looked at me. "I can't go back."

"Oh, my sweet, stupid girl." He sighed. I frowned at the insult in his otherwise heroic moment. "The days of arranged marriages are over. You can never go back."

I grimaced at the thought of never being able to return to my home planets. It was arrogant of me to think they wouldn't put me to death. I had spent so much time warning other people about my father's government, yet I forgot to heed my own words.

"Your DNA is valuable, but it's also dangerous in the wrong hands. The Coalition has recognized the futility of trying to contain you. They want you dead. No exceptions."

"My mother won't allow them to—"

"It's out of her hands now," Terrin snapped. "Your birth reunited your people, and now your dissidence has reopened old wounds. The queen has no choice but to maintain a diplomatic position or risk a hostile engagement."

"She won't help me?" I whispered.

Terrin's expression softened. "She has publicly censured the severity of the Coalition's measures, but she will not use military force to protect you."

I should have known my mother would choose the empire over her daughter. The bitter flavor of her *duty* was one of my earliest childhood lessons.

"But you came for me," I whispered and stroked his cheek.

His eyes flickered over mine and his mouth gaped. "Mallory—"

I wasn't sure what he had meant to say. Maybe he only meant to say his arms were getting tired. But I took advantage of our proximity and his defenseless position. I kissed him, drawing his face closer with a gentle pressure against his neck. His lips were resistant at first, refusing to allow a deeper kiss. But when I slipped my tongue rather forcefully through his barely parted lips, he let out a growl and fell into a heated rhythm with me.

He crushed me to his chest, and I hung from his neck. This moment—this devouring kiss was all we had. All we could ever have. If propriety and common sense hadn't kept me away from him, a room full of dead bodies certainly wouldn't.

The gun cocking in front of us, however, did put a damper on the moment.

Ahem

I stared down the barrel of Rayne's pistol. I wasn't sure what scared me more, the gun or the livid glare backing it up. "Get your hands off her, you filthy gat!" he snarled.

"Rayne—"

"Holy crap, Kit." Ayil peeked around the doorway. "What is it with this guy? Stalker."

"Where's Edric?" I asked, seeing his empty arms.

He nodded to one side. "Down here. He's seen enough today." He pointed to the dead bodies behind us.

"Oh yeah, sorry. If it makes you feel any better, Gunder is dead."

"Yeah, it does." Ayil nodded.

"Kit, I can't help but notice this green bastard is still holding you."

"I lost my shoes. He was just carrying me over the mess."

"He wasn't just carrying you." Rayne sneered, and I flushed at the accusation. I shifted to remove myself from Terrin's arms, but he gripped me tighter. "Let her go." Rayne stepped closer, pressing his gun to Terrin's chest.

"Rayne, stop! Terrin, put me down."

Terrin released me to the floor and I pushed Rayne back. "Stop! He's not the enemy."

Rayne kept his gun aimed. "Let's go." He wrapped his arm around me and pulled me into the hall with Ayil.

"I don't think so." Terrin stepped forward, ignoring Rayne's threat. "She is under my protection."

"Says who?" Ayil asked before Rayne could.

"Her mother."

"My mother?" I asked, looking back at him. "My mother sent you?"

"Yes, she may not be able to send an army to protect you, but she intends to keep you safe. She also wanted me to give you a message, but I have no intention of spanking you."

I smirked, even though I knew a spanking from Terrin would mean a significant bruise.

"We can protect her without your help," Rayne said.

"If I had waited for you to protect her, she would have been on her third rape by now." Terrin nodded to me for confirmation.

Rayne glanced at me, but before I could acknowledge the claim, Terrin was ripping the pistol from his hand. Ignited by a secondary insult to his ego, Rayne lunged at Terrin. Under normal circumstances, I would have let Terrin defend his own honor, but I knew Rayne had a lethal skillset of his own.

"Stop!" I pressed between the two men, blocking their progress with two firmly gripped collars and a ricocheting glare. "Please! I am being targeted and Ayil needs to get his son out of this situation. We need to get back to the ship.

"That sounds like a good idea," Terrin said. "I'll join you."

I turned my dipped brow at Terrin. It didn't surprise me he would come to save me, especially if my mother demanded it. I expected he might follow us until he was certain I was safe, but leaving his ship behind to join us seemed out of character.

"You aren't coming near my ship," Rayne whispered.

"Then she isn't leaving with you," Terrin stated carefully.

"Ayil, please help me. I don't even know what to say."

"Stay here, Edric. Daddy is right around this corner. No peeking," Ayil instructed his son before he came up to me. He looked at the standoff before speaking. "We... are... leaving." Ayil punctuated the words with sign language.

He grabbed my hand and pulled me along behind him into the hall. He picked up his son, who was now wearing a long t-shirt that covered him like a dress. Edric looked terrified. He clung to Ayil as if he were a life raft.

I glanced back at the stalemate in the doorway. Terrin worked his jaw while Rayne stroked his gun's trigger. I wanted to stay and tamp down their testosterone, but since I had caused it to rise in the first place, it was better I leave.

I jogged along behind Ayil, keeping a firm grip on his hand. I would not lose him this time. We had to backtrack several blocks to our transport. I kept looking back, but I didn't see Terrin or Rayne. We reached the pod and Ayil unloaded Edric before shoving me through the squat door.

I latched Edric in, keeping a smile on my face as I did. I didn't know what to say to the boy. He was so beautiful, and ugly monsters were trying to use it all up. By the time Ayil arrived to get himself situated, I hugged him.

He froze in my arms and touched my back gingerly. "Did they hurt you?" he asked, misinterpreting my emotions.

I pulled away and frowned at him. "No. I'm sorry you had to go through that again," I said. "I'm sorry you had to see that bastard again, let alone touch him."

Ayil stroked my hair. "Watching him touch you would have been a hundred times worse than doing it myself."

"I want my mommy," Edric moaned.

I glanced at him and then at Ayil. "Where *is* his mommy?" I whispered.

Ayil frowned and shook his head. "Gunder made sure I was his only chance."

"Oh." I grimaced and looked at Edric. He wasn't much older than my little sister. "Tell me what I can do." I looked at Ayil.

He furrowed his brow and shook his head. "Kit, you've already done it. You saved me. You saved my son. I can't possibly repay that... ever."

"I—"

"Strap in, you two!" Rayne shouted as he jumped into the pod.

I looked through the window outside, but I didn't see Terrin. "Where's Terrin?"

"He's too slow."

"Come on, Kit." Ayil pushed me into my seat.

"Rayne, where is he? Did you hurt him?"

"Ye of little faith," Terrin said as he popped into the hatch from the opposite side of the pod. He gave me a wink and strapped himself in.

Rayne caught the expression of relief on my face and gave me a look that evaporated my joy. Rather than start another argument or defend my desire not to lose any of my friends, I buckled myself in next to Ayil and closed my eyes.

Green

"**I** need to talk to you," Terrin said before I could leave him in his designated quarters for the evening.

"She's tired," Rayne announced from down the hall where he was waiting for me.

Terrin peeked his head out of the room to look at Rayne. "This relationship has become intimate, hasn't it?" He pointed between us.

"What does it matter to you?" Rayne asked.

"In case you haven't caught on yet, Mallory is a very special girl." Terrin stared at me. "People would kill to have what's inside of her, and now they will kill to keep anyone else from having it."

"Is that a threat?" Rayne snarled.

"You haven't explained this to him yet?" Terrin scolded me.

I shrugged. "I mentioned it, but really, who can understand my people's obsession without pictures and graphs?"

Terrin sighed and leaned his head against the doorjamb. "Have you been using protection?"

I chuckled at his bluntness, but my face blanched. We hadn't used protection. I never even thought of it. Years of careful, anguishing abstinence and I stupidly slept with a man twice without the proper protection. Forget STDs, or animal-host parasites; I could be pregnant.

"I'm sterile," Rayne said, stopping my thoughts.

I gaped at him, shocked by this development. "You are?"

"You expect me to believe that?" Terrin asked.

"Believe it; don't. I don't care. I've been sterile since... forever."

"You remember that?" I asked.

"It came up early in my development," he mumbled. "They never found a reason for it."

"I'm sorry," I said, not sure what I should say about that.

Rayne looked me over, also unsure of how to react to my apology. After the assessment, he looked at Terrin. "It's been a long day, gat."

"Terrin," I corrected him.

"Terrin," he conceded. "We should all get some rest."

"I will speak with you in the morning, Mallory." He stepped out of his room and kissed my cheek. "Goodnight."

As he stepped back behind the shield of his room, he smirked at me. He knew he was getting me in trouble, but he couldn't help but poke the man challenging his authority. Terrin wasn't above childish behavior when it came to confronting a human's ego.

Red

"Why were you kissing him?" Rayne ripped off his shirt and threw it into the bin beside his bed. He furiously removed each garment until only his underwear remained. I tucked myself behind his door, waiting for my lecture to be over. "How can you stand him touching you?"

"You and Mother would get along swimmingly," I muttered. "Look, I apologize for the kiss. I know what that must have looked like to you, but truthfully, I'm not sure when you determined my lips were solely your property."

Rayne looked back at me, surprised and hurt by my statement. "I thought you were enjoying your time with me."

"I am, but I still barely know you."

"I barely know myself!" he roared, making me jump. Memories of his improvised slap still fresh in my mind. I was over the border of uncomfortable and into fear.

I didn't wait for his apology or his explanation. I opened the door and slipped out without a word. I heard him protest as the door closed, but I was out of reach before he could stop me. Unless he wished to run around the ship in his underwear, he wouldn't be able to catch me.

Rather than go back to my quarters or involve Terrin in my love life drama, I knocked on Ayil's door. He answered the door with a frown, but he let me in. He had stowed Edric in the sleep pod next to his bed, but it wasn't on.

"What's up?" Ayil whispered as he offered me a spot under his blankets.

I slipped in beside him and tucked myself against his chest. "You do make beautiful babies, Ayil."

"Yeah, he's pretty cute, but don't change the subject. What happened with Mr. Green and Captain Rayne?"

"Nothing, but Rayne isn't happy with me. He started yelling, so I started walking."

"Mmm, he flies off the handle sometimes. He doesn't mean to."

"I've never been yelled at. Not like that. I don't even know what to do with that much anger."

"He doesn't yell when he's angry. He yells when he's frustrated. He points guns when he's angry."

"Did you see what he did back there?"

"Yeah, gotta admire a man who can point a gun at a gattaw and live to talk about it."

"No, I mean when he slit those men's throats."

"What? When was that?"

"It—" A tap on the door quieted me. "Shit," I whispered.

Ayil kissed my forehead and got back out of bed to answer it. He opened it wide enough to reveal I was there, but not wide enough to offer admittance. "Hey, Rayne."

"Hey, Ayil," he said quietly and glanced at me. "Can I talk to her?"

"Up to her," he whispered and looked at me for the answer.

I looked at Rayne. He looked genuinely contrite, but I wasn't sure if this was real or merely his acting skills. "Please, Kit," he said. The penance on his face soured into annoyance. He was no doubt embarrassed to be begging for permission to speak with me.

Rather than make him grovel, I ripped off the blankets and stepped out into the hall with him. Ayil closed the door to give us privacy, but Rayne still moved down the corridor a little to keep the conversation from seeping under the door.

He leaned against the wall, and I stayed a fairly substantial distance away on the opposite side. I waited for the apology, but it didn't come. He was just staring at the floor. Thoroughly bored by the silence, I pushed off the wall to leave.

"I need you," he said before I made it two steps.

I stopped and turned back. "What?"

"I know you want more from me, but my head is so fucked up. I know the bits and pieces of me and my childhood, but you... I don't know. Maybe it's because you slept next to me for so many years, but I can't sleep without you next to me." He looked at me, truly pained by the admission. "I haven't been sleeping since I was woken. That first night I was with you, I slept. And the other day, too."

"You want me for sex, so you can sleep."

"Do you have to make it sound so servile?" Rayne pushed off the wall and faced me. "What do you want? Do you want that *thing*?"

"Dishonoring Terrin isn't going to get me closer to your bed," I snapped.

"And kissing him isn't going to get you any closer to his."

I paused, taking in the insult. I huffed out a stuttered, emotionally-charged laugh. "Yeah, you definitely would have gotten along with my mother." I turned again to return to Ayil's room or my own—there wasn't much point in hiding now.

"Wait," he pleaded and came up behind me. I whipped around and pressed my hand to his chest to stop him from grabbing me. He stopped instantly and raised his hands in saddened surrender. "You're mad about the slap, aren't you?"

"No, you did what you had to do, but it has put a damper on my libido... and my trust."

"Tell me what I can do. I don't want to let you go, but I know holding on too tight will scare you off. You're new to all this, and let's face it, I'm pretty messed up." He stepped closer to me.

"I don't know." My bracing hand rested on his chest, between the flaps of his shirt. I could feel his heart thumping hard. "I spent a lifetime running from this. I'm not sure I can stay still."

"Give me tonight," he whispered. "Let me at least apologize." He pushed forward against my hand and kissed me. When he drew back, he gazed into my eyes. "Come with me." Without another entreaty, he turned around and walked away.

I opened my mouth to call after him, but he was already gone. If I left things as they were and ignored his request, it would send the wrong message. However, if I followed him, it would also send the wrong message. My situation was a paradox: trapped, yet free to decide.

Damn, he was good.

Surrendering to the exasperation of the day, I followed him.

"Mallory." Terrin's voice filtered down the length of the corridor.

I jumped and looked back. The dim lights hid the vague outline of Terrin's figure. "Crap, how do you do that? Have you been there the whole time?"

"I still need to speak with you," he admonished, as if I should have made him a priority over my relationship issues.

"I can't right now. I need to finish this."

"How deep are you?" He slipped out of the shadows. I could see the sternness in his face. It was hard to remember a time when he hadn't been so severe. I thought there was, but maybe I had merely projected my levity onto him.

"Deep into what?"

"In love."

I frowned as he came to me. "I don't know that I am."

"You're close, though." He stopped in front of me. The breadth of his chest was the only authority he had, but it was enough. "Do you trust him?"

I chuckled. "I assume you don't."

"I don't trust anyone completely."

"Even me?" I smirked.

"Especially you," he drawled and released his lips for a small smile.

My smile grew, and he touched my cheek. I closed my eyes and shifted into his hand. Realizing the stupidity of yet another indiscretion, I backed away. "Don't."

"Don't?" He perked a brow. "That was hardly the hello you offered me earlier."

"I know, and I'm sorry about that. I was happy to see you. I'm always happy to see you."

"So am I. Happier still that you are alive to be seen."

"Yes," I laughed. "I rather liked that part, too. Thank you for that, by the way. I take it you were the sniper." He nodded and closed the space between us again. "Terrin, I really need to not do this right now."

"You never answered me. Do you trust him?"

"Why are you asking me that?"

"Because there are a few things you need to know about him before you climb into his bed again."

I shook my head. "Unless he's gay, I think the bed should still be fine."

"I'm serious, Mallory."

"You're always serious, and so am I. I just can't pull off the stoic facade without your bone structure." He inhaled deeply. "Look, I don't know what I feel about Rayne. I don't even know where this relationship is going. What I do know is... this will never work." I motioned between us. "You have to stop coming after me."

"I saved your life and stopped those monsters from raping you," he hissed.

"Yes, and that threat has passed, but you are still here."

"The threat may have passed, but there is still danger. My job—"

"Forget your job!" I yelled. "You have to stop coming after me." I lowered my voice to a hiss. "Don't you see, Terrin? I can't be in love with Rayne, because I'm still in love with you. And the minute I get close to giving up on that fucking fairytale, you show up and make it that much harder to break free. I can escape my family, my planets, and my duty, but I can't escape you."

Terrin tipped his head up to look at the ceiling for a moment before speaking. "I understand, but I'm not leaving until you have all the information. You need to know the threats against you. After that, if you still want me to go, then I will, but I think you may want my help, despite our connection."

"Fine. We'll talk about it in the morning." I turned to leave.

"You may wish tomorrow you had heard it tonight."

"Seriously?" I turned back and shook my head. "Unless someone is going to stab me in my sleep, then I think I can make it until breakfast."

"As I said, you may wish you had decided otherwise tomorrow, but I will leave you to make your own mistakes."

I laughed. "Oh, fuck you, Terrin!"

"Hey!" Ayil scolded from down the hall. "Watch the language and keep it down."

"Sorry," I whispered and grimaced at him before he slipped back into his room.

Terrin remained impassive to my outburst, but I could tell he was restraining himself for the sake of our public position in the corridor.

"I don't know if I trust Rayne yet, but I have always trusted you, and I know you wouldn't let me go to him if you honestly thought he was going to hurt me. So, I don't see any harm in waiting until morning."

"No, you are right. The timeline for reducing pain has already come and gone. Goodnight." Terrin turned and walked back into the shadows.

"Goodnight, Terrin," I whispered after him. I stood in the hall for a moment, weighing the depth of space between Rayne and Terrin. A man I knew nothing of except his body, and a man I knew very well, but could never be intimate with. Life was definitely not a fairytale, but it sure as hell had a sense of humor.

Pink

I tapped on Rayne's door. I heard a scuffle inside and the door opened. His eyes lit as he looked at me. "I didn't think you were coming."

"I didn't know if I should."

"If you're still debating, then you shouldn't come in. I don't have the energy to be a gentleman right now."

"You mean you've been on good behavior up to this point?" I crossed my arms and leaned on the doorjamb.

"Do you want me to show you the difference?"

I bit my lip and peeked in at his bed. There was nothing special about it. I had slept in it for years, but now the ruffled sheets made me want to rip my clothes off and dive in. "Tell me one more thing about yourself. Something you remember."

"I'll tell you what my favorite color is, but you have to tell me yours first."

"Mine? Oh, I haven't had a favorite color in years. That's why I keep changing my hair. Every day I discover something new I like. I guess that means I'm flaky or something."

"I don't get that impression from you. You just like variety. Nothing wrong with that."

I smiled at the complimentary assessment. "What about you? Don't tell me your favorite color is black either; that never counts."

"No, nothing so drab. I like pink."

I frowned. "Pink? That's not usually a... manly color. Should I be worried?"

"I don't think so." He shook his head and stepped closer. "I'm not sure why more men don't like that color. There are so many pinks for men to admire." He caressed my cheek. "Rosy cheeks." He dragged his finger over my lips. "Pouty pink lips."

His finger drifted down my neck, stopping on my breast. I kept my eyes on him as he circled his finger around my nipple, drawing it to attention through the fabric. "Pert pink nipples." He looked at me fiendishly as he pulled me inside his room by my waistband. He shut the door behind me and dove his hand down below my waistband and into my underwear.

I gasped as he slipped his fingers around me and pinched. "This part is my favorite pink thing." I clasped my hands around his biceps, unsure of which side of pleasure or pain this encounter would land. The subtle pinches and fluttering fingers sent waves of pleasure through me.

I leaned against his shoulder. "Rayne." I objected to the intensity of the pleasure, but I had no desire to actually stop him. I clamped my teeth onto his shoulder and muffled my culminating pleasures.

As I panted and recovered from my ascension, he undressed me and himself. He lifted me up and dropped me onto his bed. I slid back over the cool sheets as he crawled up after me. When there was no farther to retreat to, he hovered over me, teasing me with a hint of his full potential.

"Do it," I rasped as I tried to press him into me.

He smirked at my demand, and I groaned as he provided his remaining length. His pace was painstakingly slow and methodical, despite my continued pleas for more.

"Why are you torturing me?" I finally asked in frustration.

He chuckled. "You'll thank me for it in a few minutes." He leaned in a little closer to my ear. "I want you to remember this."

"I'm not the one with amnesia."

He kissed me and I wrapped my arms around him tighter. As he predicted, a few minutes later I thanked him for the arduously slow climax.

With our bodies still entangled, he panted against my chest. I felt a drop of moisture against my breast and I shifted to look at his face.

"Rayne, are you crying?"

"No." He shifted over to his back and drew me on top of him.

I considered asking about the temporary emotional shift, but I was certain he wouldn't share the reason behind it.

Rayne drifted off to sleep, and I watched him as I had once done through the glass of his sleep pod. I wasn't sure what Terrin had intended to tell me about him, but I was now certain I was going to regret waiting to hear it after our night of lovemaking.

Lost

"What do you mean, he left?" I asked poor Aresties the same fashion of question for the third time since I discovered the missing emergency pod.

"Well," she stated more carefully so my ears could understand. "He came to see me this morning—early. He said he had some private business to take care of, and he thought he should do it alone so he didn't endanger you, and vice versa."

"What private business?" I flopped onto one of the small crates in the cargo hold. "He's got amnesia; how much private business could he have?"

"I'm sure whatever it was, it was important," Ayil said from his spot on one of the taller crates.

"Look, Daddy." Edric climbed up the netting on the side of it to reach him. He had taken to using the cargo hold as a playground. So far, he hadn't toppled off the boxes.

"You know I appreciate that you've matured into a father figure overnight, but could you be on my side for this argument?"

"What argument?" he squawked, sounding a good deal more like my Ayil. "He's not even here to argue with."

"All the more reason to be on my side."

"I'm sorry, Kit," Aresties said. "He told me not to say anything until you asked."

"Seriously! What is with the instant man-crush you both have on him? I was your captain for years. He's only been your captain for a few months."

"Says the woman who woke up in his bed this morning," Ayil mumbled.

"Daddy watch!"

"I'm watching, Edric."

"It's not that," Aresties objected. "He's just so nice to me."

"I think that's the definition of a man-crush sweetheart," Ayil contributed.

"And I'm not *nice*?" I shrieked. "When have I not been nice?"

"Says the woman shrieking at us," Ayil mumbled again.

"Shut up! Go back to being abnormally mature!"

"I might be able to shed some light on your missing lover," Terrin offered from the entryway.

"Like what?" I asked.

"Let's talk in private," he said and left without another word.

I scoffed. "Oh fine, Mr. Mysterious-o. Let's go unveil your secrets." I moved toward the exit, but Aresties caught my arm.

She nodded after Terrin. "I think he's nice, too." She smirked and giggled.

"No, no, he is not nice. I am definitely nicer than him."

"Face it, Kit, you can't please everybody." Ayil smirked at me.

"I am not mean," I murmured as I left the cargo bay to find Terrin.

After three or four rooms, I found him in the map room. The room's original purpose was 3D star map viewing, but computer updates changed its use to enjoyment, rather than plotting travel.

I stepped into the dismal gray room where Terrin was sitting at a long boardroom table. "Close the door behind you," he instructed.

"You really are getting into this bit." I shut the door and even locked it. "Why does Aresties think you are nice?"

"What?" He blinked and looked up from his electronic pad.

"Never mind." I slumped down in a chair catty corner to him, since he had naturally chosen the head of the table.

"I suppose it's because I was polite to her this morning when I asked her to give me a tour of the ship."

"Did you know he was gone?" I asked acerbically.

"What difference would my knowledge of his presence make after he was already gone?"

"Did you know he was going to leave?"

"How would I begin to predict his movements if you can't?"

"I don't know!" I threw my hands up. "I assumed you dragged me in here to help me."

"I understand you're upset about his absence, but I need you to listen to what I have to say."

"I'm here, aren't I?" I snapped.

He swiveled his chair to face me. "I need you to know what I am about to tell you is for your own good. I'm not trying to hurt you."

I frowned and glanced at his pad. "What is it?"

Terrin shifted and placed his hand on mine. "There was another reason your mother hired me to come find you. Besides the threat against your life, there was something more personal that had to be dealt with."

I stared into Terrin's eyes, wondering what could be so concerning that it would have taken precedence over my potential assassination. He moved back to his pad and clicked a few buttons to make the screen load onto the map screen. Within the foggy cube before me, a grainy image of Rayne came up.

"This camera footage was recorded at a hotel on Peloma about fifteen years ago," Terrin said. "Your mother brought me to her office and demanded to know if this was the man you had been traveling with prior to your recovery. I explained your connection as best I knew, and then she showed me this."

Terrin clicked another button on his pad and I watched video footage of a man entering a building in full black garb.

It switched to another camera, and I saw the figure stab three men in quick succession as he made his way to a locked hotel door. He bypassed the door with his own key card and entered. Without interior footage, we can only imagine what other carnage occurred inside the room. Less than a minute later, the man left the room with a briefcase in his hand.

I looked at Terrin and shook my head. "So what? I didn't see anything on that tape identifying the culprit."

"No, and neither did the other twenty videos like it. The assassin was quick, ruthless, and didn't leave any evidence behind... except once." Terrin clicked another button and an image of a woman popped up on the screen.

She was beautiful with dark features and long, umber hair. Gold and diamonds further enhanced her already flawless beauty.

"Who is she?"

"Princess Helana, the daughter of King Naadir Kapur. She was attacked ten years ago on her wedding day—an attempted assassination. She narrowly escaped him, but not before she scratched him. His genetic ID has been sitting in a computer database for the last decade, waiting for his reemergence."

Terrin pushed another button and revealed my marriage license. I recognized the signature and bloody thumbprint I provided on the day of her wedding—irrefutable proof of my identity. I hadn't even looked at the signature on the other side of the document that day. Nor did anyone else, apparently.

In his rush to get through the procedure, Rayne had signed his own name. It was sloppy and hardly legible, but, even so, his bloody thumbprint couldn't be faked.

"Your mother tested the DNA. It's a match for our assassin."

"How do you know all the assassinations were Rayne?"

"The technique is flawless. The wounds are the same, indicating the same knives."

I frowned, thinking of Rayne's extensive knife collection, not to mention his quick, lethal skill with them. "You don't actually think Rayne put himself in a ten-year coma on the off chance he might wake up and find a lucrative job holding up on his ship?"

"I don't know what I think yet," Terrin said, leaning back in his chair. "I know sleep pods can be tampered with to indicate longer sleep cycles."

"Even if that were the case, he was definitely asleep with me on board for six years. If that was anyone's plan for an assassination, then it sucks. Not to mention no one officially wanted me killed until you brought me back. They had given up finding me until then."

"You were never truly lost, Mallory." Terrin's words came out soft, but his stony gaze told me he was still bitter about the sacrifices he made to protect my freedom. "Truthfully, I have no idea why the Coalition has waited until now to act against you. I assumed they took offense to your second desertion."

I stared at the marriage license image floating in the mist in front of me. "Fuck," I scoffed. "That thing's legal. He even signed his own name." I laughed. "Well, good for me. I did wait until I was married to lose my virginity. Mother will be so proud."

My levity died down, and I stared at the floor beneath the table. I could feel Terrin watching me, but I didn't have the strength to look at him.

"Why can't I have a normal life?" I asked rhetorically. "What do I do now?" I finally turned to him. He didn't seem to have an answer. "I can't go home, can I?"

"No. That option has expired."

"I can't go home. I can't be with my husband because he might kill me in my sleep. And I can't be with you, cause..." I took a much-needed breath to calm myself. "I know I usually spend too much time wallowing in my misery and not seeing the bigger picture, but I'm not wrong this time, am I? My life really does officially suck."

Terrin shifted forward and shut off the screen. The room dimmed again. "I wish more than anything that I could change one of those burdens for you." He squeezed my hand gently before leaving the room. I wasn't sure I wanted to be alone, but he probably didn't want to hang around for the sobbing.

Found

"Kit—no, Edric!" Ayil yanked Edric's hands away from the controls and pulled him further back on his lap. "He shut the locator off. I checked that already."

"I know," I said, pushing several more buttons to find the screen I was looking for. "I'm not going to follow him; he is going to follow us, in reverse."

"You're going to make me ask what that means, aren't you?"

"I'm going to program the pod to come back to us. It will plot a path and submit it to us. But before it actually activates it, I will break the connection."

"And you don't think Rayne would have thought of that already?"

"I guarantee he hasn't."

"Why not?"

"Because he hasn't read the manual. This little nugget is pretty deep in the system. My guess is he hasn't learned anything beyond the basics of flying and shooting." I clicked the last button. A mess of data filled the screen in front of me. Rather than approve the process, I saved the map and canceled out. "Ha! There, we have it. It looks like he isn't very far away." I brought up the coordinates and scanned for the closest logical destination. "I bet he's headed here. He took a beeline toward this planet the minute he entered the solar system."

I pushed on the screen to bring up the planet. "Karthik it is." I plotted the coordinates to the planet. The autopilot's lovely event coordinator materialized on the screen as a petite blonde and began her speech about the planet's many tourist features.

"Planet Karthik is known as the garden planet, but unlike other planets with this title, Karthik is the only one to live up to the name. The planet's excess of rain leaves much of the low-lying surface as a floodplain. Rather than reroute the vacillating water levels, King Naadir has dedicated his efforts to building a series of bridges and pathways that provide dry passage throughout many of the planet's largest and most industrious cities."

"Naadir?" I questioned aloud.

The woman went on, but I ignored her litany about the capitol's remarkable water gardens.

I pressed a few more buttons and pulled up an image of King Naadir Kapur and his extraordinary daughter, Princess Helana.

"Shit." I shook my head.

"What is it?" Ayil asked. "Not a fan of water lilies?"

"Rayne is going to finish what he started ten years ago."

Another's Anguish

I sat in the cafeteria across from Ayil as he took in the videos of Rayne's assassinations on Terrin's tablet. Aresties was still shaking her head, refusing to believe any of it. The ice cream she had pulled from the freezer to eat was melting into soup.

"This can't be," Ayil repeated what Aresties had minutes earlier.

"You've seen him in action," I explained.

"No, I haven't." He bit on the technicality fervently.

"I have. There was something skilled in his movements."

"He isn't a murderer." Ayil glared at me as if I were the one who had started this vicious rumor.

"He is a murderer," Terrin stated. "The evidence is in the DNA."

"Oh, and that's never wrong."

"We are not comparing apples and oranges," Terrin explained. "It was an exact match. Short of him having a clone, he *is* the assassin."

"I knew there was something about you I didn't like." Ayil eyed Terrin carefully.

"Yes, I imagine it's difficult for you to interact with a man who doesn't lie to you."

Ayil's face blanked, and he stood slowly. I rose with him. "Ayil," I whispered, begging him not to challenge Terrin physically. Partially because I knew I would throw myself between them, and I wasn't interested in another round of bruises.

"You think you know me so damn well, don't you?"

"Mallory has told me a good deal about you. Plus, I've done my research."

"Just conversations," I interjected, lest Ayil think I divulged his background like a report.

"Research, huh?" Ayil asked. "I bet I know a thing or two about you." He brandished a sly smile at Terrin. Had he not been ready to throw a punch, I might have called it flirtatious. Maybe still.

"And what is that?" Terrin crossed his arms.

"I know you haven't told Kit about the surgery."

Terrin's controlled seething turned to momentary shock. He took a deep breath, puffing his chest before his irascible face returned.

"What surgery?" I asked.

"The spurs—" Ayil started

"Don't," Terrin objected.

"—can be removed."

I glanced at Aresties, not understanding what he meant. She raised her finger and pointed down to her lap. She smiled weakly at me as my brain translated.

I looked at Terrin. "Wait... Those spurs can be removed?"

"Oh, yeah," Ayil flaunted his revelation. "They've been working on it for the last five years. Guess maybe he's just not interested in you, Kit."

I stared at Terrin, trying to find a question to match the answers he wasn't giving. When he finally looked at me, I got my answer.

No.

I ripped myself away from the table so fast, my chair slammed into the floor. As I stormed out, I heard Terrin scolding Ayil. "Inconsiderate child! Who did you think you were hurting?"

I couldn't find any refuge on the small ship, but there was one place I knew I could at least scream and cuss without anyone hearing.

I shoved into the engine room, squirming past the stuck half-door. The hiss of the room's leaky pipes and the chug of pistons were the perfect backdrop to my frustrated scream.

I stood in the middle of the melee, panting and waiting. I finally heard the squawk of the door pushing open a little further.

Terrin maneuvered through the creative design of a refurbished muscle ship and stood before me. I waited a few moments before speaking. I wanted to say just the right thing.

"Fuck you!" Not very original, but it would have to do.

"Mallory, it's not what you think!"

"I think you've been lying to avoid your pathetic little crush." I punched his stomach. He flinched and clenched his jaw, but I knew I couldn't hurt him. As it was, my fist hurt a little. "I know you've been indulging my crush for years, but I thought things had changed between us. Oh my God, I threw myself at you! How could you let me humiliate myself like that?" I punched his chest. "You should have just told me you didn't want me!"

I moved to punch him again, but he halted my fist with his firm grip. "Because that would be the lie," he said.

"Why did you tell me you loved me?" I whispered.

His next movement had me spinning, falling, and landing in his arms. "Because I do," he rasped and then his mouth was on mine. His hand slid away from my face and roamed over my breast. He continued to explore down my stomach until he reached the waist of my pants, but he had no intention of stopping there. He undid the snaps and zipper.

Was this really happening?

We still couldn't have sex, but that didn't mean we couldn't give each other pleasure. Hands, lips, fingers, tongues, very progressive adult toys.

This could work.

This could... be another in a very long list of bad decisions.

My mind was in a frenzy of debate. If it had been a few weeks ago, or maybe even just yesterday, I would have braced myself for the pleasurable depredations Terrin could provide and begged him for more. But today, it felt like I was doing something wrong.

I had Rayne, or at least I did. He was a human man with a socially approved, biologically compatible penis. That was what I needed. And it should have been what I wanted.

And mature women should want what is best for them.

Right?

Terrin's fingers slipped past the elastic band of my panties, but I grabbed his hand. He stopped.

"No." I uttered the word mournfully when he released my lips. "I can't," I said without truly understanding the emotion, which had overcome my oldest desire.

Terrin looked disappointed, and I felt guilty for baiting his attentions only to reject them. He put me down on my feet and I stayed close to him for a moment, touching his chest. I hated to withdraw. There was no way to balance what I felt for him. My connection to him was so strong it was hard to interpret it as anything but lust.

And yet, it was so much more than that.

He was... in me. To the point that I wouldn't be the person I had become without him.

I finally backed away and leaned my head against a pipe, while I snapped my pants and composed myself. "I don't understand, Terrin. If you felt this way, why did you wait until now to tell me? Did you even consider the surgery before you left me to suffer a loveless arranged marriage?" I asked, wiping away a tear I couldn't contain.

"Yes." His jaw clenched before he spoke again. "You're right. I have long indulged your crush. I used it to keep you under control in a way your parents had been unsuccessful. It was perhaps inappropriate, but I never had any designs on you beyond my duty and our unusual friendship. Then something changed." He stared at me, as if I were solely to blame for his shift in attraction.

"I grew up." I shrugged, defending my lack of control for my aging.

"You kissed me," he said, slightly dazed. "I admit it wasn't so much the kiss as the defiance following it that changed my opinion of you, but in the end, it was transformative for me.

"When I saw you again on that roof, I felt relieved and betrayed all over again. I knew I cared for you, but I didn't know how much my attraction had grown until you kissed me again. At that moment, you were no longer a girl, or a job, or an incompatible species. You were just a woman, and I was a man." Terrin's eyes closed as if he was still getting his desires under control.

"Why didn't you tell me about the surgery, then?"

"Even with five years of research, the risk of impotency is about 15%. Nearly a quarter of the *successful* patients report lowered sensation. As much as I wanted you, I wasn't sure if I wanted to risk it."

I nodded, finally understanding. I loved Terrin unconditionally, but to ask him to gamble with his sexual vitality was too selfish. Not to mention, if he lost his function, we would be back to just being friends, anyway. The only difference would be the escalating resentment he would have for me. "I'm sorry, Terrin. I wouldn't want you to limit your own pleasure in exchange for mine."

"That wasn't why I decided not to do the surgery."

I furrowed my brow. I was pretty sure a 15% chance of erectile dysfunction was a good enough reason not to do the surgery. "Please don't tell me it was my mother."

"It was the same reason I didn't break up your wedding and take you for myself." I smiled, thinking how furious my mother would have been.

"It was Elizandra."

"My sister?" I frowned in confusion.

He sat on the main exhaust pipe—his pants were ruined. He raised his hand to me. I slid my fingers between his and he tugged me over and sat me on his knee. He caressed my cheek before he spoke.

"I was considering the surgery. I want you to know that. I do love you, Mallory, and if things were different, then..." He chuckled. "If things were different, we could finish those sentences without hurting each other.

"The reason I decided to let you go was because I remembered how you looked at your little sister. That sweet little girl is the spitting image of you, and she could have just as easily been your daughter as your sister."

I gulped, thinking of what had run through my mind when I first saw her. For a split second, I think I *did* think she might have been mine. A runaway egg, come back to haunt me.

"I can't give you a child, Mallory," Terrin admitted, as if I hadn't known that already.

"Oh, Terrin, I don't care about that. All they've ever wanted from me is to be a baby-making machine."

"I thought you should still have the option. Especially since you would make an excellent mother."

"Really?" I wrinkled my nose at him.

"Yes. Imagine my disappointment when I realized you chose the only naturally sterile man in the galaxy as your lover."

I chuckled. "Don't worry, there is plenty of me out in the world to satisfy that damned prophecy."

He brushed my hair back behind my ear, and I could see the hunger return to his gaze. "I suppose my reasons for not being with you have—" His hand dropped to his lap and his eyes narrowed on me. "What do mean there is plenty of you to satisfy the prophecy?"

My eyes flickered over his, and I tried to find an answer that wouldn't anger him.

Eggs

"What the hell were you thinking?" Terrin yelled, storming through the ship after me. I had told him the truth, but unfortunately, I had *not* figured out a way to say it without pissing him off.

"Initially, I was thinking I needed money! I had to get started somehow."

"How many times have you done it?" Terrin asked.

"I don't know, fifty or sixty times by now."

"So, you are endangering the lives of hundreds of people because you needed money?" he yelled behind me as I slid down the stairs to get away from him.

"Hundreds?" I squawked. "I don't have hundreds of children out there. At best, maybe *one* hundred."

"What is it now?" Ayil barked as I veered into the cargo bay—aka Edric's playground.

"Oh, sorry, Ayil." I turned to leave again, but Terrin's finger was in my face.

"If anyone finds out about them, they will be killed, along with their mother and father and any of their siblings. That blood will now be on your hands!"

"Who's killing who?" Ayil asked.

"What about yours?" I batted his hand away. "What about my parents? I have obligations and a duty, remember? Was I supposed to just discount the potential to ease human suffering with my super awesome DNA? Like that burden hasn't been resting on my shoulders since birth. I may have been careless by selling my eggs, but you and my parents were the ones who guilted me into that decision."

"I don't think the prophecy includes the option of surrogate eggs," Terrin snapped.

"Those were egg banks you were going to?" Ayil asked behind me.

"The prophecy is bullshit. The only part of this I am remotely on board for is the science. Do you think I should have ignored my potential because the science of it wasn't romantic enough?"

"If you were interested in any part of the prophecy, you should have stayed on your home planets and done your duty the proper way, but that was too much to ask."

"That argument is six years too late!"

"I never got to have that argument with you. You just left, remember?"

"I was never *allowed* to have that argument with you." I pushed into Terrin's space. "Or don't *you* remember?"

Terrin stiffened, to maintain at least the appearance of superiority. I stared at him, double-dog daring him to tell me more about my unfulfilled destiny, so I could tell him about my unfulfilling childhood.

Ayil jumped down from his crate and rested his arm on my shoulder. I wasn't sure if he meant to dispel the tension or establish support. "What's the big deal? She donated some eggs. Aside from there being a resurgence of cute, funny-haired little girls, who cares?" He poked my nose, and I batted him away.

"Terrin believes if all the competing interests find out about my eggs, they will start killing or kidnapping the resulting children to get access to their DNA."

"Who knows about the egg bank except us?" Ayil asked.

"No one," I said to Terrin.

"You used an alias, right?" Ayil asked.

"Of course."

"A different name at each bank?"

"Yes."

"That's my brainy girl." Ayil squeezed my shoulder and kissed the top of my head. "So, this isn't really a big deal." He looked at Terrin. "I mean, not enough for you to be having a catastrophic conniption and blaming her for hundreds of deaths that haven't even happened yet."

"Someone will figure it out. Mallory isn't quite so lucky. We need to do something to stop this, before it becomes a catastrophe." Terrin eyed Ayil sternly.

"Okay, so let's step back and look at my to-do list. I need to avoid being assassinated by my parents' governments. Avoid being taken hostage and dissected by the competing governments. Protect my friends from the crossfire of said assaults. Plus, I need to save my potential and existing offspring from extermination, just in case someone finds out about them. And stop my husband from returning to his assassin ways." I raised my hands. "Is that about everything, or did I miss anything?"

"This isn't a joke, Mallory."

"Of course it's not a joke, Terrin, but what do you want me to do? There is only one thing on that list I have an increment of control of at the moment. You can lecture me about the past as long as you want, but in the end, we are stuck with the decisions I have made. You can either stand by my side and help, or you can judge me from afar."

"Are you asking me to leave?" Terrin stared me down.

I frowned and blinked at him. "Actually, I was asking you to shut the hell up and help me, but... it's your choice."

Terrin crossed his arms. "How long until we reach the planet?"

Water Gardens

Since the emergency pods weren't quick, we not only arrived on Karthik before him, but we had plenty of time to find the palace and get situated for our intervention.

I should have been immune to anything as gaudy as an alabaster brick building surrounded by ornamental gardens, but apparently I wasn't. I couldn't keep my eyes from wandering to the endless fountains, interpretive sculptures, and the nude statues of godlike beings.

"Did you see that one?" I asked, peeking from behind my pillar-o-bush. "Is she eating a snake?"

"I think it's a representation of Eve succumbing to the influence of Satan," Ayil surmised from his own hiding spot behind a memorial altar.

"Really?" I asked.

"No, Kit, it's a dick reference. They're all dick references. This is a garden of blooming flowers and stone-hard statues. Trust me, everything in here is about sex."

"Quiet, you two!" Terrin hissed from behind me. "Someone is coming."

I angled myself to see through to the path on the other side. "Holy shit, that's her," I whispered. "She certainly doesn't fail to impress, does she?"

Two attendants accompanied the princess: one to hold a parasol to shade her, another to wave a frond as she walked.

I grimaced and looked at Terrin. "Please tell me I have never looked that snooty."

He smiled at me and brought his finger to his lips to hush me.

As she passed by, I could see the wide hem of her ivory pants, trimmed with diamond embellishments. I saw that white lace tattoos covered her arms and bare midriff. Either they were decorative, or her father was far more lenient than mine.

A waft of lavender overpowered the already fragrant gardens. It reminded me of my father's house and, for the first time since I had been told, I realized what it meant to be locked out of my home forever.

I looked at Terrin and he seemed to know what I was thinking, or at least the generalized emotion. He looked back at the path and his brow furrowed. He stood up, and I raised my hand to stop him.

I peeked out and spotted Rayne stalking down the path toward us.

"I want to see for sure," I whispered. "Maybe he just wants to talk to her."

"Mallory, don't be naïve," Terrin scolded.

"I'm not, but I have to know for sure."

Terrin simmered down, and we all hid while Rayne's boots tapped past us. I stepped out onto the path and followed him. I darted in and out of the tacky bush animals on the way.

I could see the princess up ahead. She turned a corner but hadn't noticed Rayne gaining on her. He stopped and reached down to his boot. He pulled out a knife, which glinted in the sunlight.

"Shit," I whispered. "He's going to do it right now," I hissed back to the undersized green elephant behind me.

"Now?" Terrin popped his head up from behind the leafy pachyderm. He moved to me and yanked the pulse pistol off my belt before dashing after Rayne.

"Don't kill him," Ayil hissed and ran after Terrin.

I followed right after them, but my short strides left me trailing, with or without the speed. After one or two turns, I was into a maze of greenery and had no idea which path anyone had taken. I shuffled along the brick paths and found a gazebo with kissing lovers—not just statues—a butterfly sanctuary, more rose bushes than any garden should have.

Finally, I popped out of the mess and arrived back in the flood plains of the garden. In place of bushes, there were shallow water ponds filled with lily pads and a dizzying matrix of stone bridges.

I could see the princess and her entourage passing over a covered columned bridge ahead of me and I ran toward her. I didn't know why Rayne felt compelled to kill this woman, but I refused to watch her die. And more importantly, I wouldn't let him fall back into old habits.

Part of me wanted Rayne to be a good guy. Part of me also needed him to be. I was prepared to overlook his questionable career choice, but I couldn't be with someone who enjoyed killing enough to complete a ten-year-old contract.

I sprinted silently down my low bridge, unnoticed by the passing princess or the man stalking her in broad daylight. I closed in as he raised his knife.

I skipped the war cry as I reached the intersection of my path and the covered bridge. I rammed into Rayne before he could pounce. He let out an *"uff"* before we both toppled between the columns and into the frog sanctuary below.

Pond Scum

After a brief struggle, I was beneath Rayne, under the water, grasping at his arms. He held me down, pressing me into the slimy bed of the pond.

The water lilies floated in the path of my blurry vision, blocking his face from view, and mine from his. Or perhaps he didn't need to see my face. Maybe he already recognized me.

I squeezed his arms rhythmically, begging for air. When I had no more breath left, and I was certain I was about to die, I gave up my plead for air, and just flipped him off with both hands. I may not have been able to fight off an assassin, but damn if I wouldn't get the last word in.

Rayne pulled me up, and I sucked in a breath, part air, and part water lettuce. I spluttered and spat out the foliage. "Please don't kill me," I panted and blinked away my water blur.

"Kit?" Rayne questioned. "What are you doing here?" He pushed my hair out of my face.

"I'm here—" I let out a necessary burp. "To stop you from making a horrible mistake."

"What do you mean?" he asked suspiciously.

I opened my eyes and stared at him. I was very aware he was still straddling me, and it would only take the press of his hand to put me under the water and silence me forever. I wanted to chastise him for stupidity and ego, but I was honestly afraid of him.

"Please don't do this, Rayne."

"What is it you think I am here to do?" he asked.

I shook my head. "I saw you. Don't lie to me, okay? I know what you are, what you were, but you don't have to be that man anymore."

Rayne frowned and looked toward the palace. The sun was shifting into its evening position, casting slanted shadows across the grounds. "You don't know the whole truth."

"I know you were an assassin, but you don't have to kill the princess. That job is over."

Rayne's jaw clenched. "The princess was never a job for me. That one was my choice. A choice I was robbed of ten years ago."

"It doesn't have to be like this, Rayne. Let's just leave. We can go anywhere you want. We can lie on a beach and have sandy, sunburned sex all day long."

He smiled down at me. "I'd like that. But first I have to kill a princess." He got up, but I grabbed his arm.

"Rayne, if you continue to pursue this, I'm going to have to stop you," I said with a measure of backbone in my voice.

He shifted back down, looming over me. I flinched as he reached his hands toward my face. He cupped my cheeks and leaned down close to look at me. "You can try." He smiled and dragged his nose over mine. "You might even succeed. You are pretty clever, but remember... no matter what happens, by the end of this day, either the princess will be dead, or I will."

Rayne leaned down and kissed me. He deepened the kiss, calling to every part of my body. When he had thoroughly liquefied me into a puddle of goo, he released me and stood up. "I know you'll make the right decision," he whispered and hopped onto the nearest bridge and disappeared into the vining foliage of the upside-down garden section.

"Well, he doesn't know me at all," I grumbled and extricated myself from the frog pond.

Starla

"He is continuing with the assassination?" Ayil asked as he pulled a cluster of duckweed out of my hair.

"Yes."

"But why? What the hell for? He's been legally dead ten flippin' years."

"The princess isn't a job. He *wants* to kill her." I glanced at Terrin to see what he thought of that. He didn't bother to express his irritation verbally, he just started walking toward the palace. "Terrin?"

"We have to stop this, Mallory," he hollered back to me.

"Don't you think I know that?" I took off after him, with Ayil right beside me.

"I think your judgment is clouded right now, or you wouldn't have let him walk away the first time."

"Oh, excuse me for being terrified of my armed, lethally trained assassin husband! I'm new to this whole marriage thing."

"Did he tell you why he wanted her dead?" Terrin shifted to look back at me.

"No, he just said it was his choice. He said..." I frowned, thinking about what the next few minutes were going to involve.

"What is it?" Terrin stopped and turned to me.

"He said one of them was going to be dead by the end of the day, either him or her."

Terrin looked at Ayil. "Do you know anything about this?"

"What?" I scoffed. "Don't be ridiculous, Terrin. Ayil just found out about all this."

"Do you?" Terrin asked again, and I looked at Ayil, since he hadn't denied it yet.

He glanced at me and shook his head. "He never mentioned the princess, but he did say something strange when we were installing the new pilot's counsel. He got really serious and said, 'I won't forget again.' Then he touched that name on the old panel."

"Starla," I verified.

"Starla?" Terrin asked. He grimaced and took off for the palace again. "Let's go, hurry."

"What does that mean?" I asked, trying to keep up with him.

"Starla is Princess Helana's mother," Ayil answered.

"How do you know that?" I asked.

"I finished listening to the tourism ad," he said.

"Terrin, what does that mean?"

"It means Rayne may be covering up his tracks. Starla Kapur was murdered the day of her daughter's wedding. The same day Helana was attacked. I think he screwed up and left a witness, and until he kills her, he isn't going to be unidentifiable."

I looked at Ayil. He had the same expression of disappointment on his face that I felt. I didn't want to believe it, but it was true. Rayne was a cold-blooded murderer, and we had to stop him.

The Princess

It was no surprise the doorman looked at us like we were beatniks selling vacuum cleaners. The fact that we had *talked* our way through the guarded gate was a miracle in and of itself. Hopefully, no one would notice the three unconscious men in the courtyard before we explained ourselves.

The doorman shook his head and closed the door. I stepped forward, putting my foot in its path. "How *dare* you close a door on royalty?" I seethed with pomposity.

The elderly man was astonished.

"As if it isn't bad enough, I have to travel through your precarious water traps to reach this palace." I squeezed a little more water out of my hair. "Now I have to explain to yet another minion who I am."

"Princess Kit, don't trouble yourself." Ayil jumped to my side, prepared to play his part in my impromptu performance. "Sir, this is Princess Kit Mallory of Brahama. She has traveled far from her home to meet with Princess Helana to discuss a potential marriage to join their houses politically and spiritually." Ayil clasped his hands together and smiled as if a prayer or a single tear should mark the occasion.

"But Princess Helana has no siblings, and her only unwed cousins are female."

Ayil and I glanced at each other and crossed our arms simultaneously. "So?" we asked.

Desperate not to offend, the doorman led us inside to a room my mother would have politely called the drawing room, and in private called the sweeper room. It was where she placed guests she didn't actually want in our house. It would have to do. All we needed was an audience with the princess.

Ayil sat down on the beautiful but hard furniture. After discovering it served no other purpose but to fill the room, he stood up again. He moved over next to me to examine a portrait of the king and his daughter—or was that the queen? I gazed up at the beautiful woman, who was no doubt responsible for the creation of Helana. They could have easily named her Helen of Troy.

"So, is this what your palace looks like?"

"Uptight and uselessly expensive? Yes."

"Come on." Ayil nudged me. "Tell me it wasn't a little fun living in a place like this."

"I spent most of my time outside in the gardens, or in my room. Look around, Ayil. This isn't a place meant for children. Everything is expensive and breakable. It's meant for uptight dignitaries and their snobby wives."

"Is that so?" a silky voice said behind me.

"Shit," I mumbled and turned around. "Princess Helana." I bowed.

"We don't bow here. What kind of backwards nation do you think we run here?" Helana snapped and stepped further into the room with her human footstools in tow. She was still in her ivory pant suit, but she had added a translucent cardigan to *cover* her exposed midriff and arms. "What is this about you wanting to marry my cousin?"

"Princess, this isn't about your cousin. I am here to warn you about—"

"Christ, who let the fucking gat in here?" Helana squawked when she got a full inventory of the room.

"He's mine—my bodyguard..." I stumbled on my words, unprepared for the audacity of her rudeness. Despite my explanation, she kept snarling at Terrin. He took it in stride, as he did everyone who insulted his species on a daily basis. "Princess Helana." I cleared my throat, but she continued to glare at my friend. "Keep looking at him like that and I will give him permission to punch your teeth in."

The two footstools on either side of her jumped to attention, prepared for a threat from Terrin. However, he was the only one not provoked by the situation.

"Whoa!" The princess gawked at me with wide eyes, and room to rent in her open mouth. "Look who thinks they can play with the big kids."

"Oh, shut up!" I screamed at her. "You are the reason I can't stand people like us. Would you just listen? Rayne is coming to assassinate you."

Helana's slack-jawed attitude dissolved as she took in what I was saying. Her face contorted back into arrogance, and she shook her head. "That's not possible."

"He's probably already here. You need to search the palace. He could be hiding anywhere."

"Rayne is dead."

"No, he's not. He's—wait, why do you think he's dead?"

Helana stood up and walked toward me, but she was looking at the picture on the wall. "That bastard killed my mother, and then he tried to kill me, but I wasn't as easily done in." She turned away from the picture and looked at me. "I scratched him." She flipped up her finger for me to see the bladed fingernail on her index finger.

"You think a scratch would kill him?"

"If my nail polish was made of cat's fever, it would."

"What is that?"

Helana rolled her eyes. "It's a very common plant in our gardens. It's a potent poison. Lethal, if introduced into the bloodstream by, say, a scratch. So, you see, even though he got away from my guards, I know he is dead."

"Unless he found a way to counteract the poison," Terrin surmised and joined me. "By, say, going into a long-term hypersleep."

"Impossible," Helana dismissed the idea, but her mouth was already contorting into a snarl.

"The sleep pod would have slowed down his heart, giving the bio-filters enough time to identify a problem in the blood and repair the damage."

"Son of a bitch," Helana murmured as her eyes glazed.

"We believe he has returned to eliminate the only witness to your mother's murder," Terrin explained.

Helana drew her eyes to Terrin and then to me. She erupted into a tearful vocalization and threw her hand over her face. "Oh, God, why?" she wailed. "How can this be happening again? I just want to be free of this man and his violence!"

She ripped her hand from her face and grabbed me. "We are all in great danger. If he knows that you know about him, he will kill you, too." She looked around the room. "This isn't safe. There are too many windows here. Come with me. I know where we can be safe."

The Bitch

"This doesn't feel right," I whispered to Terrin as Helana and her guards led us to a safe room.

"I agree," he answered. I glanced at him, surprised he was agreeing with me. "She's suddenly interested in saving the gat?"

"She wasn't even crying before. This is all an act."

"I think I may have been too quick to judge Rayne," Terrin admitted.

"But he didn't deny being an assassin."

"He's an assassin, alright, but I'm not so sure he killed Starla."

A knot settled in my gut as we arrived at the so-called safe room, deep at the center of the palace. We might as well have been in a basement with heavy ceiling insulation.

Helana turned back to offer us passage into the room. "Here we—where's the third one?"

I looked back and saw that Ayil was indeed gone. I wasn't sure when he had slipped away.

"Where is he?" Helana asked again, losing her *pleasant* demeanor.

"Maybe Rayne has already struck. Perhaps you and your guards should wait in there while we go get help," I suggested.

"I wouldn't think of putting my guests in danger."

"I think the most important thing is that *you* stay safe."

"Just get in the room, you stupid bitch." Helana waved us in while her armed guards drew their weapons.

"I hate being right at the wrong times," I grumbled and did as I was told.

Terrin and I entered the vacant room with no windows. The fire in the hearth was the only light in the room.

The door shut and latched behind us. I looked back, disappointed to see that Helana and her brutes were inside with us. I preferred lonesome captivity.

One guard held me at gunpoint while the other relieved Terrin of my borrowed pulse pistol and his short copper sword. He slipped the pistol into his belt, but tossed the sword away as if it were useless. Terrin's eyes followed the blade as it skidded across the floor. I didn't know the full history behind the weapon, but I got the sense he didn't appreciate being separated from it.

The guards disappeared into a darkened corner of the room and returned with a pair of wooden chairs. They set them to face the fireplace and stood behind them.

"Sit down." Helana waved to the chairs. Neither one of us moved. "Go on, don't make it harder on yourself. Cooperation is the key in all negotiations."

"What exactly are we negotiating?" I asked stupidly.

"We are negotiating for information." She slipped a fire poker off the ledge of the mantel and started heating it in the flames below. "If you give it to me, I give you less pain."

I looked at Terrin, hoping we weren't in as much trouble as I suspected, but I could see his discomfort with this development. I shifted closer to him.

"Or I could kill you right now."

The men raised their weapons in unison and pointed them at me.

Terrin pulled me back behind him. "No. We'll answer your questions."

"Good. Sit down."

I was too terrified to move, but Terrin pushed me forward. I surmised there was no point in pinning myself to his chest and weeping like a baby. We could save that for later, if we survived.

I sat down in one chair and Terrin sat in the other. The man behind mine pressed down on my shoulders to keep me still. I waited for the other guard to do the same for Terrin. I relished the idea of watching a cocky idiot trying to hold down a gattaw. Unfortunately, the guard wasn't an idiot. He shifted his gun and shot Terrin in the leg.

Revenge

"**N**o!" I shrieked and lunged for Terrin. The man behind me pinned my shoulders back and pressed me down harder. "Terrin!" I cried and futilely reached for him.

He leaned over his leg, holding the seeping wound as best he could. He turned to look at me, but he couldn't quite muster the strength to dismiss my concerns. Things were escalating faster than either of us could have predictable.

"What do you want?" I screamed at Helana.

She pulled the fire poker out of the fire and turned to me. "I want to know everything you know about Rayne."

I stared at the tip of the hot poker. "I don't know as much as you think I do. I bought his ship six years ago, and he was still on it, in hypersleep. I didn't shut him down. He woke up recently and long story short. Here we are, trying to stop him from assassinating you." I frowned. "Turns out you're a psycho bitch. Strange how first impressions are so... accurate."

"Funny. Care to know what impression I got from you?" I didn't bother to answer. "I know this gat is more than your bodyguard." She shifted her hot poker over to him and stabbed it into his bleeding wound. Terrin screamed as the poker cauterized his flesh and irritated the already painful injury.

"Stop!" I struggled again, but this time, I wriggled out from under the guard. I didn't waste a moment of my freedom.

I bulldozed the princess bitch and toppled her to the floor. She was a wiry thing, but I got in one good punch before she got a hold of my neck.

Her men dragged us apart, pulling me back to my chair. Helana adjusted her clothes and hair, snarling at me as hard as I was at her. "You'll pay for that." She retrieved her downed fire poker.

"Tell me something, Helana." I tried to change the subject. "Since we're negotiating. What's the whole story? The truth."

"Didn't Rayne tell you?" She stepped back in front of me, examining me like a bug.

"Rayne didn't remember shit when he woke up. I don't even know how you two are connected to begin with."

"That's unfortunate, but allow me to enlighten you." Before the generous enlightenment could begin, she whipped the fire poker around and smacked me in the face with the end.

The heat had since reduced, but the impact felt like it had cracked my cheek bone. I didn't cry out, but only because the pain had taken my breath away. My eyes watered from the impact, but even without that involuntary response, I was pretty sure I would still be crying.

I mustered the courage and turned to face her again. Terrin struggled to free himself, much as I had when he was being abused.

"Just wait, gat. We'll get back to you." Helana stuck her poker back into the fire and leaned on the decorative marble pillar to watch me. "Our family hired Rayne during a time of great unrest in our rule. Our legacy was in dispute by more than one of our charter planets. My mother and father weren't necessarily in danger of being overthrown. But they were in danger of being assassinated.

"Naturally, my parents weren't going to stand by and wait for someone to kill them. They made a preemptive strike. That strike came at the hands of a highly trained hitman named Rayne.

"Not only was he a good killer, but he was a good lover." I frowned at any suggestion of this woman sleeping with Rayne. "Or so I gathered from the sounds coming from my mother's bedroom when he visited to *report* on his missions."

"Is that why you killed her?" Terrin asked.

I looked at him. He seemed to have cracked the case.

"Oh, please." Helana chuckled. "Do you really think I gave a damn who my mother was fucking? Infidelity was as ubiquitous as toilet paper in this house.

"No, I killed her because none of the other assassins I hired could get past Rayne." Helana chuckled. "The bastard was too damn good. So, I had to resort to alternate means. He never thought to protect her from her own daughter, but, of course, he had to walk in on me cleaning off the knife.

"Bastard knocked it out of my hand and pinned me to the floor. He was screaming at me about betrayal and motherly love. Blah! Blah! Blah! So, I used my natural defenses and scratched the shit out of his face.

"He didn't even flinch at the pain, but when he started to feel a little off, I explained what was happening to him." Helana pouted. "He didn't appreciate being outsmarted by a little girl. Too bad, so sad. He's gonna be pissed when he finds out I outsmarted him again."

She grabbed the poker and started toward me. I took in a deep breath and braced myself for another hit, but this time, she raised the poker high with both hands. She stabbed the hot poker toward my leg. I whimpered and pinched my eyes so I didn't have to see and feel the damage.

The impact didn't come.

When I open my eyes, I saw Helana struggling against Terrin's grip on the poker. His hand was sizzling and I could smell the burned flesh. The men were hitting his arm, demanding he let go.

"Shoot him," Helana ordered.

"No! No! Please!" I begged.

One man repositioned his gun to fire, but a knock at the door interrupted him. He glanced at his mistress for further orders. She waved away the attack, staving off Terrin's execution by at least a few minutes.

Helana yanked the poker from Terrin's hand, which was now bloody. He wouldn't have much luck with that stunt the second time around.

"Hello?" Ayil's voice filtered in before Helana could reach the door. "Where did you guys go?"

"Ayil run!" I screamed, but a hand smothered my voice. Terrin called out too, but the gun shoved in his cheek silenced his warnings.

Helana chuckled and moved to the door. "What an idiot." She peeked through the peephole in the door before opening it.

"Hey, where did you guys go?" Ayil's voice seeped in from the opening.

I was about to let out a muffled scream, but something landed on my head, distracting me. More light, warm pressure to the sensation, and then my captor released me.

I turned to see what had caused him to release, and I saw blood pouring from his throat. He stumbled back.

As his body cleared my view, I saw Terrin gripping the gun hand of his captor, while Rayne covered his mouth and slashed his throat open. Blood splattered across Terrin, but he didn't flinch.

As Rayne eased the dying man to the ground, Terrin twisted the gun out of his grip and attempted to stand. I rushed to his side to hold him up and he graciously accepted the help, despite his crutch being a few inches too short.

"Look who made it," Helana said cheerfully as she returned to the scene of her torture with Ayil in tow. "What the... Rayne?" Her eyes settled on him as he stepped up to face off with her.

Ayil snatched the fire poker from her grip. "You won't be needing this." He wiggled it in front of her. She dove for the metal rod, but Ayil whipped it across her face like a bat. The cracking impact made me jump. It frightened me to see that level of violence from Ayil, but I was definitely glad to see the skank get a little of her own back. "That's for hurting my friend, you prissy, pretentious bitch."

Helana stumbled back, grasping her face. She nearly backed herself into the fireplace, but no one warned her. If she fell in, it would be a rather fitting end for the witch.

"Ayil, help with Terrin," Rayne instructed, and he ran over to help me.

Ayil pulled Terrin's arm over his shoulder and helped support a good deal more of his weight than I could. "Come on, Kit, we're out of here." Ayil maneuvered us forward.

"Use the other door." Rayne pointed to the back of the room. I could barely see through the shadows, but I was certain there wasn't a door back there.

When we reached the back wall, Ayil pulled open a door disguised perfectly as a section of the wall. It led into an internal passageway between the walls.

"Wait," Terrin rasped and pointed to the floor. "My sword."

I slipped out from under his arm and retrieved his fallen weapon. I restored it to its rightful place in the sheath on his belt. He looked relieved to have it back.

"We have to get out of here." Ayil urged Terrin to move again, with or without my help.

I looked at Rayne to see if he had any intention of coming with us. He was still staring Helana down with deadly intent as she recovered from Ayil's punishment. With two bodies bleeding on the floor, there wasn't a question of what his intentions were. However, since he was waiting until we were gone to carry them out did concern me. "Rayne?" I called back to him.

He looked at me. The satisfaction of revenge marred his features, but I could also see agony. He had loved Starla, and because of that, he wouldn't avenge her with a broken jaw and a slit throat. He had far more inventive ways to deal with Helana's betrayal.

Ways I didn't want to know about, let alone see.

"Come on, Kit," Ayil insisted behind me.

Rayne didn't take his eyes off me, nor did he say anything to me. I followed Ayil into the corridor and took my place to help support Terrin. Ayil shut the door behind us and we staggered down the hidden passage. After several yards, I heard a scream. It didn't last long, but that didn't mean it would be the last one.

Tbe Assassin

It was an effort to get clear of the massive gardens without being noticed by anyone. Several times we had to sit Terrin on a bench, with me in his lap, to hide his wound.

I wasn't sure what the punishment would be for assisting the assassination of a princess, but I was pretty sure we didn't want to find out. I was certain there was going to be another bounty added to my head, but what was one more?

When we arrived back at the ship, my first instinct was to wait for Rayne, but Ayil insisted we didn't. He seemed to be privy to more of the man's intentions than I was, but I didn't ask what they were. I already had my suspicions I would never see Rayne again. Somehow that sounded on par for my life.

When we were clear of the planet, I left Ayil to pilot us while I played nurse for Terrin.

"It is situated wrong!" Terrin yelled at me, tugging on the shrapnel extractor.

"No, it isn't!" I yelled back. "It is telling me to put it here." I adjusted the suction device toward the side of his leg.

"If you put it there, the bullet will be yanked out the side of my leg."

"I know, but it is saying the bullet fragments are underpinned by the quadriceps and the shortest vector is through the side." I pointed out the words on the screen at the top of the device. "That means less pain—"

"I am already in pain!" he panted and squirmed on the tiny bed the medical station offered him. The room was basically a storage closet with an endless amount of gauze, but there were a few self-help devices that kept space travel reasonably safe.

"I know you are." I set the extractor down and I moved up the bed. I touched his forehead, which was burning up. "You're getting overheated. I need to get the bullet out, and get you cooled down, or you are going to have a stroke."

"I know what my condition is," he grumbled.

"I know you're mad about getting shot, but you could hardly have predicted how much of a lunatic that woman was."

"I should have fought back right away."

"You and I both know you held back because you were worried about me getting hurt in the crossfire. Now stop beating yourself up."

"I nearly got you killed."

"I don't even know how you came to that conclusion. We were all in agreement that Rayne needed to be stopped. Granted, that decision was overthrown the minute Helana opened her mouth, but whatever."

"You must be relieved to know he was justified in trying to kill her the first time."

"Yes, but he is still an assassin. He is no different from all those other yahoos who are plotting to kill me."

"So, if he comes back, you aren't going to receive him."

"I don't know." I shook my head. "I don't want to talk about him right now. All I care about is getting you better. Are you going to let me do that, knucklehead?" I leaned forward and tugged his horns.

"Hands off the horns, girl." He smiled through narrowing eyes.

I leaned forward and kissed his forehead. "This is going to hurt. Are you sure you don't want anything?"

"No. Painkillers rarely work on gattaw, anyway."

"Okay." I picked up the machine and strapped it to his sterilized leg. After about thirty seconds of preparation and warning bleeps, the magnetism started dragging the bullet fragments out of his leg.

Terrin did his best to bite back his pain, but there was no room for ego during a slow-motion reverse buckshot.

I patched up his leg and placed ice packs around his body to reduce his fever until it could stabilize on its own.

I woke by his side in the middle of the night and checked his vitals. He was out cold, but his temperature was normal and he was clotting.

I dragged myself off the cot and returned to my bed. I took a quick peek in at the autopilot, but everything seemed in order. We were on a direct path away from the planet at high speed. It wasn't a practical long-term pace, and I knew it guaranteed that Rayne wouldn't be able to catch up to us in the emergency pod.

I should have been relieved, but there was still a part of me that wanted him back. It wasn't about good guy or bad guy anymore. It was about the fact that he was the only man I had ever been intimate with. We may not have known each other as well as Ayil and I did, but we knew deeper things about one another. Private things. That was still something special. Something worth pursuing.

I slipped into my bedroom—Rayne's bedroom. Despite my understanding of the emergency pod's capability and the distance we had put between us and it, I was still disappointed to see the bed empty.

I stepped toward it, but arms wrapped around me from behind. Still stuck in a fantasy, I hoped Rayne was back after all, but when a wire hit my throat, cutting deep into my skin, I reversed my hopes.

I screamed and grappled to get my fingers behind the metal cord. The tension was enough to cut me, but I pulled it off enough to breathe and scream for help. There wasn't much hope that anyone would hear me, but I had to try.

As I struggled to get free of the wire, I realized the body at my back was not Rayne's. It was a relief, but that only meant a stranger had gotten onto my ship and into my room. That wasn't a good sign if the assassins could reach me that easily.

I kicked and headbutted my attacker. He faltered. I slipped out of the garrote and fell to the floor. I whipped around to face the assailant. At first I didn't recognize him, but then I realized he was one of the new crew members Rayne had hired while I was in Terrin's custody.

"You?" I asked and scrambled to my feet. "You're an assassin?"

"I am now." He shrugged. "That's a lot of money you got on your head."

"Yeah, a head I fully intend to keep, you murderous bastard."

He lunged at me, and I jumped on the bed. I grabbed one trophy on the shelf over the bed and rammed it against his head. I wasn't sure it was enough to knock him out, but he froze as it impacted him.

Blood dripped from his head.

I tried to pull the gold metal pie slice away, but it was stuck. I looked back at the shelf and found the wooden base for Rayne's pie-eating trophy still sitting there.

I gave the trophy top a firmer tug, and I withdrew a slender sharp blade from the man's skull. He flopped down at my feet, and I kicked his body off the bed to save my sheets from the stains.

I looked at the bloody weapon in my hand and turned back to the shelf. I picked up another trophy. The top popped off, revealing a blade. Two more and I had determined the shelf had nothing to do with bragging. This was his emergency defense stash.

I wiped off the blade, put it back in place, and hunted down Ayil to help me dispose of the body.

Choose

"Oh, my God!" Aresties stared across the table in the cafeteria kitchenette. "I can't believe it. Are you okay?"

"Just some cuts on my hands and one on my neck." I showed her the wounds.

"You got lucky," Terrin said from his spot at the head of the table. He wasn't in any condition to be moving around, but he insisted movement would accelerate his healing. Rather than argue the virtues of sleep, I had helped him to breakfast.

"Thank you, Captain Obvious. I wasn't quite aware I almost died last night."

"I can't believe that prick tried something so... prickish," Ayil fumed. "It's a good thing he's dead. I can tell you that much."

"Did you talk to the others?" I asked Ayil.

"I explained what happened and told them if they tried to hurt you, they would be shoved out of the garbage port."

"How's Edric?" I looked around for him.

"He's playing in the cargo hold."

I shook my head. "I wish you wouldn't let him do that. Climbing can be dangerous."

"I recall you being an avid tree climber," Terrin chided and gave me a sly smirk that I returned.

"What are we going to do about all the people trying to kill you?" Aresties asked, returning me to the sour mood I had started with that morning.

"Stop sleeping," I joked, but no one laughed.

"She's right." Ayil leaned over and took my hand. He rubbed my fingers. "This guy was an amateur. If he had been a real assassin, you'd be dead and gone before any of us could stop it."

"Yes. Once again, thank you everyone for reminding me I am severely incapable of dealing with the threat against me."

"I'm just saying we should get some plans together. Emergency, *oh-shit* plans, you know?"

"Ayil, the only plans you should be making is getting your son the hell away from me." He shook his head. "I'm serious, Ayil. I am not safe."

"And where the hell do you think I'm going to go, Kit?" Ayil dropped my hand. "I don't have any family other than what is sitting right at this table. I certainly don't have a home to live in."

"But your son—"

"Is going to grow up with his aunties right by his side." Ayil stood up and left the room. I must have hurt him pretty deep. I wasn't sure I was wrong to suggest it, but Ayil was probably the one person whose life kind of did revolve around me. We were very much a family now. Just because the danger of bounty hunters had escalated to assassins didn't mean we should abandon each other.

"I'll go check on him." Aresties stood from the table and went after him. Hopefully, she would plead my ignorance and make him understand. I only wanted to protect him, not reject him.

I looked at Terrin and swallowed hard. "What about you, crocodile toes? What do you want to do?"

He shook his head at my forced humor. "What do you want me to do?"

"You know what I want you to do."

"I'm not sure I do. I thought I did, but you turned me down." I met his eyes, but I soon dipped my head, ashamed of my contradictory signals. "What do you really want, Mallory?"

I sighed. "I want you to stay with me. I want you to protect me and keep all the bad men away." I frowned. "But I can't ask you to do that."

"Why not?"

"Because it's selfish. I can't ask you to leave everything behind to tag along with me indefinitely."

"I can collect bounties and protect you at the same time. In fact, the two might not be mutually exclusive." He paused and tipped his head. "Do you want to be with me?"

I looked up at him, fearful of the direction the conversation was heading. "I can't ask you to do that either, Terrin."

"That's not what I'm asking. I'm asking you if you want my bed or his."

"It doesn't matter anymore."

"It matters a lot, Mallory. I want you to say it, if not for me, for yourself. Whose arms are you missing when you lie in bed at night?"

My eyes blurred a little with tears as I thought about my empty bed. I was almost ashamed to admit the real answer. I insisted it was selfish to take Terrin away from his life, and yet I still didn't want to release him from my overbearing crush. As if breaking my connection with him would sever our friendship, too.

"His," I whispered and looked at my lap. "I didn't mean to lead you on, it's just..."

"You're in love with him," Terrin answered for me.

I looked at him and frowned. "How is that possible? I spent eight years pining for a man I couldn't be with and now that there is even the slightest chance we *could* be together, I'm in love with a man I'll probably never see again."

"Why are you so sure he won't return?"

I shrugged. "It was in the way he spoke to me. And how he looked at me that last time. He has no intention of coming back here."

"Then I guess we will have to go find him."

"What? Why would we do that?"

"Because I think I am going to need help to protect you. All respect to Ayil—I know he would throw himself on a bomb for you—but I agree he needs to take a step back from the danger while his son is at risk. Not to mention, judging by the audacity of our crew member, we are going to need eyes on you 24-7 to keep you alive. Since you've selected your bedmate, we just need to find him to take his rightful place. You can reverse track him again, can't you?"

"Yeah, assuming he took the pod."

"Well, get on it. And tell Ayil to come fetch me."

I stood up and tugged on his horns, which he only ever barely tolerated. I looked down at his slightly scolding face and smiled. "It's not that he has more of my heart. You know that, right?"

He raised his hand and rested it on my hip. "Part of you will always be mine, Mallory. If Rayne can accept that, then I can respect your choice."

I headed out to fetch Ayil, but stopped in the doorway. "What if he doesn't want to come back?" I looked at Terrin. "What if he doesn't want me?"

"I hardly think that's a concern."

Muddy

"You've got to be kidding me!" Ayil yelled at the sluicing mud, sucking his boots in about three inches shy of touching his pant leg. I couldn't really begrudge his complaints. I knew how much he'd paid for them. "Who lives in a place like this?"

"People who want to hide." Terrin trudged along ahead of us, keeping a decent pace despite his leg injury. We had only been on the planet for a few minutes, but I was already sick of the endless mudscape. "Who would bother trudging through this crap to find someone?" Terrin said.

"No one but us," I murmured.

I looked around the foggy swampland. It was after sunset, but there was enough light from the three tiny moons above to illuminate the trees lining our *trail*. I kept thinking I was seeing movement amongst the trees, but so far, nothing living had revealed itself.

Rayne's had hidden his emergency pod in a gully a few hundred yards back. Since we had no way of tracking him, we headed to the nearest known town to start our search.

The planet had a small mining community, which scavenged the mud for minerals. There wasn't a lot of money in it, but there was plenty of money in hiding the workers of said community. If I had predicted correctly, Rayne had arrived with every intention of disappearing forever.

We pushed on through the mud until we reached an archaic settlement laughably called a town. Since the wood-constructed buildings provided planked pathways to get us up out of the mud, I had to give it the small credit of civilized.

"Oh, thank God." Ayil climbed onto the wood pavement and scraped his shoes on one of the many mud scrapers lining the path.

"Now what?" I asked Terrin.

He looked over the small town carefully, inspecting the many dark corners for signs of threat. "We start asking questions at the only reputable establishment in town. The bar."

As much as I should have taken the settlement seriously, the smoke-filled saloon we walked into only exacerbated the old cow town motif. The tinny sound of rustic live instruments took the place of the piano player. The band didn't sing so much as howl in a semi-melodic way. I couldn't say it was unappealing, but it definitely wasn't music.

More than a few faces looked up as we entered. Several sizable men were playing a game of cards at the table nearest the door. They turned to examine each of us.

Ayil sidled up next to me and spoke out of the corner of his mouth. "We are so going to die."

"Oh, yeah, without a doubt," I agreed without hesitation.

A waitress passed by us, rolling her toothless jaw as she evaluated us. I was pleased to see I wasn't the only woman on the planet. At least I wouldn't be gang-raped *before* I reached the bar.

Ayil and I huddled close behind Terrin as he strode through the saloon. More eyes took notice of our group, but Terrin didn't seem to mind. He propped his arm on the bar and looked back at all the inquisitive faces with a slow head turn.

"We don't serve gats here," the bartender drawled from his spot behind the bar. He stood with one foot perched on the liquor shelf, which took up most of the back wall. He puffed on smoke from a long cylinder containing God knows what narcotic or hallucinogen. I wanted to defend Terrin, but for several reasons, it would be pointless and dangerous.

"Doesn't much matter, since I don't partake." Terrin shifted closer to him. "I'm not here for the liquor. I'm looking for someone."

The collective bar shifted, reaching for their guns and blades. I looked around at the paused faces that were waiting to find out who we were there for. Not that it much mattered. I got the feeling they would kill us for the presumption of the inquiry, anyway.

"We aren't here for a bounty." Terrin spoke a little louder to ease the armada at his back. "We are here for personal reasons."

"What's the name?" the bartender asked.

"Rayne," Terrin answered.

"How badly you want to know?" a man asked behind us. We all shifted and saw the biggest of the burly poker players standing up.

"Enough to ask," Terrin answered.

"Ain't nothing free here. Least of all to a gat."

Terrin's jaw clenched, and he stepped forward. "Then perhaps you should let me know what I owe you." Terrin pulled the short copper sword from his belt. I wasn't sure I had seen him draw it since he cut my hair with it.

Before the men could even meet for their battle, a fight erupted everywhere. A new man, not even involved in the verbal riposte, jumped on Terrin's back.

I yelped as he spun, sending bucking feet right at me. I backed into Ayil and he shoved me back as the next man arrived for the impromptu fight. Ayil punched the man and flattened him. The next, however, was not so easily downed.

I reached over the bar and grabbed a bottle of something. Terrin's offender flew over the bar, careening into the back shelf of liquor bottles.

I turned back and raised my bottle to hit Ayil's determined opponent. My hand snagged before I could make contact. The bartender dragged me over the counter.

Once I was on the other side, I kicked away from the bar, pushing him into the wall. He stumbled over the man at his feet and lost his grip on me.

I yanked free and noted the three men surrounding Terrin with knives. They were dancing, anticipating his every move. Despite the numbers, none of them wanted to take the first jab.

I threw my still gripped bottle at the one closest to me, hitting him in the head. Terrin immediately sensed the shift and reached for the other two. He yanked their heads together, giving them both an audible knock before releasing them to pass out against each other.

He turned back to the third and punched him. One hit from a gattaw was all it took to break jaws, and this was no exception. I smiled stupidly at the minor triumph before leaping out of the way of the pursuing bartender.

With little room to run, and Terrin already surrounded by a new band of jackasses trying to prove they could compete with a gattaw, I had to fend the guy off myself. I grabbed another random bottle and threw it at him. He raised his arm to defend his face, and it shattered on his wrist.

Barely affected, he lunged again. I saw his smoking pipe lying on the counter and I tossed it to him. Rather than let the precious dope go to waste, he caught it.

The pipe's ember erupted, the liquor drenching his arm. The flames lapped up his elbow, and he screamed in horror as his shirt caught next.

He ran past me to a barrel at the far end of the bar. He turned a crank and started dousing himself with a drizzle of water from its tap.

By the time I could give my attention back to Terrin and Ayil, they were both surrounded by the gun-toting card players. I could see they were both ready to continue the fight, but neither one could compete with the threat of bullets against them. Terrin had already learned that the hard way.

"Wait!" I raised my hands before anyone could punch, shoot, or stab anyone else.

The biggest man looked over at me and furrowed his brow at the partially burned man behind me. "What is it, girl?"

"You don't understand. We aren't here for a bounty. Rayne is my... husband."

The man narrowed his eyes at me, trying to see the lie. I crunched through the glass behind the bar to get closer to him. He watched me cautiously, so I kept my hands high.

"I'm serious."

"Is that true, Rayne?" the man called out loudly, but didn't turn to see the recipient of his question.

I looked around the bar for his face, but I didn't see him.

"I suppose it is." Rayne's voice filtered down from the loft. It still took me a moment to locate him among the curious faces leaning over the balcony. He looked like the other men in the bar—burly, overgrown beard, and unavoidably muddy.

He looked down at me with the same hard stare he had left me with weeks earlier. I couldn't tell if he was mad, but his face definitely didn't show any joy.

"Hello, wife."

DIRTBAG

The bartender slammed my drink down in front of me, making me jump. Most of its contents splashed onto the table. He stopped to glare at me, shrinking me a little deeper into my chair.

"Back off, Lily," Rayne scolded, and the man reluctantly headed back to his bar—and his ice packs.

Terrin reached across the round table and took my drink. He didn't bother to smell it or taste it before dumping it on the floor. He replaced the mug and turned to Rayne. "Lovely group of friends you have here."

"We keep each other safe." He took a sip of his beer. "They don't like gats much, though."

"That's unfortunate, seeing as I was enjoying their company so much."

"Why are you here—how the hell did you find me, anyway? Again?" Rayne looked at me.

"I reverse-tracked the emergency pod."

"That's not possible."

"Clearly, that's why we *aren't* here," I said peevishly.

Rayne shook his head. "You shouldn't have followed me. This planet is not the safest place for someone of your... value." Rayne glanced around to check the neighboring tables for eavesdroppers.

"That's why we came," Terrin said. "We need your help."

"Help with what?"

"Mallory had another attempt on her life." Rayne looked at me, but there wasn't any sign of concern in his eyes. He was stone cold, but I wasn't sure it was an act anymore. Maybe the gentle, generous lovemaking had been the act. A very, very good act. "It was a crewman you hired," Terrin added, and Rayne's face snapped back to him.

"I hope you ripped his arms out of their sockets."

"As tempting as that was, he was already dead. Mallory killed him."

Rayne's brow dipped as he looked me over. "You killed him?"

"I stabbed him. With one of your *trophies*. Thanks for that, by the way."

A tiny smile warmed his hard eyes and for a moment, I thought we might make progress toward luring him back to the land of living and out of the depths of *Dickville*. Unfortunately, Rayne's amusement died, and he turned back to Terrin.

"What do you need from me, then?"

"I need your help to protect her."

A low rumbling laugh emerged from Rayne's chest. "I'm an assassin. I kill people for money. Don't you think that's a little ironic?"

"It's extremely ironic," Terrin admitted. "But that's why you are the best man for the job. You know how these people think. You know how to protect her from them."

Rayne stared at me, debating—I hoped. "As you can see, I also literally know these people. I might actually be killing my friends if I took the job."

"You can't be serious." Ayil finally spoke up and Rayne looked at his disappointed face. "*We* are your friends. Are you saying you would choose to protect them over her, or me, or my son?"

Rayne's blank-faced stare didn't waver at Ayil's accusation. That was when I knew it was hopeless.

"We're done here." I stood from the table.

"Damn straight we are." Ayil stood with me.

"Let's go," I said when Terrin didn't move. He stared across the table at Rayne, meeting his gaze with equal ferocity. He eventually stood slowly, never taking his eyes off him.

"Do you know why people like you hate gats so much?"

Rayne offered a slight smirk that might have been more contempt than amusement. "Enlighten me."

"Because we have integrity and loyalty, traits that are as weak in humans as their muscles."

Rayne stood up, meeting him nearly eye to eye. "You know nothing about me, Terrin. Least of all my motivations. I would advise you to follow Kit's lead and get out of here."

I touched Terrin's arm, not because I was concerned they might stoke another bar brawl, but because I was on the verge of tears and I couldn't bear the thought of showing Rayne how much he was hurting me. I should have left him in my rearview mirror where he belonged. Where all flings belonged.

Stuck

"Push it again," I requested from the control panel, while Ayil and Terrin tried to engage the gravity lift on the shuttle pod. An hour after leaving the bar, we were still trying to get off the godforsaken mud-puddle planet, but the water was dampening our boosters. So far, the pressure ejection was worthless since the ground wasn't solid enough to push off of. We could only spread the mud and let in more water.

The shuttle pod popped and dropped, as it had the first ten times. I slammed the console—which hurt like hell—and sat back in my seat.

I wanted so much to be off the planet and back to my ship so I could cuddle in my bed and cry like a normal heartbroken woman. The only thing barring my tears was the fact that I was refusing to think about how Rayne was abandoning me to get murdered.

Terrin touched my shoulder, and I jumped. "What is it?"

"I asked if you wanted me to call Aresties. She could send down the other pod."

"Why, so we can have two pods stuck?" I snapped and jumped out of the seat. "I just need to think. If we can't pop it, we'll have to ignite the boosters."

"How do we do that?" Ayil grimaced. "We are knee deep in watery sludge."

I pinched the bridge of my nose and shook my head. Years of data, ever at my fingertips, were floating away as I tried to grab it. "There's a section in the base of the booster where a manual fire can be produced. It will evaporate the moisture on the spark plugs. If we do a super-heated burst, we should be able to displace the remaining water on takeoff. It makes for a puke-worthy takeoff, but it'll get us off this hellhole."

"What do we need to do?" Terrin asked, ready to follow my orders.

"I need wood and kindling."

"Are you shittin' me? Kit, it's a swamp." Ayil motioned through the pod window.

"I know it's a swamp, Ayil! I want to get the hell out of here, though."

"Okay, okay, I'm sorry."

I moved to the door and looked back. "I'm going to go look for some wood. If we can't find any, then you two are going to hand over your pants."

"I'll go find some firewood." Ayil sprang into action and bounded out the door ahead of me.

I turned to follow him, but Terrin grabbed my shoulder. "Are you okay?"

"Fine."

"You can't fool me, Mallory. I know what you must be feeling right now."

I looked back at him. "I'm not trying to fool you, Terrin. I'm trying to fool myself." I pulled away and set out to find something dry enough to burn.

Fool

I gave the search a good half hour, but with only a few dry sticks in my hand, I gave up the hunt for more and headed back to the shuttle.

I was tired from trekking through the mud, but I had to keep a steady pace or risk losing my shoes entirely.

Once the pod was in view, I called over to Ayil and Terrin. "Did you find any?"

"Not much." Ayil waved his measly handful of sticks.

"Same here." I waved my sticks. "Maybe we should—" My next step dropped through a weak top layer of mud. I toppled over and sank below the surface of the sludge. I scrambled in the darkness and silence for several seconds before I felt my body being heaved upward by knobby ropes.

Blinded by mud-shut eyes, I heard the muffled sound of Terrin and Ayil yelling below me. I announced I was alive, albeit in an awkward spot. They continued to talk, but I could hardly interpret the words through mud-filled ears.

I shook away the excess muck and wiped my eyes off. I looked down between the ropes of my net cage and saw both Ayil and Terrin staring at something. Terrin had once again drawn his copper blade. I twisted around to see our new enemy.

A short, stocky man covered in furs was pointing up at me. "It's my land. My traps!"

"She's not an animal!" Terrin yelled back at him. "She is a human being!"

The trapper looked up at me, evaluating me through the ropes. "That's even better. Worth more."

"You son of a bitch!" Ayil yelled and leaped forward. Had it not been for the mud, he might have made a dent in the man's skull, but as it was, the slow-motion attack left the trapper time to pull a gun from his fur poncho.

"No, no, no. I don't think so. She belongs to me now. You go run along."

"That's not happening," Ayil growled.

"Then I shoot you both and be done with you."

"Don't even think about it, Marcus!" Rayne's voice emerged from the trees shortly before he did. He moved through the mud with a little more ease, since he had snowshoes on to keep him from sinking. "You aren't taking her."

"She fell into my trap."

"That doesn't make her property."

"My trap," Marcus petitioned again. "My catch. Mine!"

"Not yours. Not now. Not ever," Rayne stated clearly. Marcus shifted slightly, not entirely threatening, but enough that Rayne tensed. "Don't do it, Marcus. She's just a girl. Not worth dying for."

There was another slight shift, then Marcus turned his gun to aim at him. Rayne's recourse was so quick, my eyes couldn't register it until it was already over.

Marcus wobbled and looked down at his chest. The knife embedded in it must have been razor sharp. Poised in his crouched position, Rayne waited to see if further retaliation was needed.

The trapper toppled to the ground, dead, and I exhaled in relief. This planet was too dangerous. I needed to get out of here before someone found out I was the most valuable hit bid in the entire galaxy.

For a moment, I wondered if I was being completely selfish and unrealistic in asking Rayne to protect me from all the Marcuses of the universe. Or anyone, for that matter. This was going to be my life from now on. Perpetually hiding from the next threat. I would never be free from danger. Was my friendship really worth all the trouble it came with? My DNA was worth killing for, but was I worth dying for?

Not according to Rayne.

Wortbless

"**I**t won't work," Rayne muttered from his spot, leaning on the hull.

After dumping Marcus's body in his own mud trap, Rayne helped Terrin and Ayil get me out of my net. However, he was still hanging around, and I didn't really understand why.

"You don't even know what I'm doing," I snarled as I tried to dig the boosters out with my hands. Since I was already covered in mud, I didn't bother asking anyone else to do it.

"Do you know how many shuttles have come to visit this planet, and made it their permanent home?"

"How does anyone ever leave, then?"

"They use the elevated parking stand." He smirked.

I frowned. "I didn't know the mud was this deep," I defended.

"It's okay, no one does. I can get you out, but it won't be until morning. We have a sort of tow truck service, but the guy who owns it is three sheets to the wind right now. He won't be functional until morning."

"I can't wait that long. I want off this planet."

"It won't work, Kit." He shifted his foot and pressed his snowshoe against my arm, interrupting my digging.

"You don't know what I'm doing!"

"You're trying to dry out the ignitions so you can do a forced combustion burst." I stared blankly at him. "I read some of the books." He rolled his eyes.

"Why won't it work?"

He moved his foot and crouched down. "You're not sitting in water. You're sitting in mud. The fire will dry the ignitions, but they will still be covered in dirt, along with the vents and the fuel pores. When you go to make the burst, the clogged ducts will back-fill and when it finally busts loose, you'll explode the entire booster. Best-case scenario, your pod is trashed. Worst-case scenario, the entire pod explodes with you in it."

I frowned and looked at the ground. He was right, of course. I had almost blown myself up. "How do you even know all that? The books certainly don't get that specific."

"It happens all the time around here."

I scratched my face, dusting away another smattering of dried mud. "How long until sunrise?"

"Still another six hours. Probably another eight until Lyle is functional."

I pinched my eyes shut in frustration. I stood and nearly fell over since my knees didn't readily release from the mud. Rayne put out a hand to steady me, but I braced my hand on the pod rather than get his help.

I moved around to the pod door. Terrin was patiently waiting by the controls. Ayil was sitting beside him, pouting. I wasn't sure he could have been more hurt by Rayne's behavior than me, but I was pretty sure he was more pissed than me. Rayne was probably the first man to treat him with any respect or dignity. That was a heavy burden to live up to. Much too easily dropped.

"Looks like we can't get out until morning," I announced.

"What?" Ayil groaned. "We have to sleep in here?"

"We don't really have a choice," I said.

"You do," Rayne said from right behind me. "You can come back to my place." I turned to stare at him with narrowed eyes—fickle much? "It's not much, but it's safer than staying here. No one will bother you if you're under my roof."

"That's not necessary," I said.

"It is if you want to be protected," Rayne said.

"As I recall, you turned down that job." I crossed my arms and leaned on the door. "You recall that, don't you? About two hours ago, you declared I was less important to you than a band of murdering assholes."

"I never said that." He frowned.

"Implied then."

"Image is everything in a place like this."

"So, what, that was an act?"

"An exaggeration."

"It doesn't matter, Rayne. You can say it loud; you can say it in a whisper, but your answer was no. I heard it just fine, and then I stopped listening." I stepped into the pod and slid the door shut right in his face.

Rayne peered through the tiny window, a glare perched on his face, but I all but stuck my tongue out at him. As I expected, he disappeared from view to trudge back to the hole he had crawled out of. No doubt a fairly accurate description of this planet.

I turned back to my crew. Ayil was still pouting, but Terrin looked a little disappointed. "What?"

"Are you really going to risk our safety because of a breakup?"

"What? We... He... We will be fine in here. It's only eight hours."

"The door lock is broken on this pod."

I glanced back at the potentially dangerous kink in my foot-stomping plan. "I don't care. I already slammed the door. It would be degrading to give in now."

Terrin shook his head and stood up. "Then I will degrade myself and you two can pout over your lost boyfriend."

"Bite me, lizard-breath," Ayil groused.

"I don't doubt you would enjoy that, Ayil, but now is hardly the time."

Ayil looked up from his chair, stunned by the borderline flirtation.

Terrin moved to the door I was still blocking. I crossed my arms and shook my head. I was mad, but the quiver in my lip wasn't portraying it very well.

"I'm sorry, Mallory." Terrin reached around me and tugged open the door. "Rayne, wait," he called out.

Shower

I couldn't claim that Rayne had done well for himself. His shack was little more than the name implied, but it had a shower, and that was enough to make it a mansion to me. I didn't bother to strip, since my clothes were the culprits of the mud adhesion.

I tucked into the little alcove off the bedroom—aka a cot with a sheet separating it from the rest of the shack. I let the gravity-fed water drain the mud through the grate beneath me.

Once I was sufficiently less muddy, I slipped off my shirt and pants to rinse out my bra and underwear. I shut off the water and squeezed the excess water out of my clothes before hanging them over the enclosure. I stepped out of the shower and searched for a towel to wrap myself in until my clothes had dried. I nearly ran into Rayne as he came around from the curtained entrance. He froze and stared at me. His eyes skirted my nearly nude state and his jaw tensed tight.

I wasn't sure my sopping wet under garments were leaving anything to the imagination, but since he had seen it all before, he didn't need one. As hunger bloomed in his eyes, I almost wished I had elected to take the bra and underwear off. The distance between nude and sex was so short.

Then, of course, I remembered I didn't *want* sex from him, because he was a lousy jerk-head with no heart. Strong sturdy shoulders, ample biceps, and an ass to weep for, but no... no heart to speak of.

"I thought I should bring you some clean clothes." He raised a stack of clothes I hadn't noticed. He tossed it on his bed. "I'm sure they won't fit, but they'll be dry." He turned and walked out without another word.

So much for this being a social visit.

Dogfights

Fully clothed in clothes that smelled like Rayne, I sucked in every measurable breath I could before joining the others in the living room—aka the other side of the sheet.

Terrin was sitting in one of Rayne's wooden chairs, sipping on a cup of something—coffee, tea, or perhaps just more mud. Ayil was washing his boots in what I would have called Rayne's kitchen sink.

"Ayil, we are going to be walking back through it eventually anyway," I said.

"I will go barefoot before I put these shoes through that again." He continued to scrub at the details on his footwear.

I sat at the table across from Rayne. He immediately stood up and I couldn't help but feel rejected again. This time, however, his movements seemed almost uneasy. His cool, calm, I-could-kill-you-with-my-bare-hands demeanor was waning. I could only assume being back in his own home was making it harder to amplify his indifference to me.

Rayne poured another mug of hot liquid from the kettle on his potbelly wood stove. He brought it over to me. When I reached for the cup, he put his hand up. "Careful, it's hot." He set it down and twisted the handle to face me. It was a sweet gesture, I thought. Naturally, my mind boomeranged between several sarcastic responses, highlighting the absurdity of a man more concerned with my burned fingers than my shattered heart.

"Thank you," I said politely, rather than voicing the raging lunatic stuff.

"I take it you've been a resident of this planet for some time?" Terrin inquired as he looked over the room.

"Yes." Rayne sat down and leaned back in his chair. "My father was a miner here." I glanced up, intrigued by anything resembling a piece of Rayne's past. "One of the few straight-and-narrow ones. He was a hard worker, and he wanted to teach me that with hard work, I could have a good life."

"What about your mother?" I asked.

"She was long gone—dead or just gone. He never told me."

"What about the horse? You said you remembered..." Rayne shook his head and took a sip of his drink. I frowned and did the same. The sweet taste was a surprise. A pleasant change from the bitterness I was feeling.

"How did you get involved with hits?" Terrin asked.

Rayne cleared his throat and looked back at me. "Are you sure you want to hear this?"

I looked at Terrin as if he might have the answer. He raised his brow—almost a shrug at my question. I wasn't sure I *wanted* to hear Rayne's climb to murderous stardom, but I *needed* to hear it. If I presumed to be in love with him, then I needed to know who I was in love with.

"Go ahead," I answered. "It doesn't much matter anymore."

Rayne stared at me a moment before he continued to relay his story to Terrin. "As you've seen, this place is dangerous. When I got older, I was no longer safe because I was a child. At first it was only a matter of self-defense—beating down the boys who had a beef with me. I was fast, though, and strong. I never lost. Cocky as I was, I picked the fights. I was more than willing to brawl with anyone twice my size, and eventually someone took notice.

"That big burly guy in the bar? We call him Bear. He was my father's friend. I never knew how they met, but I always assumed my father had a history he didn't want to admit to.

"He took me under his wing, so to speak. The first time I left the planet in my whole life; he took me to Miorita."

"The gattaw home planet?" I asked.

"Yes." Rayne looked at me. "Even decades after the rebellion dismantled the slave trade operations, there were a few distasteful traditions that were kept."

"What traditions?" I asked, but Rayne looked at Terrin as if it was his answer to give.

"I believe Rayne is referring to the *dogfights*." It's an underground gambling operation. It was something my people excelled at. There was a lot of money involved for the winners. It was no surprise we kept them going, since the gattaw never lost."

"Rarely lost," Rayne corrected.

"Very rarely," Terrin re-corrected.

"Your father's friend took you there to fight a gattaw?" I asked.

"Not at first. First, he had me watch. We watched maybe a dozen matches before he took me down to enter the contest. I was young, and as I mentioned, cocky. I thought I was going to clobber a gat my first time out."

"Foolish," Terrin scoffed.

"And I did."

"That's a lie." Terrin shifted suddenly, as if he might need to jump up and defend himself. His knee hit the table, shaking the contents of my mug. I grabbed it up lest I lose more of the yummy goodness.

"It was a lie," Rayne readily agreed. "A ruse. Bear had paid my opponent a significant amount to take it easy on me. High on false arrogance, I was prepared to fight every gat on the planet. We stayed on the planet and I fought whoever or whatever they put in the ring with me. My payments became increasingly lower as time went on. Eventually, I was fighting for the sake of pride."

"And how did you fare against your competitors?" Terrin asked smugly. I was surprised to see this particular topic elicited his pride.

Rayne chuckled. "When Bear wasn't paying them to take a fall? Let's just say I was on Miorita for nearly a year, and six months of that time, I was healing from injuries. I was oblivious to the financial aspect of the game. I hadn't realized Bear was making a fortune off me. Every time I competed, he made money, because he already knew what the outcome would be. Since I was too stupid to see that I was being used, I kept going back for more. Eventually, the greedy bastard had the odds he wanted. That's when the game changed."

"He put you in a death match," Terrin suggested. "Higher stakes, higher gains."

Rayne nodded and shifted in his chair. A small smile crept onto his face.

"Are you really that pleased with your first kill?" I asked.

"No." Rayne pinned his gaze on me. "I had never killed a man before that day and I had never thought about killing a man either. My pleasure was in the conquest. The strength and competition. I only wanted to win."

"And you did," Terrin said with a gleam of amusement in his eyes.

Rayne smirked at him. "And I did."

I glanced between the two men, not understanding their enjoyment of the topic, or the intrigue that backed it. "I don't understand. What's the joke?"

Terrin looked at me, and the subtle delight on his face bloomed a little bigger at seeing my befuddlement. "Bear bet against him."

I looked at Rayne. "He put you in there hoping you would die?"

"Yes, and I have no doubt I would have, except they gave me a weapon. The gat had a traditional short sword, and they handed me a knife instead. I suspect the imbalance of weapons was also Bear's money at play, but he denies it to this day."

"Not as imbalanced as he hoped," Terrin teased.

"No." Rayne chuckled. "The second that blade hit my hand; I knew how to use it. I had always been faster than my gattaw opponents, but never strong enough. But with a knife, it didn't matter. I embedded it in the back of his neck before a single hit landed on either of us. The crowd—mostly gattaw, as you might imagine—went silent. They booed and jeered. They dragged me off the court and nearly beat me to death for the offense of winning.

"I did get a substantial amount for winning, though. That was when I realized hard work truly did pay off."

AIR

I had to leave the room. It took a while to come to terms with Rayne being an assassin the first time around. Hearing about the murderous competitions that gained him his deadly skills was discomforting. It only made sense that his reputation would eventually provide him with work as a hitman. In fact, after years of fighting the gattaw, killing humans was probably an easy income.

I stared out at the muddy, tree-filled landscape. There was nothing beautiful about the planet. Not the view, not the smell, and certainly not the people. I couldn't imagine a childhood of muck and abuse.

Ayil stepped outside, too. His bare feet stopped on the wood plank porch next to me. "Pretty wicked childhood," he commented.

"Yeah."

"Sure beats being sold into sex slavery, though."

I scoffed. "I think you can still keep the title of shittiest childhood."

"Thank God for that," he said. I looked at him to see how amused he was. He looked back at me, probably trying to discern the same thing. "How are you doing?" he asked.

"Me?" I chuckled. "Oh, I don't know. I feel like the odd man out. Terrin's in there sharing stories of combat like Rayne's his new best friend. I'm... so confused." I shook my head. "I just really want to get out of here."

"I know."

"No, I mean…" I huffed and turned to him. "I don't want to hear any more about him. I don't want to get to know him better and then have to leave him again." I groaned and rubbed my forehead. "This is so messed up and backward. I get married to a man I hardly know. I sleep with him, then fall in love with him. Then I get to know him, so I can break up with him. There is something seriously wrong with my decision-making abilities."

"I'm telling you; you should have made babies with me."

"Yeah!" I agreed.

Ayil laughed at my enthusiastic annoyance and pulled me into a hug. "Oh, Kit, it'll be alright. You'll get it right someday. I promise. Maybe one of your other assassins will want to marry you."

I laughed into his shoulder and hugged him back. He was right, it was going to be okay. I had too many friends not to survive a messy breakup.

Crushed

When I finally came back in, the "war stories" were coming to a close by the stove. The three men had taken up residence in the comfy patchwork chairs. I debated getting a chair from the table, but I wasn't entirely sure I wanted to stay.

The decision between chair arms was a little more difficult than I expected. Obviously, Rayne was out. He was off the list for a lot of things at the moment. Sprawled across his chair, Ayil was nearly asleep, and I didn't want to disturb him. Since Terrin's chair had little for an arm ledge, and also because I wanted to make Rayne a little jealous, I sat on Terrin's leg.

The bad one.

Terrin grunted and shifted forward to intercept me. "Sorry, sorry, sorry." I grimaced.

"It's fine, Mallory, but how about you take the other knee?" He directed me to his other leg, and I snuggled back into his bracing arm. It was strange, being in his embrace so casually after everything that had transpired between us. But our bond was stronger than awkward silences and emotional breakdowns. A few ill-timed kisses wouldn't break our friendship, either.

"How is the leg?" Rayne asked.

"Still a little touchy, but much better." Terrin smiled at me. "I was fortunate to have a good nurse."

"I was the one dragging your ass to the pisser," Ayil objected without opening his eyes.

I chuckled while Terrin took a cleansing breath. "Yes, well, I wasn't sure if such a private detail needed to be mentioned."

"Screw that, I want credit."

Terrin cleared his throat and looked at Rayne. "Ayil has also been very helpful during my healing."

A small smile perked on Rayne's lips. He was at least amused by Ayil's antics. Terrin was still finding a happy medium with my best friend.

"Speaking of my leg, Helana explained how she poisoned you. I assumed you were able to make it back to your sleep pod before the poison could kill you, but why did you stay under so long?"

"Good question." Rayne raised his brow. "I'm not really sure either. I think it was a fluke. The poison should have been cleansed out within a few days. At worst, a few weeks. All I can think of is that I was closer to death than I thought. I may have been teetering on the brink of death for years. My body just wouldn't wake until I was better."

"You're very lucky to be alive. If your ship had been found by marauders, you would surely have been unplugged."

"I plotted a course as far into dead space as possible. Still, I was surprised the pod hadn't crapped out. Turns out someone rerouted the power into an ionic battery cell."

Rayne looked at me, already guessing it was me. "The old one was beeping." I shrugged. "Had to do something to shut it up."

"Why did you keep me alive?" Rayne asked.

"Why not?"

"Because it's a drain on the system. Because an ionic battery costs a fortune."

"I tried to talk her out of it," Ayil mumbled sleepily. "Poor girl couldn't let you go. Been in love with you since the day she peered through that glass."

My face instantly heated. I wanted to scream at Ayil, but he was scarcely conscious, let alone aware of the massive embarrassment he was causing me. I looked back at Rayne to see what he thought of that statement. He looked sad, and I realized he didn't feel the same way.

I could easily assume his desire for sex had led him to seduce me. The little lies and anything resembling sentiment were a manipulation to draw me back in for more. Even his territorial displays were just that—anger at someone threatening to take his cock's toy. There was no specific devotion to me.

My fairytale crush on sleeping beauty was turning out to be a bust, too. No one ever tells the bedtime stories that way. Snow White wakes from the brink of death and tells the prince she's just not that into him. Cinderella turns out to be a gold-digging con-artist. Ariel gets stuck as a mermaid, and Eric dumps her for a chick with an accessible vagina. That's what all the fairy tales are missing. Real problems. Real emotions. Real life.

But who wants that?

When it was clear my face was going to be red for the rest of my life, I buried it in Terrin's neck. He shifted to accommodate me and rubbed my arm. The gentle movement was as good as being rocked. I was down to half steam and seconds from snoring when the conversation about ships and weapons turned to something more private.

"You must have been devastated to find Helana had killed her." Terrin's volume lowered to a soft whisper.

"She was always power hungry. Her mother was strict. She had rules and morality. She was an amazing woman."

"You loved her?"

"Yes."

My heart clenched. I didn't want to think about Rayne in love with anyone, but that was what stilled my transition to sleep. He loved the woman, and right on the brink of her being murdered, he was forced into a long hypersleep. Ten years later, he was finally dealing with the grief of her death, which, from his perspective, was only moments behind him.

"I was meant to protect her," Rayne mumbled. "I couldn't."

"You could hardly know her own daughter would be the assassin," Terrin rationalized.

"I suspected it, and told her as much, but she didn't believe me. I think what bothers me the most is that I was so incapacitated by her death a pampered little bitch beat me. Took me ten years to get my revenge, and I made it count."

"I'm sure you did. As was your right." There was a long pause. I imagined Rayne was brooding about his lost love. "Have you reconsidered coming back with us?"

Another long pause.

"I can't," was all Rayne would offer. I heard movement and footsteps. Terrin took in a deep breath, kissed my forehead, and shifted slightly in the chair.

I didn't remember falling asleep, but I remembered giving up.

White Flag

"**M**ust you disagree with everything I say?" Terrin scolded Ayil as he stepped off the porch into the mud barefooted with no pants.

"I am not risking my shoes again."

"Shoes are not necessary. Your feet are. This bog must be crawling with parasites."

I couldn't help but laugh at the situation. I knew Terrin was honestly trying to look out for Ayil's safety, and had Terrin simply pointed out his concerns to Ayil, he might have listened. As things were, though, Ayil was fighting being put under another man's thumb, and Terrin was unhappy with his lack of control.

"Unless you plan on carrying me, then this is how I am getting to the pod." Ayil raised his arms, effectively displaying his exposed underwear proudly.

Terrin turned to glare at my giggle before storming off the porch after Ayil. I waited for them to disappear into the tree line before I turned to speak with Rayne. I knew things wouldn't end happily ever after for us, but I wanted him to know I didn't blame him for wanting to mourn his former lover.

Before I could offer my condolences in the form of a white flag, Rayne dove at me and kissed me. He picked me up and steered us back against his house. I helplessly endured the wanton kiss that begged me to submit to my desires.

Somewhere between being lifted off my feet, his body grinding into mine, and our deepening kiss, I realized he was just trying to get another round in before he lost the chance. I pushed him away, but he wouldn't budge. I bit him and he drew back to look at me.

"What the hell, Rayne!" I gasped for much-needed air. His eyes looked me over, still lustful, still oblivious to the pain his waffling desires had caused me. It was poetic, I suppose, since I had done the same damn thing to Terrin.

"I've wanted to do that since the minute I saw you." Rayne leaned forward again to kiss me. His attempt to bypass my anger infuriated me. Since I wasn't at the right angle to slap him, I spat in his face.

That finally brought him out of his arousal. He released my legs, letting my feet drop to the porch. For a moment, he simply stared at me.

"And to think I was going to apologize for not being more sensitive to your bereavement. I guess your cock is already done grieving."

"It's not like that. I just thought—"

"What, that I should give you a goodbye present? Why did you even bother including me? You could have asked me to get on my knees. We could have snapped one out in under a minute." I snapped my fingers for emphasis.

"Don't do this." Rayne shook his head. "Don't belittle everything we had because it didn't turn out the way you wanted it to."

"What we had was sex. I just didn't know it until last night."

"It wasn't just sex."

"It wasn't love."

"And how do you know that?"

"Because you are still in love with Starla." Rayne's jaw tensed at hearing her name. "Or was it just sex with her, too?" I shouldn't have said it, and I knew I would come to regret it, but I wanted to hurt him.

Rayne stepped forward, and I tensed, ready to take the slap, or whatever he had planned as punishment. I almost wanted him to. Something, anything, to help dissolve this heartbreak into hatred.

His face towered over me; eyes ablaze with lethal fury. "You should go," he whispered.

"Yeah." I backed away. "My exit is long overdue." I stepped off the porch and gave him a blind overhead wave. "Have a good life. Thanks for not killing me in my sleep."

Start Over

I stared out the cockpit window at the stars. It had been two weeks since we left the muddy planet. Two weeks since I had booted Rayne out of my heart. Two weeks since I had put my heart in a box and shoved it into a dark hole where no one else could hurt it.

I hadn't even heard Terrin arrive before he sat on the arm of the copilot chair. He stared at me, but I said nothing. I already knew the question and one more prescribed "fine" wouldn't change the fact that I still had a lot of healing to do before it wasn't a lie anymore.

"You don't have to hide your feelings from me, Mallory," Terrin finally said. "It is my deepest wish for you to be happy. I want so much to help make that happen, in whatever capacity I can."

I reached out and touched his hand. "You and those other yokels out there are 90% of my happiness."

"I feel the same way—about you, anyway. I may have to strangle Ayil. He is even more trying to my patience than you."

I chuckled. "No killing my friends. Why don't you make him a list of rules to follow? I'm sure that will help."

"Mmm, yes, that was so helpful in the initial stages of our relationship." He smiled at me.

"Can I ask you something?"

"Certainly."

I swallowed hard, not wanting to ask, but almost needing to. "When I chose Rayne over you... Did I hurt you this much?"

"Are you asking because you want to avail yourself of guilt, or because you want to know how deeply I love you?"

"Both." I chuckled and shook my head. "I'm still dragging you in two different directions, aren't I?"

"Not really. You just have a tendency to hang on tighter when you think you're going to lose me. I know you're separated from your family; I know Rayne has stupidly let you go, and I know you want to push us all away to protect us from your trail of assassins, but it is not going to happen. You are never going to lose me, Mallory. I am your friend. I am here to offer you love and receive your love, without the stipulation of a bed to bind us."

I gazed up at him, nearly in tears for the sentiment. He stood up and kissed the top of my head. "Go to sleep, Mallory. You'll feel better in the morning." He brushed his finger down my cheek. "I promise."

I nodded, and he left.

I stared out at the stars a little longer, before I put on the autopilot and headed to bed.

I slipped into my room, noting the empty space behind my door before I undressed.

I picked up Rayne's shirt off the floor—the one I had borrowed and never given back because my clothes were still sopping wet when we prepared to leave. I took another sniff of it. I had been wearing it as a nightgown, so almost all the male scent was gone. I had considered shoving it over a pillow and cuddling with it, but I wasn't sure how healthy that was. I flopped the shirt over my shoulder as I removed the rest of my clothes for bed.

Freshly naked as a jaybird, I felt a familiar creepiness in my peripheral vision. I looked over to the blob that might have been an assassin in my bed. He lunged toward me and I screamed.

I had no time to react before he covered my mouth and threw me onto the mattress. I bit his hand and screamed through the smothering palm.

I could see the face above me and feel the naked body pressing against mine. It was Rayne. As terrified as I was before, I still wasn't sure if I was in danger. He shushed me and removed his hand from my mouth. He clicked his tongue at me.

"You need some lessons on how to avoid being assassinated."

"You son of a bitch!"

"Rule number one: always turn on your lights before entering a room."

"Get off me!"

"Rule number two: look before you start stripping naked. A lesser assassin might be inclined to abuse a woman before he killed her."

"That is not funny!"

"You're right, it's not. So, start paying attention." I threw a fist at him, but he dodged it and pinned my arm back. I bucked against him. "Rule number three: never let him get on top of you."

"Knock it off. Why are you even back here? How did you get on the ship without anyone seeing?"

"Terrin knows I'm here."

"What? He didn't tell me that."

"I asked him not to."

"He let you walk back in here without a word of complaint?"

"No, we had a very long conversation man to man. Mostly about how my face would look if I ever hurt you."

"Okay, I guess you've got the job then. You can stand outside my door and watch for someone who looks like you." He chuckled. "Seriously, Rayne, if you want back in my bed again, then you can earn it."

He sighed and climbed off me, releasing me completely. I stood up and searched for the t-shirt where I had dropped it. I found it and turned back to brandish more accusations at him.

"What the hell are you doing?" I asked when I saw him shifting under the sheets again. "Get out!"

"My room, you get out." He smirked.

"Oh, hell no, you left." I came around the side of the bed to dispute his claim. "You were dust in the fucking wind. This is *my* ship!"

"My ship," he added between my territorial rant.

"My room!"

"My room."

"My bed!"

"My bed and" He leaned over and ripped the t-shirt from my hands, leaving me naked again. "My shirt."

I shook my head and bit my cheek. He, however, was pleased as punch to be right back where we had started. He leaned back and propped his arms behind his head.

"While you're at it, why don't you bring me the rest of what's mine?" He gave me a rogue smile.

"What?" I asked, knowing he wanted me to ask.

"My wife." He perked his brow and for a moment I was lost, back into the muddy depths of passion versus pride.

He leaned forward, reaching his hand out to me. I shook my head, fighting to keep hold of the pride. He scooted forward and tugged my hand. I was still glaring at him, but I moved, succumbing to the passion. He guided me onto the bed and into his lap. "Rule number four: if you have a chance to get away, take it. Don't wait to see what he has planned next." He rolled me over and started kissing my neck.

"Do you not get that you hurt me?" I asked solemnly.

He froze and lifted his head to look down at me. "Yes, I do, but I needed time. Time to deal with my shit... and think. I know that to you, I've been awake for months, but I really didn't start remembering my past until a few weeks in."

Rayne pushed my hair out of my face. "Ayil and Aresties turned out to be very helpful. His willingness to work and her generosity. I know you basically threatened me to keep them on, but I'm glad you did."

"They're good people," I agreed.

"When we went back to rescue you, or kidnap you, it was all to help Ayil. I thought nothing of you one way or another—actually, I thought you were a bit of a pain in the ass."

I smiled. "Little did you know I was a *big* pain in the ass."

He chuckled. "Yes, you are difficult at times." His smile faded, and he kissed me. His hips pressed against me, trying to start more.

I pressed him away, and he looked devastated that I wasn't ready to give in yet. "You were saying something about when you guys came to my rescue."

His eyes glazed in thought, and then a small smile played over his lips. "I was going to reveal my identity to you after the chaperones had left, but you pulled your veil off, and... you were perfect. The hair, the makeup, the dress. Still, I wasn't a slobbering teenage boy anymore; I intended to be a gentleman. Then you closed your eyes and opened yourself up for a kiss. I thought to myself: no bride should be disappointed on her honeymoon." Rayne's hips shifted against me, and I let out a groan of appreciation. He dipped down, kissing my breasts.

"Please don't stop talking. This is the most you've ever spoken to me."

"I'll talk after," he mumbled into my flesh.

"No, you won't. You'll just fall asleep."

Rayne chuckled against my chest before looking up. "I hope you know it's a compliment. I really can't sleep for shit unless I've had you in my arms."

"Don't you mean unless you've had me, period?"

"Actually, I sleep better next to you than any woman I've been with."

"Really?" My brow dipped.

"Like I said, it's a compliment. Hopefully, it means you put me at ease."

"I thought I was a pain in the ass. How is that sleep-inducing?"

"Maybe that's the point. You exhaust me during the day." I gave his shoulder a playful punch, and he smiled at me. "Are you going to let me make love to you yet?"

"Finish your story."

"Would you like me to retell the part where I coaxed you into bed the first time?"

"No, I remember just fine. I was weak and vulnerable."

"Bullshit." Rayne laughed and propped himself a little higher. "You wanted your honeymoon. Arranged marriage or not, you wanted to know what it felt like to have a man pressing inside you. Pleasuring himself with your body and, in turn, pleasing you." A shiver went through my body as I thought about it.

"Yes, I did want that. I wanted you. I haven't stopped wanting you since the moment I saw you inside that damn pod."

"You poor thing. You had to wait six long years for me to wake up and show you what a man can be to a woman."

"Don't you think that's a little pathetic? Me lusting after a dead man?"

"I wasn't dead. I was waiting. I just didn't know I was waiting for you." He kissed me again, but this time I didn't stop him from slipping between my legs and pushing himself inside of me.

He looked down at me as he moved inside of me. The focus was unnerving, but I liked that he was intent on making the moment important.

After an arduously slow rise to the summit, I tumbled over the side, with Rayne right after me. He shifted to lie down beside me, holding me in a close embrace. I waited to hear his soft snores.

"When those goons took you into that van," he said, surprising me with his lucid conversation, "I was furious I had let it happen."

"You didn't really have a choice."

"I should have protected you. I should have stayed close to you. My priorities were split. Ayil was blind, the child was screaming—"

"Rayne, it's okay. I don't blame you."

"I followed the van until I couldn't run anymore. I broke into a vehicle, went back for Ayil, and searched for the van. By the time we arrived, we were too late to partake in the violence. I was, however, in time to see that kiss."

I moved my hand up to touch his, reminding him I was still in his bed, despite anything that had happened.

"I was so jealous. For years, I had loved a woman who I could never call my own. I didn't even know until then I had any designs to make *you* my own."

Rayne pulled away from me and sat up on the edge of the bed. He shoved his fingers through his hair. "That's when I realized I was starting to fall for you." He stood up and moved to lean on the sleep pod. I didn't dare follow him.

"I did love Starla. She was the only real joy in my life, and then I let her get killed. Ten years later, I woke. I mourned her before I even understood who she was. I started to remember the details of her murder. I felt guilty I was sleeping with another woman instead of avenging Starla's death." Rayne slammed his fist into the sleep pod, then turned to face me.

"I didn't want to leave you, but I couldn't let her murderer go free any longer." I nodded in agreement. "I didn't truly feel her loss until I was face to face with Helana. After it was over, everything was fresh again. My open wounds were full of salt. I was angry, ashamed, and I didn't want to put you through that. I thought if I stayed away, it would be better for both of us.

"Then you had to go and show up in that bar, like the pain in the ass you are. You said you were looking for your husband, and I realized we were technically married."

"Serves you right impersonating a groom."

Rayne moved back to the bed and got back into position with me. "I did my best to push you away, and you did your best to push me away."

I nodded, remembering the hurtful things I said to him. "Why did you come back? What changed your mind?"

"It was that flippant little thing you said when you left."

"What, thanks for not killing me in my sleep? I was actually grateful for that; I mean, you are an assassin."

"It's not a habitual tick." He pinched me playfully, making me squirm.

"Why did that convince you to come back to me?"

"It reminded me that you kept me alive for six years. You wasted resources and money on a man you had never met."

"What can I say? I'm a sucker for unavailable men."

"I thought about everything you had done for me. Forcing me to take on Ayil and Aresties. Coming after me when I left the first time. Coming after me the second time."

"I was just being nosy the first time."

"You were trying to save me from myself." He kissed my temple. "I thought about what you had done for Ayil. Saving him from Gunder, twice. You were even willing to hand yourself over to those assholes in the suckerfish to save all of us."

"So, you realized I'm a glutton for danger and I'm going to need all the help I can get to stay alive?"

"Can you be serious for one second? I'm trying to tell you that I love you."

"You do?"

"Yes, you troublesome woman. After you left, I realized the only reason I was saying no to protecting you was because I was afraid of failing you like I did Starla. I was afraid of feeling that pain again. Then I realized if you were killed and I wasn't there to stop it, I would still feel that pain." He frowned at me. "You were already in too deep." He tapped his chest.

I smiled and touched the same spot. "I know the feeling."

Love

Love had to be the strangest invention of the gods. Hate made sense. Somebody pisses you off, you hate them, but of course, the severity of that hate fades in time. Love, however... Well, that's an addiction, a parasite, and a survivor all in one.

My love for my family was definitely a parasitic kind.

"Mom, Mom!" I yelled at the monitor with her fuzzy face on it. I smacked the side of the box, hoping to make her grating lecture stop. "I don't have time for this. You know we can only stay on for a few minutes."

"And whose fault is that?" she asked smugly.

"Mine!" I raised my hands in surrender. "I take full responsibility. I ruined my life. I've made horrible decisions, and it's cost me my future. Put Elizandra on. I only have a few seconds."

My mother lifted my little sister on her lap and she squealed at my image and hugged the screen. "Kit!"

"Hey, little sis. I don't have much time, I just wanted to tell you how much I love you, and I miss you so so so so much!

"I miss you too. When are you coming home?"

"Probably not for a really long time."

"Why?" she pouted.

"Because I didn't listen to Mommy's advice." I smirked at my mother, who smiled slightly at my effort to suck up.

"Is it because you played in the mud?"

"Yes, as a matter of fact. Just a few weeks ago, I was playing on a planet covered almost entirely in mud."

Elizandra clicked her tongue and shook her finger at me. I laughed. My beeper started going off and my mother frowned, almost breaking into tears. Rather than let her get carried away, I proceeded with the pretense of a casual goodbye.

"Okay, I have to go. I love you both. Tell Daddy I'll call as soon as I have a safe channel."

"I will. I love you too, Kit," she squawked over her emotions and the monitor clicked off.

"Damn," I whispered, wishing we could talk longer even though I dreaded making the call every time. It was a strange situation, but in truth, I had spoken to my parents more in the last few weeks than in the entire six years of my absence. It was better than nothing.

"How did it go?" Ayil peeked over the receptionist's desk to gauge my mood.

"Great, I feel like a jerk and I'm on the verge of tears."

"Sounds about right for a family call."

"Yup."

"Are you two ready?" Terrin called into the darkened waiting room from the hall. "Let's get this going before someone catches us."

"We're coming. Don't get your horns in a twist." Ayil winked at me and headed out of the room after him.

"My horns are not twisted," I heard Terrin say as I made it out of the receptionist's area to meet them in the hall. "I don't want to get into a situation like last week."

"What? That went super well!"

Terrin turned to face Ayil. "You seducing a night watchman to get access to the labs is not my idea of a professional operation."

"Professional? Who the hell do you think we are? We're criminals now, Terrin. We are glorified cat burglars, and by the way, seducing that dude was my pleasure."

"You are disgusting." Terrin walked away.

Ayil looked back at me. "I'm really starting to like him. I can see what you see in him."

"Mmm, just be careful how many of those nerves you want to tug on. He's only being this generous with his patience for me. You wear him thin enough, he could snap... your neck."

Ayil chuckled, indifferent to the threat. "There it is, Brainiac." He pointed to a door labeled *Records*.

After a quick pick of the lock, we entered the room, and I sat down at the computer. It took less than a minute to bypass their password.

"Why do these places always make their password 'baby'?" I asked.

"It's a fertility clinic. Maybe they're being positive. It's better than using something tacky like *man juice* or *jizz factory* or—"

"Stop making sperm references. Go tell Terrin the name on the specimen will be Kate Darrow."

"Gotcha." Ayil headed out the door.

"Tell him to relabel it!" I called after him. "Pour my little egglets down the sink," I mumbled. "So rude."

I finished deleting my file and the existence of anything that could link to my ID scan, DNA, or general direction, thereby saving my potential offspring from being hunted down and killed if anyone found out I had donated eggs.

I tiptoed down the hall to the lab, where Terrin and Ayil were silently arguing behind a frosted glass window. Ayil rubbed his arms furiously, trying to ease the cold of the freezer room. Terrin didn't seem to be affected by the temperature, but I knew from experience he was highly susceptible to the cold. He just couldn't feel it until he was in danger of hypothermia.

I hopped onto a spinning chair and spun as one must. After a few too many head rushes, I dug into the drawers of the counter next to me.

I pulled out several technical devices before I found a packaged lollipop. "Sweet tooth much?" I turned the package over and read the instructions. "Open package and lick. Duh, you think?" I opened the package and stuck the candy in my mouth.

I immediately spat it back out and the remaining flavor it left. "Gross. What kind of candy is that?"

"It's not candy, Kit, it's a pregnancy test." Rayne came through the door, shaking his head at me. "It's a litmus lollipop."

"Aren't you supposed to be watching the front door?"

"You guys are taking too long. I wanted to check on you."

"Ahh, you missed me."

Rayne smirked and sat down on a twirly stool beside me. "Yes, but that doesn't change the fact that you guys suck at this."

"We were doing fine before you came along."

"Yeah, I heard about Ayil's side-show blow job. That's not how to keep a low profile."

"Oh, should I have done the blow job instead?"

Rayne smirked and shook his head. "I thought you didn't want me to kill anyone unless you were in danger."

"It was just a thought. I mean, I want to be a team player."

Rayne pulled my chair forward with his legs, and I bit my lip to control my smile. "Not a good idea to tease a former assassin, honey."

I chuckled and kissed him. As I leaned back, his eyes drifted off behind me. He frowned and reached for something. He picked up the litmus lollipop and examined it.

"No seriously, it doesn't taste good," I said as he examined the flat blue *candy*.

"It's blue," he commented.

"Yeah, so?"

"It was red before."

I narrowed my eyes, trying to remember what flavor I had expected. Cherry maybe.

I snatched the wrapper from the counter and read the fine print.

"Ah, crap."

FELICIA JEDLICKA

Destiny Reclaimed

BOOK 2 IN THE DESTINY SERIES

Destiny Reclaimed

Felicia Jedlicka

Book 2

With a baby on board, Kit Mallory's DNA just went from valuable to priceless.

The genetic gold mine growing in her belly is getting difficult to hide and the bounty on her head has just turned from "dead or alive" to "preferably dead."

For years, her father's government has failed to retain her DNA which will supposedly bring about the next evolution of mankind. Fearing the devaluation of a viccenial investment, the Coalition has deemed Kit a traitor and an apostate. With access to the most advanced military force in the universe, they will stop at nothing to prevent her genes from ending in the hands. Even if that means eliminating her.

Thank you so much for reading. I hope you
enjoyed the ride and if you aren't getting off here,
I encourage you to sign up for my newsletter
so I can return your generosity with new release
updates and special offers.

Sign-Up

You can also find me on Facebook or visit my
website. Keep reading!

Website

Facebook

About the Author

As a Nebraska native, and a small-town girl at that, I have very little to occupy my time beyond imagining a world outside of my own reality. By the grace of God and the seat of my pants, I have kept my waning attention span on the task of becoming an author.

So here I am, an indie author, peddling my words in cyberspace and enduring my comeuppances with an unwavering determination. I may not be a professional, and I certainly am not perfect, but if you've made it this far, you have to admit, this smartass yokel does spin quite a yarn.

From the self-inflicted sweatshop conditions of my unairconditioned childhood home, to the arthritis reaping positions of a sedentary lifestyle, I bring to you: my sarcasm, my oddity, and my heart. Take it with a grain of salt or a teaspoon of sugar, but take it for what it is: a story born of the mind, translated to paper, and gifted to you.

I thank you for your readership and even more for your support. Please recommend this book to your friends and family via any social media that you use. Word of mouth is still the best advertising and is greatly appreciated.

Most importantly, keep reading. I'll keep writing.

www.ingramcontent.com/pod-product-compliance
Lightning Source LLC
Chambersburg PA
CBHW010640190726
48289CB00009B/2789